Praise for *Monarchs of the Northeast Kingdom*

"Lush and evocative . . . A highly satisfying, delicately woven story about loss, loneliness, life, and death."

—*KIRKUS REVIEWS*

"Infused with the hypnotic tone of a dream and rich evocation of place . . . utterly affecting."

—LIAM DURCAN, author of *The Measure of Darkness*

"An astonishingly mature first novel, suspenseful, haunted—and haunting—from start to finish."

—A. G. MOJTABAI, author of *Shine on Me*

"Ominous from its opening image, *Monarchs of the Northeast Kingdom* is a haunting beauty. A quiet madness unfolds and the narrative forces the reader to look and see what the most fragile among us are capable of."

—KELLY SOKOL, author of *The Unprotected*

"Every sentence sings with grace and music . . . a book you don't read so much as savor."

—RICHARD KRAWIEC, author of *Time Sharing*

"An intimate portrait of one woman's grief and journey towards self-sufficiency . . . raw, emotional, and poignant."

—Burrowing Owl Books

Monarchs

of the

Northeast Kingdom

Monarchs
of the
Northeast Kingdom

a novel

Chera Hammons

TORREY HOUSE PRESS

SALT LAKE CITY • TORREY

First Torrey House Press Edition, May 2020
Copyright © 2020 by Chera Hammons

Published by Torrey House Press
Salt Lake City, Utah
www.torreyhouse.org

International Standard Book Number: 978-1-948814-21-8
E-book ISBN: 978-1-948814-22-5
Library of Congress Control Number: 2019952018

Cover design by Kathleen Metcalf
Interior design by Rachel Davis
Distributed to the trade by Consortium Book Sales and Distribution

Torrey House Press offices in Salt Lake City sit on the homelands of Ute, Goshute, Shoshone, and Paiute nations. Offices in Torrey are in homelands of Paiute, Ute, and Navajo nations.

NATIONAL ENDOWMENT for the ARTS
arts.gov

This project is supported in part by the National Endowment for the Arts. To find out more about how National Endowment for the Arts grants impact individuals and communities, visit www.arts.gov.

"Fresh, untouched, green, lovely. Untrammeled, except by ourselves. A lifetime of warmth and beauty and fertility. The kind of life and world people have been dreaming about ever since they first began fouling this one. I can sometimes catch glimpses of what it will be like, and they are tantalizing—"

"I have seen it, you forget," Gloria said. "In the mirror. It is more beautiful than you can believe."

—Shirley Jackson, *The Sundial*

1

The first thing John says when he comes inside is that he has seen blood in the new snow.

"Blood?" Anna muses over her coffee, not awake enough yet to feel alarm.

"Yes, beside the driveway." He hits the newspaper against his leg to get the ice off of the orange plastic wrapper. It's a habit Anna hates because it leaves cold, clear pools on the kitchen tile that seep even through her thick winter socks. "Just a few drops, not a lot. Still . . ."

Blood. How stark it would look against the crystallized white, like rubies loosened from a ring and fallen into a white fur pelt. "Where could it have come from?"

"A deer, I think," John says. "There were tracks going off into the trees."

"Oh," Anna says. "Again?"

"It looks like it," John says. "They didn't get a clean kill this time." He sits in one of the worn oak chairs and unfolds the paper. "I'll take Charlie out later and try to find it."

"Why? What good will it do?" She wants it to be spoken.

"Well." He clears his throat. "It might be suffering."

She nods. They can't allow anything to die slowly in the cold, bleeding to death. Not on their land. They're decent people.

She asks, as she did the last time, "Should we call the game warden?"

He looks at her over the paper for a moment, thinking. "Let's wait," he says. "I want to make sure there's a good reason first."

They are, after all, used to keeping their own counsel. Neither of them has any interest in hunting or knows anything of hunting laws, though they have read stories about these subjects in the *Gazette* and notice generally when hunting season falls. It hasn't yet started this year, but it will soon. Anna doesn't even know how to find the number for a game warden if she needs to call one. She assumes John knows, though he has never called one, either.

They eat in easy silence. Anna picks at her eggs and sips her coffee while John reads his paper. Every once in a while, he frowns; he must be reading bad news: obituaries, politics, crime, fracking, reports of invasive species that could kill the trees. That's all the paper ever has in it besides births and weddings.

Anna tries not to think of the blood. It's nice to watch John without his noticing. She studies his eyes, the pleasing wrinkles at their sides that mean that he has laughed a lot. Nearly everything he does possesses an air of benign absentmindedness that has only increased over time. He taps his foot as he reads. Anna can tell from the squeak that he has forgotten to take off his boots again; the snow will soon be melting onto the kitchen floor in dirty rings. She sighs. Still, staying annoyed with him is hard; he's easygoing and tends to take good care of her.

She stands and begins to do the dishes while he finishes the paper. The window over the sink lets chilly air seep in that makes the metal faucet handle cold. The taps sputter at first. As she waits for the water to run hot, she looks at the naked maples and tall thin evergreens at the edge of the yard. The snow has clumped on the needles, making them droop. The trees look heavy, gray, depressed.

It's still only the middle of autumn, and it has been harder than most. The ground will be white and blank for months yet. The floor under her feet leeches cold, making her heels ache. She's glad there isn't much to wash. The soap bubbles burst in the sink in tiny rainbows. The almost-translucent, spotted skin on her hands turns pink. The blue veins at the tops spread like roots.

As she dries her hands and slides her wedding ring back on, John stands and stretches, yawning wide and slow like a bear. "Well," he says.

"Are you going out now?" Anna asks.

"I guess I'd better," he says. "Who knows how far it might have gone." He kisses her on the cheek.

"Be careful."

"Old Charlie hasn't thrown me yet," he says.

She stands at the kitchen counter and listens to him rummage in the hall closet for the rifle. The rifle is only a secondhand .22 they purchased years ago, when they'd first bought their property, but it does well enough at close range. They both hate the gun and know nothing of killing except that it should be both careful and quick. They had originally been driven to buy it for protection of their livestock from wildlife and dogs, and it comes out only in emergencies.

Anna has never used the rifle, and has seen John shoot it exactly three times. Once at a tree trunk to warn off a couple of coyotes that had been prowling near the chicken pen. Once to put down the Hansons' gelding, which had gotten loose and been struck by a car. She can sometimes still hear the horse screaming in her memory; she had called their own vet to ask where in the forehead to shoot it for a clean kill, shaking so badly that she had misdialed several times. And once to kill a dog with distemper that someone had dumped off near their house.

If you live out of town, you have to get used to some killing. That's the way of things. But that doesn't mean you have to like it.

Anna is sorry that John needs to take the rifle with him. He tries not to seem bothered by it. "Take your cell phone," she tells him. "I'll be in the tub for a while, but I can help you after I get dressed if you need it."

But she is still at the kitchen window watching twenty minutes later when he leads the ageing mule, Charlie, out of the barn and toward the woods. The mule is, as always, beautifully rigged with one of John's handmade saddles. John specializes in custom orders, hard-to-fit horses, the short-backed quarter horse sore from trees that bridge, the wide table back of a paint with no withers, the large flat shoulders of a Tennessee walker, the slab-sides of mammoth donkeys. John sometimes has Anna help him with the leather tooling when orders pile up in the spring. To her, it feels clumsy, unnatural, knocking the stamp into the unyielding hide, and the leather sewing machine with its noise and strength frightens her, makes her hold her breath while her heart pounds. She sometimes finds herself in awe of John, who is comfortable around such industry.

He checks his girth and swings up on Charlie's back. The mule's ears flick back and forth, listening. John pats the mule and speaks to him, then reaches back to check the rifle in the scabbard. Charlie looks thick and warm in his winter coat. John kisses the air, their signal to the mule to go ahead. It's strange to see the expression from far away without sound. Charlie tucks his nose and strides forward, and they're soon lost in the horizon of slim trunks. At least one out of every ten of the trees in Vermont forests stands tall even though the tree is actually dead, though it's harder to spot the dead ones in winter. Going into the woods is a little like walking among ghosts. Anna pictures not only the spirits of trees, but caribou, mastodons. Lives that passed through the land before hers and will never come back.

As she waits for her bath to run, she thinks of all she ought to do that day. She keeps a list stuck with a magnet to the fridge, ticking chores off as she goes, but today is a good day, and she can remember much of what the list contains. The barn needs to be mucked out, more hay dropped from the loft, the chickens fed and watered. The cold often makes these tasks seem impossible. There are some bills to pay, and the house, of course, could always stand a cleaning. The Epsom salts swirl and vanish in the steaming water roaring from the faucet.

She tests it first with her foot, then stands in the tub, acclimating herself to the heat. She ran it hotter than she was supposed to. It turns her skin red, and sometimes it hurts. The hotter the bath starts out, though, the longer she can stay in, weightless and untethered to her unwieldy body. She holds on to the sides of the tub and lowers herself inch by inch. She can feel her joints loosen, relax, and the pain soon seems to float around her, no longer a part of her, but a part of the water. The ache hovers around her wrists, hips, fingers, and knees in filmy clouds. She closes her eyes.

Once the cold starts to spill into the bath, too, Anna pulls herself up and wraps herself in a towel. She dresses in faded jeans and a sweater that is too big for her. Her once-brown hair, she pulls into a tight ponytail. Older women, she has been taught, are supposed to keep short hair, but she's used to the low-maintenance, collarbone-length style and can't bring herself to cut it.

She doesn't like growing older, though she doesn't try to fight it; there's no point. Appraising herself in the mirror, she tries to judge her reflection as a stranger might, but she doesn't allow herself to focus on her wrinkles, the sagging lines of her neck; she looks instead at the dark brown eyes, which still have some of the depth and sparkle they had when she was a girl. She rubs moisturizer into her skin, enjoying the feeling of softness and luxury that comes from it. She doesn't bother with makeup anymore.

There have been no missed calls. John likely doesn't have a signal, which is spotty even on the best days so close to the ranges. The Green Mountains and White Mountains together are like two hands cradling the Kingdom between them, isolating the region from the rest of the state, making it colder and lonelier, but also protecting it—giving it a history all its own. Its inaccessibility has become part of what she likes about it. She texts John so that he'll have a message to respond to when he can: "Is everything okay? Find the deer?"

It's hard to stay motivated when John is gone; with so much to do, she doesn't know where to start. He has a way of streamlining tasks and making them seem easier. Without him, she too easily falls into the trap of resting through the moods of the arthritis.

Anna decides to go into the barn first and throw more hay down for the week. They are on track so far this year, only about 15 percent of the way through their winter supply, which they'd bought over the brief summer at a low price and stored in the loft. The sweet mild smell of it usually soothes her, reminds her of the soft green breezes of an easier season. She sometimes wants to lie in it and dream the way she did when she was young, but it could prickle through her clothing and leave welts on her skin.

She plunges through the deep snow into the warm cloud of her breath, the barn tipping up and down in front of her as she tries to step into the footprints John left, struggling to match his wider, straighter stride. The snow and the white-veiled trees muffle every sound, the bright summer birds have long since moved south, the animals all huddle somewhere in burrows; against the silence of the hibernating forest, her breath seems loud and uneven.

She opens the barn door. Dust motes swirl and rise, but they soon settle and hover in the cold light that comes in through the planks. Her short, gentle Icelandic horse, the one they named Keeper, their only riding animal now besides the mule, whickers and bumps its head against its stall door as if asking her to open it. The only other inhabitant of the barn is the border collie that stretches from its bed and pads up to her, tail wagging in slow arcs.

She pats the horse and speaks to it for a while in low, singsong tones. It has been cribbing on the edge of the stall door; the wood there is splintered and pale. A quick-natured horse, it has difficulty staying inside all winter. She checks its hay and water.

She needs to take it out for a ride, give it some exercise. She mentally adds that to the list.

The dog whines when she begins to climb up the ladder to the hayloft. She looks down at the pale wolfish eyes and reassures it. "Good girl," she soothes. "Good girl. I won't be long."

The dog never whines when John climbs the ladder, as if it, too, views him as the stronger member of the household and her as the weaker. In the same way, the house cat never leaves its toys in her shoes, only John's. She wonders how they know, what it is about her that they read as submissive, as lesser.

Anna takes the smooth tan cowhide gloves off the hook at the top of the ladder and puts them on. The fingers, too big for her, hold bits of hay that have broken off and fallen to the tips to lodge in the stitching. They prick her as she opens and closes her hands. She tosses the hay down in the easy rhythm she learned long ago, swinging it by the baling twine to get momentum and letting go at the top of the swing to throw it over the edge. She throws down three before a hitch in her hip nearly knocks her over. She leans over a bale, breathless, holding her hip and trying not to look down. The dog whines. She should leave the loft while she still can, in case the hip locks up. She hasn't done as much as she'd intended, but it's something.

The dog circles the ladder as she comes back down, and when she steps off the ladder and lets go of it, the dog bumps her legs, sniffing. She pets it to calm it down, holding its head to look into the sharp, intelligent face and rubbing its warm ears. It barks after her in staccato yelps after she closes the barn door.

She checks her phone where it charges in the kitchen; still no messages. John didn't pack a lunch. It's 11:38. Maybe he is nearly back home. Or maybe the wounded deer has gone farther than he guessed it would. Perhaps it's really okay and he won't find it at all. He will get to a place where the snow shows that the bleeding has stopped and the deer has run off, tracks wide apart and blurred with speed, indicating the deer has disappeared into the wilderness, as it is meant to do. The rifle will hang cold and still in its scabbard, unnecessary weight. And John will turn around.

Anna eats canned tomato soup and watches the local news. Cold, cold, and more cold. More snow. It never changes. Winters are always the same. Each winter runs into the next in her memory, a dashed line of frozen pipes and raw throats and the smell of space heaters burning off their dust. Even in spring and summer, the sun rarely breaks through such a landscape, one hewn by clouds and glaciers.

She puts her bowl in the sink and runs water into it. She doesn't bother to wait for it to get hot before she washes the bowl. She scrubs the red line on the side until it has disappeared, then rinses it and sets it on the drying rack.

She looks up. Movement at the edge of the window catches her eye.

It's Charlie, pawing desperately in the snow in front of the barn. He raises his head and calls with his strange sound, the noise somewhere between a whinny and a bray. He takes a step and trips; his leg is between the reins, which drag on the ground. There's a white froth of sweat like foam along his neck.

He is riderless.

2

Anna runs outside without her coat. She stumbles through the snow all the way to the barn, growing hot and clumsy with the exertion, though her cheeks numb with the cold. Pain shoots through her hip, but she ignores it.

Her floundering movement and her rasping breaths frighten the mule, and he startles and backs away from her as she approaches. The reins jerk the noseband of his hackamore when he steps on them, pulling his head down. His eyes are wide and afraid.

Anna makes herself stop and slows her breathing. Inhale, exhale. Inhale. She has stopped running but her heart hasn't. Her pulse pounds in her ears. "Whoa, Charlie. Whoa," she says, low in her throat. He holds his head as high as he can, the muscles of his neck hard and tense; he is the statue of a mule. He doesn't look at her, but over her; she may as well be invisible. She makes her way to his side, speaking consolingly to him as she picks up the dragging reins. She holds her palm open to him. He flicks his ears toward her, then back toward the gray forest. She tells him it's all right, rubs his neck, and he begins to soften. Of course animals never want to be afraid, any more than people do.

With shaking hands, Anna undoes the knot in the reins and frees his leg. She strokes Charlie on the shoulder. He's trembling, and he leans against her with a sigh. She feels the vibration all through his big warm body. Dried sweat runs from under the saddle pad down to his belly in a crust of salt. The rifle scabbard is empty.

"John," she calls, turning to look around the yard. Then louder, "John!" There isn't any answer. The watching trees swallow what's left of her voice. The snow is churned down to black dirt where Charlie pawed at it, but there are no new boot prints that she can see. It doesn't matter anyway; she knows with strange certainty that John didn't come back with the mule.

Anna leads Charlie into the barn, strips off his saddle, and lays it down on the floor of the tack room. She hurries him into his stall while the border collie crisscrosses behind them, believing as it always does that it herds the mule in itself.

Anna shoves a square of hay into the mule's feeder and leaves him to settle. She pulls the barn door closed against the reassuring sound of the mule beginning to lip the hay from the net. At least he isn't so upset that he can't eat.

Anna stands with her back to the barn, facing the trees, the wintery sky seeming darker than it had a few minutes before. The clouds have gathered into a close bundle and are growing dense and wet. Charlie's trail in the snow leads from where Anna stands to the line of pines, where she loses sight of it.

Heart still pounding, Anna makes herself walk back to the empty kitchen to pick up her cell phone (fully charged now, still no messages) and winter coat. She shoves her hands into the thick ski gloves that don't allow her fingers much mobility, but will keep them from frostbite. She looks around the room, hesitant to leave its safety, suspecting that she is forgetting something, but unsure what it could be.

Following Charlie's deep tracks is easy. They cut across the clean snow like sutures. He had come from the trees in the same place he had gone in, along the familiar trail; he had probably followed the trail as long as he possibly could have. People and mules are the same that way, relying on their habits. She wonders if she ought to ride the Icelandic horse instead of walk but doesn't want to use the time and energy saddling it. Not when John is probably not far off.

Just before she reaches the tree line, Anna turns and looks back. Small and lonely, the house nestles in the clearing against its backdrop of trees and boulders. The mountain crouches like an ancient god over it, shaggy with rock and earth, higher than anyone would care to reach, sometimes with an attitude like brooding anger, sometimes benevolence. Now, it sleeps, blanketed with snow and clouds, waiting.

It has gotten dark enough for her to see that she left the kitchen light on, and even from that far off she can see the chairs pulled out from the table unevenly, as though she and John had only just finished breakfast and gone off to their separate, but intersecting, days. The outlying trees hover over her, watching what she does likes spies, roots whispering to each other below the soil while the trunks slumber. They tell the forest to expect her, a stranger, to enter its wilderness. She wonders which seems more beautiful to them—the bare, still winter season or the summer with its birds and leaves and life. The evergreens are always the same, no matter the weather.

She steps into the dusk of the trees, leaving the house behind her.

The path takes Anna ahead with a slowness that is almost cruel. The whiteness and monotony of the trunks make the horizon a dreamscape that moves by as if on a reel while she stands still. She fights her way down the trail on cold, unfeeling legs where the snow has drifted. Steady walking will eventually warm her up, so she focuses on the ground instead of looking forward, marking each step before she takes it, trying only to follow the trail without slipping.

The clouds grow so heavy above Anna it seems she could hit her head on them. The ground and sky press her between them, and the air tastes moist. Maybe she should have ridden the horse.

Even in the low light, she can see that the nature of the tracks going and coming differs. Heading out, Charlie had, of course, been walking, unconcerned. He had picked up his big hooves in no apparent hurry, and set them nearly straight down. Those tracks are almost circles.

He had returned to the barn at a full run, strides far apart and stretched at the edges where his legs had been at more of an angle. Those tracks are ink smeared across a page in carelessness. His run had chopped the ground. Did something spook him? Anna wonders. Had he actually thrown John, or maybe just run off after John had dismounted? John is a good rider, though not perhaps as good as she is. Or used to be. But then, he had started later in life. She expects any moment to hear her husband wading through the snow around the bend, cursing the mule in his gentle but persistent way. That gentleness that means no one takes him seriously when he loses his temper. She feels the warmth start to grow in her stomach and spread to her chest; the exercise is working.

Here and there, too: the scattering of blood, the stray sharp print of the wounded deer. The same signs that John had followed. It is more blood than she expected.

Anna stops, realizing what bothered her when she stood in the kitchen, what she is forgetting. Not just the empty saddle—the empty scabbard. *Where is the rifle?* The more she tries to imagine what happened, the more she worries. It means John had a reason to take the gun out of the scabbard before he was thrown. Or maybe it had simply fallen from the scabbard as the mule galloped and bucked toward home. If John doesn't have it with him when they find each other, they will have to look for it. It isn't the sort of thing someone should leave lying around in the woods.

Anna doesn't know how long she walks. The snow makes for slow and clumsy going, and she stumbles many times. It's deep enough snow for martens to tunnel in, hunting for mice. The toothy, mink-like animals are returning, she has read. First the trees came back, then martens; maybe, one day, wolves.

Anna shivers. Her hips and knees ache, a pain somewhere between fire and needles. She has grown warm and then cold and then warm again. She rests on fallen trees, brushing the snow off of them with hands that feel huge and numb in the neon blue and black ski gloves. Her face has grown so stiff that it seems unable to hold any expression. She wonders if her nose is running, as it often does in the cold, but she doesn't have enough feeling in it to tell.

The watery light that was left after the clouds gathered has quietly ebbed, but the clouds' full bases and the white ground still hold enough luminosity between them for Anna to make out shapes without much difficulty. She keeps on, growing miserable with hunger and fatigue. *I shouldn't be out here.*

At a place in the trail where the tracks abruptly split, Anna hesitates. The morning version of Charlie had continued at its measured pace along the path; the later, frightened Charlie had come from the south and rejoined the path to run home. Following either track should get her to John, in theory, but which will be faster? *Don't panic.* She should have found John by now. He should have passed her on the way home.

Then again, maybe not. John doesn't get disoriented in the woods as she sometimes does. He might not rely on the trail to get back. He could go straight through the trees. Maybe he is home, looking for her. Returning home to warm rooms with John waiting would be the answer to every prayer she's ever had. But she can't be sure he's there.

She checks her phone again, fumbling to get it out of her pocket and get the screen to turn on, but it shows she has no signal.

"John!" she calls to nothing. She waits, watching her breath melt into the air.

She turns down the mule track that leaves the trail. It might be nice to walk a different direction for a while. It's marked only by the mule's tracks, no sort of boundary. Quiet makes the forest seem darker, emptier the farther she gets from the path. A few white flakes fall like ash between the trees. She shivers. She walks into her own silence, like she is the only person left on earth. "John!" she cries again.

Through her gloves, Anna can barely feel the outline of the button that illuminates her cell phone screen. She presses it and shines the mild light away from her so that she can better see the uneven going. Though dim, the blue light comforts her. Every few seconds, she hits the button again to keep it on. With some steps, her feet sink into snow up to her knees; with others, the ground sits closer to the surface and she steps too hard and trips. Her jeans stiffen with caked ice.

Anna works far beyond the level of exertion she normally allows herself. Under her determination boils a desperation borne from the inability to change where she is. There is no easy way back. She doesn't know when to stop, can't stop until she finds John. For all she knows, she is closer to him than to the warm kitchen.

The trees stand dark and quiet over her while the tracks go on and on, as far as she can see. Anna wonders if she has gotten lost, if she is even still on their own land. Getting lost had been impossible in the place they lived before. *Getting lost is good*, Anna tells herself. The ability to get lost is what they had wanted.

The snow keeps secrets from her. Anna is stumbling forward half-asleep when the toe of her left boot catches on a covered tree branch and she falls hard onto her side, wrenching her ankle. She curses and sucks in the cold air. For a moment she lies on her back and looks at the clear stars frozen in the spaces between low clouds, which are breaking and floating off from each other like calving ice.

Her phone, which has landed beside her, buzzes.

She scrambles to pick it up and pulls off her gloves to unlock it. With her numb fingers, it takes several tries. The message appears on the screen, and she mouths *Thank you* to the darkness. It's from John.

The floating words make her dizzy with relief. "Nearly there." She reads it three times. *Nearly there, nearly there, nearly there.* She blinks tears out of her eyes. They could be caused by the cold; she isn't sure.

So John really has passed her in the woods. She tries to respond, but the signal has dropped again, and the message fails. She wonders how far he is from home. He will get there before her, see she is gone, and worry. But there is no help for that.

Anna stands up, ignoring the pain in her ankle, and turns back the way she came. Everything seems easier now that she's going back. She limps a little, but as she walks she supports herself on the trees, leaning against the rough trunks. How cozy the wood-burning stove will be, her slippers, the cat curled in her lap, a hot cup of chamomile tea. She and John will sleep late in the morning after such a day as this one, wake when the sunlight falls too strongly between the gaps in the curtains for them to stay in bed any longer, make steaming coffee and read the paper and listen to the peace of the woods, snow dropping off the branches.

The main trail appears before she expects to see it. It's trickier here to walk on the ankle, the trees spaced farther apart, but she manages. It's only a minor sprain; once she gets home, she'll wrap it with the same bright elastic material she uses on the horses. What color will she choose? Electric pink? Neon green? Behind her, the snow proves that she walks unevenly, dragging the foot. The forest is silent except for the sounds of her progress, her ragged panting and the scrape of her boots in the thick, soft ground.

She must be getting close; she has been walking now her entire life.

A chilling howl breaks from the darkness to her left, beginning with some high-pitched yips, like someone trying to choke off a sob. Then it finds itself, pure and tonal, and rises up and up through the bare canopy of the trees and hangs there. She stops to listen, pinpricks on her arms and neck. It can't really be wolves; they've been extinct in Vermont for years. Hybrids? Coyotes can possess wolf DNA. This is surely only what is left of the wolves, their residue, some kind of memory or ghost of them, something that stalks and haunts, then disappears.

The entire forest has stopped to listen with her. The melody threads the trunks, moves darkness over the moon, and drops, and then there are cries and laughter all around her, many sharp voices begging and threatening and laughing and arguing at once without listening to each other, exactly what humanity must sound like from far away; she is sure then that it is coyotes, many of them together. Nearby.

Anna glances back, but there is nothing behind her. Nothing she can see. Coyotes are common and she's never been frightened by them, but she's never encountered a pack of them at night on her own before, either. Only one or two at a time, in daylight that shows the texture of their sand and cream and black coats. She forces herself to walk faster until she can go no farther. Lungs stinging like sunburn, she rests, sitting with her back to the wide trunk of an old maple. The song of the coyotes ends, leaving no trace of them. She may as well have imagined it. Still, they have taken her calm from her. She takes off her glove to feel her cheeks and is surprised to find that they are still wet. She can see her breath, how quick and white and hollow it is.

If I were going to freeze to death, this is where I would stop . . .

Where is John? She wonders it with irritation. He should have found her by now, shouldn't he? It is awful for her to be out in the winter at night this way. But time feels strange, moves strangely in situations like these, and she has no idea how long she has been out, or how long she should expect such an errand to take.

The cold grips her legs, pulls her down again, since she has stopped walking. It pains her. She has always considered it a mercy that, before people die of hypothermia, their bodies feel warm to them one last time. She wonders if that means they stop shivering.

Don't be dramatic, she tells herself. *You're not freezing to death. Home is just around the corner.* She counts to four for each inhale, slowing her breath down.

Using the trunk for leverage, Anna drags herself to her feet and goes on. Two hundred and fifty feet farther down the trail, she emerges into her clearing, hers and John's, the little board house still standing against the darkness with the yellow kitchen light still shining through the windows and the chairs pushed back.

3

Anna fumbles with the doorknob. She opens the door too hard, and it bounces off of the stop. The knob makes a dent in the wall behind it that John will have to fix. She walks into a wave of heat and feels the door shut out the cold silence behind her.

"John! John!" she calls, throwing her wet gloves on the table. The ice maker in the refrigerator drops ice; the heater hums. She limps into the living room half expecting to find the television turned low, but it's off. "John?" Back in the kitchen, she glances into the mudroom, looking for his boots. Where they should have been, there is a smear of old mud and meltwater.

Anna half runs, half pulls herself up the stairs with the worn banister, calling John's name every few steps. The second floor is dark, but perhaps he's in bed, warming up and resting, waiting for her to get back. She opens their bedroom door and flicks on the light. The old four-post sits empty, the wedding ring quilt smooth. Untouched since that morning.

All of the rooms upstairs, bathrooms, closets, all are dark, all empty. Anna's skin tingles with the heat returning to its surface.

Moving more quickly now, fighting panic, Anna makes her way back down the stairs to the ground floor. The house cat chirps at her inquisitively but she pushes it away with her foot. She returns to the mudroom and listens for a few seconds at the door that leads to the cellar. It always sounds like water is dripping down the cinder blocks, though John swears nothing leaks down there. It is, more likely, the groans and pings of an old house settling. On nights John works late in his shop, Anna can almost believe she hears voices, but she can get carried away with her imaginings. It's really only mice.

She opens the white wooden door and tugs on the chain attached to the bare bulb overhead. The stairs stretch before her like a perspective drawing, all lines and shading. At the bottom, they disappear in shadow. She never goes into the cellar; it makes her dizzy, that feeling of being underground with no exit, that buried-alive feeling. It is older than the house and damp and has an earthen floor that has never been covered by any of its long history of owners. She doesn't descend this time, either; her hurt ankle causes her to be unsteady, and the darkness at the bottom of the stairs tells her that John isn't there.

There are still three places John could be. Anna decides to check the barn first. It would be just like John to get home and make sure Charlie was okay before anything else. He would want to know that the mule hadn't been injured in its wild flight through the trees. Anna turns on all of the remaining downstairs lights in the house before she leaves it, then pushes her aching body through the churned snow for what seems like the hundredth time that weary day.

She opens the barn door to find that the tack room light is already on. She switches on the fluorescents; they sizzle to life and hum. There's the sound of cloth and movement, and her heart leaps. But it is only the border collie, which has stood from its bed and stretched, and now trots toward her, wagging its tail and blinking against the sudden brightness of the overhead bulbs. Charlie is in his stall as she left him so long ago; he and the Icelandic horse, Keeper, look at her with too-bright eyes reflecting the glow of the light. Anna checks the tack room. She must be the one who left the light on there. The mule's saddle still sits on the floor where she threw it. With shaking hands, she replaces it on a saddle rack, its proper place.

She allows the border collie to come with her to check John's workshop, the old sugarhouse. The dog cavorts around her in uneven curves, leaping into the drifts, sometimes burying its face in the snow and grunting, snapping its teeth. She gets to the door and calls the dog toward her. Its tail hits her leg in a steady cadence as she turns the bolt. She feels braver with the dog beside her as she steps inside. The air is cold and still, smells of leather and oil and maple and winter. No one has been there for many hours.

As in the barn, the lights come on with a low buzz, dim at first. Everything in John's shop looks in order, just the way it had been the last time she'd sat with him and helped him to stamp a trail saddle with basketweave. The heavy-duty leather sewing machines sit covered and quiet. There are saddle trees arranged by material, type, and size on shelves along the wall. Rawhide stretches across the work table with patterns arranged across it. Anna recognizes most of the shapes—fenders, cantle, skirt. Shears, pliers, screwdrivers, and other tools are arranged in large coffee cans, the old metal kind that used to be in every grocery store. An antique potbellied wood-burning stove, not the kind with a window for viewing the fire, but the kind meant only for heat, sits in the center of the room. Anna touches the cold metal as she walks past. The dog follows her, leaving balls of snow from its pads on the wooden floor.

A phone and a well-used gray computer are in the corner alongside the safe. John reluctantly got internet only after one of his clients suggested they market their saddles online. Now most of their orders come through the computer. A once-colorful banner that says *Northeast Kingdom Saddle Co.* drapes across the wall over it—their way of trying to make the technology seem friendlier.

The message light on the shop phone blinks red. Despite their website's order form, John still averages about one phone order every week or two. Some people still like to do business the old way, he'd told her, preferred a voice to a screen. John's favorite customers are the locals, though—the people he meets in person and befriends.

The dog whines and pushes against her leg. Anna has been standing still for some time. She takes one last, long look around the sugarhouse before she turns off the light. Without John, the shop is just waiting for John, as if he has merely stepped out.

Anna makes her way to the detached garage, their only remaining outbuilding, slowly. Twenty feet from the house, it has the space for two cars if they are parked carefully, and both the four-wheel-drive farm truck and the hybrid car they use for rare road trips are kept within it. A thin layer of snow-covered ice coats the driveway, just enough to make it slick. Anna doesn't recall how long ago measurable snow fell, but it holds no tire tracks. She fights with the garage's walk-through door, which expands and jams into its frame every winter. It opens so suddenly, with the scrape of wood against wood, that Anna must catch herself to keep from falling.

Like the workshop, the dark garage has an air of waiting, but it has a dankness that the shop didn't have. Anna hesitates, hand on the light switch. She tries to feel the space around her and how much of it has been taken up. It smells faintly of gasoline and mildew. The concrete would be gritty if she bent to touch it, would dirty her fingers with motor oil. She can feel the grit under her feet. If the truck is gone, if John has come home and taken it, there will be an oil stain in a ragged oval where it was parked, with a few drops of fresher, darker oil from a slow leak covering it.

The border collie's tags clink from somewhere in the darkness as it sniffs past the corners of a room it is seldom allowed to enter. Anna turns on the light.

The truck and the small car are parked side by side, too large and quiet, taking up all the space between the walls.

Anna looks at them for a long time, then whistles for the dog, and it bounds past her and out into the night.

4

What bothers Anna most is that John will be hungry. Cold, too, but it won't be his first time caught overnight in the forest, and, as a rule, he learned in his younger days as a hiker and camper to carry his well-used pocket knife and a book of matches alongside the ink pen and notepad in his shirt pocket. He will know how to stay warm enough to survive. According to the morning's paper, the forecast low for the night is fifteen degrees Fahrenheit. They are only a few hours away from dawn.

Though resuming the search for John while it's dark would be fruitless, Anna can't make herself sleep. She lies down, then gets back up. Her whole body feels as though it's buzzing; the fatigue disorients, dizzies her. She fights the resulting nausea by chewing on a piece of ginger root. Her ankle throbs. Instead of resting, she packs and repacks saddle bags until she gets all she might need: John's winter socks and ski gloves, hand warmer packets, glow sticks, lip balm, snack-sized bags of mixed nuts, a bottle of water, a thermos of coffee that sticks a fair amount out of the top of the buckled bag, but not enough to tip. And she will bring her cell phone, still plugged in though the charge has been at 100 percent for some time.

Exhausted, Anna wipes down the kitchen counters, then waits at the table for the darkness to lessen. She pours the scalding coffee that remains at the bottom of the carafe into a mug and gulps it. The heat makes her cough, and she spills some of the dark liquid on her shirt and onto the table, where it spreads until she wipes it with her sleeve. The pain of it has jolted her awake, though her tongue turns to cotton with the burn.

She can't wait any longer.

She finds Keeper lying down when she enters the barn. She pauses outside his stall. He stands and shakes the straw bedding off his coat. He looks at her with large dark eyes, showing crescents of white at the edges, and nods his head. Charlie drowses with his chin resting on the stall door. Anna learned long ago how intuitive horses are—a mule even more so, since it has a share of the donkey's more agile mind. She wonders if Charlie might understand on some level what has happened, might know where to find John.

"Wake up, old boy," she says. He blinks at her, and she rubs his forehead. He flicks his long ears back and nudges her shoulder. She leans against him for just a moment, swallows the lump in her throat, then goes to the tack room. Saddle, blanket, bridle, brushes—Anna, already cold through her muscle and down to her bones, fumbles for everything she needs and sets it all in a pile outside of Charlie's stall.

The mule sighs and turns to look at her, but doesn't object, as Anna throws the saddle pad over the dried sweat mark from the day before. His coat is dull with the salt she hasn't taken the time to scrub away with the rubber curry, chalky where it is thickest. His back doesn't seem tender; she had pressed it before doing anything else, running her thumb and forefinger hard down both sides of his spine to see if he'd flinch. That at least is a good sign.

She swings up onto him as soon as they are outside the barn, leaving the mounting block standing like a small black buoy against the snow. She doesn't ride the mule often; he is wider than Keeper, and she has to open her hips painfully and twist her thighs inward to sit in a way that feels at all secure. She lets her foot with the swollen ankle hang outside its stirrup while she guides Charlie toward the barely visible gap in the trees.

The entrance to the path is like a blank window in a bedroom at night, a darker shade in a tableau of darkness. Knowing that Charlie can see far better than she can in low light, she keeps the reins loose and lets him find his own way through the frozen ground.

The mule begins to tense about twenty feet from the tree line. He stops hard, startling her. He lifts his head, ears pricked forward, listening. His stance is such that, if she had been riding a horse, Anna would have prepared for a spook. But Charlie almost never spooks. That's one reason John likes him. Anna holds the pommel of the saddle with one hand and concentrates on making herself relax while the mule stares into the woods and huffs his breath. His ribs move in and out, in and out under her legs. He feels unwieldy. She reaches down to stroke Charlie's neck, but it's as hard and cool as a slab of granite. "Come on," she tells the mule. She kisses to him, urges him forward with greater energy, pushing with her seat bones. He flips his nose in the air twice to tell her no, scratches the reins through the grip of her gloves, and plants his feet.

Anna knows she can't make a mule do anything it doesn't want to do. But Charlie hasn't balked before, and it frightens her. She takes a tighter hold on the pommel and tries wiggling her hanging foot to get it into the stirrup, to give her more to brace against if anything happens, but it hurts too badly to force her foot in, so she settles as deep into the seat as she can with her toes barely on the stirrup's edge. She seesaws the reins and nudges the mule with her heels, trying to get him off-balance enough to step forward, but he resists. If she didn't know him so well, she would call him dumb, unwilling, a coward. Against her better judgment, she pony-kicks the mule, bringing her legs hard to his sides to surprise him forward. He flinches and grunts with each kick, but he doesn't budge.

I don't have time for this. Anna drops the rein on one side and Charlie turns without hesitation and trots back the way they came. She slides off his back at the barn door, removes his bridle, and loops it over the saddle horn so that he carries it, tying a rope halter onto his head instead. She lets the lead rope drop to the ground. He stands ground-tied outside of the barn, eating snow while Anna saddles Keeper.

Maybe it makes more sense to take both the horse and mule, anyway, she reasons. John will need something to ride back, after all. If he is injured, she can tie him into Charlie's saddle to keep him steady, draped over his neck, the way she has seen in old Westerns. John will know how to tell her to do that, which knots to tie. In a past life, Charlie had been used to pack out elk for hunters. He would likely carry a hurt man gently despite an awkward distribution of loadweight. Anna doesn't wonder how she will heft an injured man onto a mule in the first place, only trusts that she can when the time comes, because she will have to. She ties a frayed lariat rope onto Keeper's saddle in case she needs it.

When she points him toward the barn door, Keeper nearly pulls Anna outside into the yard himself; the little horse is sharp and ready in the cold dawn air. His breath appears in a warm mist and dissolves again, steadily as the soft ticking of a watch; soon, ice will coat the guard hairs around his nose and mouth. She picks up Charlie's lead rope and holds it while she scrambles onto Keeper's back. She tells Keeper to walk. As the slack comes out of the lead rope, Charlie starts to walk, too, adjusting his strides to match the horse's, and Anna shortens the rope until the big mule's head is alongside her knee.

Soon they are facing the path again, the opening in the trees flat and ominous in the new gray light. Anna braces herself, expecting the mule to balk again and unseat her as she tries to hold on to the rope while Keeper walks on. Instead, the mule moves closer to the horse, nuzzling his large, honest face against Keeper's shoulder. Anna tugs the rope to back him up, worried he'll press too hard on her leg.

Keeper enters the woods with his ears pricked and neck arched. Anna has to keep a hold on his reins to keep him from breaking into a faster gait. She is amazed how much easier the path is to follow by the weak morning sun despite the way her blunders of the night before have confused the tracks. The horse beneath her loans her its courage and some of its warmth, and she feels comfortable bundled in her winter clothing in the crisp air. Less tired than she should be. Charlie occasionally hangs back, and Anna sometimes has to stop and pull on him to get him to catch up, especially where the path narrows between the trees. Beneath the creak and metal clink of the tack and the breath of the animals, Anna hears clumps of snow falling in cascades from branches too far in the woods for her to see.

They make good time to the place the tracks split.

The strengthening daylight causes the trees to cast deep blue shadows. Anna decides to stay on the trail this time and guides Keeper straight ahead, past her own footprints leaving the straightaway like a spirit's, footprints that she almost doesn't remember leaving, as if she had watched someone else do it. The snow is cleaner before them, and the tracks of the almost-forgotten injured deer sometimes cross the old, deep tracks of the mule. Behind Keeper, Charlie walks with lowered head, swiveling his ears forward and backward, listening to something only he can hear.

It's Charlie who tells Anna that she has found John. They have been walking for a while lulled into calm, enjoying the warmth of the sun on their backs in the clearings. Keeper has settled, too, and is striding out well but not rushing or pulling on the reins.

Without warning, the mule grunts low in his throat and sits back hard, pulling the lead rope through Anna's hand fast enough to burn a patch of material off the palm of her glove. Keeper spooks and jumps forward; Anna drops the end of Charlie's rope and grabs for her horse's mane as he spins and rears, snorting. The trees flash by in dizzying arcs. Anna feels like nothing at all is underneath her. She doesn't know how long she can hold on; her hands slip. Keeper stops and she slams back into the saddle crooked.

The horse snorts and blows, then stands trembling while Anna tries to gather herself. Her legs shake and she can put no weight on either ankle; doing so causes her feet to spasm in the stirrups. She can hear Charlie crashing back through the forest farther and farther away, and then he's gone. Anna curses. She has never liked the mule as much as John does.

Anna swings off of Keeper, needing to catch her breath and feel solid ground. She has forgotten about her injury and lands on the wrong foot. Pain shoots up her calf into her back, and she falls sideways against the horse. She stands still, heart pounding in her ears, and buries her face in his mane. His warmth and softness reassure her. She keeps a hand on his neck for stability even as he grows impatient with her and sidesteps away.

Something is ahead of them. Something that badly frightened the mule.

At first, all she can see atop the gentle rise in the small clearing is color, a shock against the monochromatic white and gray landscape. Rust, black, orange, blue. It has been arranged together like it has some kind of intention. It's almost beautiful. It reminds her of an amateur abstract painting she once saw in a local gallery, the tableau of shapes something fascinating, obscene, and obscure at the same time. She hadn't been able to look away from it. She blinks, trying to focus, and hobbles closer. There are pieces of color radiating off the center like waves of heat.

A plaid scrap of fabric, ragged at the edges, stained with brown, arranges itself at her feet. Anna takes her gloves off and picks it up. It is both wet and stiff; something is wrong about it, and her brain screams for her to drop it, but she holds it closer and makes herself look, turning it over and over in her hands. It's familiar. *Drop it*, she thinks.

It's from John's shirt.

She follows the pieces at her feet, her mind a cold blank. She can't make herself look ahead. When she does, the colors are too bright all the way to the center, a mass of reddish brown in the reaches of endless white. The coyotes had found him before her—him and what was left of the deer; a glance tells her that the backstraps and tenderloin have probably been stripped from the deer cleanly, with a knife, the head removed, and the rest torn and left ragged by teeth. She knows how hunger looks. The deer still has skin over its neck, fawn fur, a white tail that looks yellow against the white ground. And the body that is in the middle, the one she can't look at. How could something so awful exist?

"John?" Anna says. But it doesn't move, not even to breathe. Not even to look at her. She had known it wouldn't. It has too many holes in it.

Anna closes her eyes and counts, then opens them. It is still there. She has fallen to her knees, and the melting snow seeps into her jeans, spreads to her calves and thighs, a tide of cold and numb. Keeping her head turned to the side, gulping back bile, Anna bends and touches the trousers that are coated with ice. Her hand finds a sock, then a leg, the skin cold and stiff and smooth. She retches beside it, clutching the fabric helplessly.

Choking, swallowing in gulps, she feels her way to John's back pocket. His wallet is there, right where it ought to be. With trembling fingers, she opens it and looks at the thumb-sized photograph of the face she knows so well. It's too thin, too pale, too flat. She grips it so hard it could cut through her palm. They hadn't taken his "eating-out money," ten or fifteen dollars he kept for when he and Anna didn't want to cook.

An urge to turn the body seizes her. She can't stand to lift it where she will see the face. She worries the face has somehow vanished, become a blur, is featureless. But maybe she can roll the body toward her and keep her eyes at the waist and be okay. She grabs the tattered clothing on the right arm and leg and pulls. It is frozen to the ground and won't yield; she slips and falls backward twice.

She digs her feet deep into the snow to brace her lower legs. She pulls as hard as she can in jerks, but she can't get enough leverage. The motion has, however, worked the trinkets of John's shirt pocket out onto the ground. Shivering, Anna gathers the knife with the notched blade, the spoiled matches, John's cell phone (she flips it open, but it is dead, with droplets of moisture along the screen), and the pad of paper he kept for notes and ideas, which has a hole in the side and is glued closed with blood, ruined.

She sits back on her heels for a long time and watches the light changing over the body, how the shadows go from one side to the other, as if it is a tree or a stone. She is as chilled as the air and can't separate from it. Her legs fall asleep.

After a while, she tries to lie down beside John, but the position is too awkward. She doesn't want to touch him, he isn't real, but she takes his hand out of habit, tries to send her heat into it. She studies the rounded nails, the white scars where the awl and needle had slipped over the years and he had healed. She has no other place to be, no direction. Without him there, home is an empty box.

There's a shuffling behind her; Keeper nudges her hard in the back, and she looks up at him blearily; she had forgotten him. He snuffles her clothes, nuzzles her cheek, warming her in little disconnected patches. She touches his forehead with its star in the shape of Alaska. She has always liked his star. Of course, he will want his evening feed. She stands and gazes at him. He looks back at her with eyes as deep and calm as the night sky.

There must be the prints of a stranger's boots in the snow, a line going parallel to their own as he had tracked the deer by sight, waiting for it to weaken. Somewhere beside where she stands, there will be tire tracks, probably from an ATV, going off into the woods, venison in freezer bags in a cooler, the deer's head packed in ice. She doesn't search for the evidence; it must be so.

Sometime not long ago the poacher who had killed her husband would have flown through the darkness, getting far away from the woods where John had lived. Far away from her. But he wouldn't have gone so fast he'd get caught with the spoils of an untagged deer. He'd do that carefully, the way he had trimmed the deer's body to get what he wanted from it. John must have surprised him in his work, or just after he'd finished.

Later, she is glad she wasn't able to see John's eyes empty and meaningless, as they would have been without his life illuminating them. That she has no memory of that emptiness to carry.

She doesn't want to find the gun and doesn't search for it.

5

A nna wakes in bed, uncertain how she got there. She blinks against the insistent white light that spills through the open curtains. She awakes with the same feeling she has after a realistic nightmare, when she leaves sleep relieved to find that she hasn't taken the wrong plane after all, that she hasn't forgotten to pay an important bill, that she hasn't set the house on fire with the stove or run over the neighbor's cat, that she hasn't made some other disastrous and irrevocable mistake. Daylight usually corrects the dread of such a dream. But the feeling of wrongness lingers this time. Something is off. She feels so hot and uncomfortable, clammy, like she has been sick. She still wears her clothes from the day before.

John. She sits up too quickly, and her stomach lurches.

With one hand on the wall to steady herself, she limps down the stairs, her swollen ankle sometimes banging against the lip of a step and causing her to wince. It alternates between numbness and pain, but the numbness is worse. Her head aches. In the kitchen, the previous day's damp supplies are spread across the tile in muddy piles to dry. John's phone sits on the counter in a bowl of dried white rice. She hasn't tried to turn it on.

Anna can't get her boot over her ankle, so she tapes plastic trash bags over her socks and struggles outside. Though still cold enough to sting her skin, the air is warmer than it was the day before. The ground under its white blanket squelches as she makes her way across it. The mud feels lumpy and thick beneath her toes. She slips and catches herself several times. The choppy snow in front of the barn has begun to transition into slush.

She wrestles the barn door open, and the border collie runs to greet her, frantic in its enthusiasm. Keeper whinnies and hits his stall door with his hoof, a bad habit he resorts to if she is late to feed him. The sound cracks and echoes in the barn aisle; Anna cringes and covers her ears until it stops. Keeper seems too alert. It seems strange to Anna that she is alive and safe and in the barn. Everything looks too bright, sounds too loud.

Charlie sulks in his stall with his rump toward her. He doesn't look at her though she pauses and speaks to him. What has happened? Her memory has chasms. She must have found him after he had taken off. No one else would have caught him, stripped him of tack, and deposited him in his stall. Only her. He hasn't been groomed; neither has Keeper. But they do have water. She must have seen to that, at least.

Anna moves through sand, unable to make herself focus. It's as though her vision has slanted; she has no balance. She walks from Keeper's stall to the tack room several times, forgetting what she is doing. The undeterred dog weaves around her legs. Keeper paws at his stall door again, and she sets out the buckets.

While their beet pulp soaks, Anna tidies the tack room. All of the tack has been dumped beside the door in a pile. Barn dust and prickly bits of hay coat the saddles and pads, and the pads are still wet. She grows frustrated trying to untangle the bridles—the buckles and straps of leather seem like they have turned inside out and fastened together somehow. The cheek of Charlie's halter has caught on something and torn so that the leather is held to itself by a bare fiber. In frustration, she lays the dirtiest tack on the table to clean later. The feed is ready.

Anna brushes the animals as they eat. Charlie only picks at his feed, but Keeper has a good appetite. Dried foam streaks

Keeper's sides, and he pins his ears if she presses too hard on his ribs. They must have had a hard ride home, she and the little horse. She tries again to remember it, but her effort only makes the headache worse.

Charlie has small scratches down his sides from branches, and a tender nose, probably because he had stepped on his lead rope and jerked his head down while he had run. He chews slowly and watches Anna with one eye while she brushes him. She doesn't quite trust him not to bite or kick her. Every time his ears go back, she holds her breath. Is he angry or just listening? They will have to learn to trust each other again, and the thought makes Anna tired. It was John who had wanted a mule. Anna had argued that they were not as simple as horses—had longer memories, nursed tempers, held grudges, could be quirky or aggressive if not handled carefully. But that was exactly why John had wanted one. Because mules can be so incredibly loyal. But you have to earn everything they give you. You have to work to deserve a good mule.

It's as if Charlie resents Anna for taking him back to a man that wasn't really his version of John.

John. As she cares for the horse and mule, Anna's day starts to feel to her almost the same as every other day. But it isn't the same. She can see the body spread in the snow as clearly as if she still stood before it. That rough, broken shape, empty now, had been John.

She can pretend it is like every other day for a while, if she wants. She could spend hours waiting for John's work in the shop to end, watch for him to come back inside to where she waits, where she looks through the window and feigns being busy at his approach. Her reliance on him was a secret she had kept from him, knowing he wouldn't approve. He had probably kept small secrets from her, too; it was only natural. He probably would have told her anything, if she'd asked, but that wasn't their way.

Anna knows she will have to learn to stop waiting for him. If she keeps waiting now, she will wait forever. She will never see him walk into the kitchen again.

She gives the horse and mule enough hay to keep them content until morning. When she leaves the barn, she calls the border collie, and it runs after her.

There is so much to do, and she doesn't know where to start. The immensity of it overwhelms her. The coldness of her feet travels up her legs as she pushes through the sludge back to the house, wobbling on the swollen ankle. In the mudroom, she sits on the dirty floor and peels off the plastic bags, leaving them balled up by the door. She goes into the kitchen and begins to put the dried outerwear and contents of the saddlebags away. The border collie, which has never been allowed into the house, runs from room to room in a frenzy, sniffing and sneezing in the corners.

Once she finishes tidying up, Anna sits at the table and looks around the space, clean and quiet but for the hum of the refrigerator. *When will John come in?* He will want something hot for dinner on a day like this—she takes leftover hamburger patties from the fridge—then she glances out the window toward the shop, is ashamed and chastises herself for forgetting so quickly. Strange that nothing will change in the house now unless she changes it; she won't find snacks left out or mysterious trackings of dirt on the tile. All waste and effort will belong to her.

The cat jumps into her lap, and she strokes it down the spine so that it lifts its back and purrs. She sees herself as if from far away, a tiny aging woman alone in a diorama, a little isolated container with toy furniture. Outside, the shadowed mountains on either side mean she lives in the tense place between colliding plates of earth, and there are spreads of kettles and kames like burial mounds, too, left by frozen rivers gone extinct, and somewhere in the stands of elm and maple, ash and pine, there are teeth. There is a gun. She shudders. Her body is dull and buzzy;

she's probably in shock. She is supposed to drink something with sugar in it for shock, isn't she? But she can't make herself move. It's all right now, really, this lack of feeling.

She has other chores, and so much to do. Someone ought to call the sheriff. But she doesn't have the energy for it just yet, doesn't know how to say to someone else that John is gone, can't imagine leading uniformed men back down the path with their stretcher and questions and tape. And then, to see him again . . . to know that he isn't really there. That somehow, he isn't there. She is tired.

The dog snores near her feet, where it lies curled and twitching its paws. Anna sits still until it gets dark outside, then she sits in darkness. She has never liked darkness before, but now it almost seems merciful, blind. *When is John coming in?*

The sound of plastic sliding across the countertop startles her, then the muffled thud and rainstick sound of rice spilling across the tile. The cat has knocked John's phone onto the floor. *John.* Anna gasps, gropes her way out of the chair, and limps to the light switch.

The light fills the room with yellow and makes the night outside the windows look flat and black. Anna's face floats pale against the glass. She closes the curtains and turns to the mess. She picks the phone up out of the spilled rice and studies it. White rice dust and patches of sticky grime coat it unevenly, but it doesn't appear to be damaged. She plugs the charger in, hesitates while the kitchen clock loudly counts off the seconds, then flips it open and tries to turn it on.

At first, the trick seems like it didn't work. She holds the power button down and counts to three, but upon its release, the screen stays black. She tries it again, holds the button for what seems like far too long. Finally, the phone sounds a metallic tone. A circle in the center of the screen spins and spins while the phone recalls itself. A notification of missed calls pops up, and Anna selects it. All of them are from her. If she selects voicemails, they will all be from her, too. The phone is slow, but it functions.

She clears the notifications and finds the texts. She has left notifications for John there, as well. The last one John sent was the one to her. It has a timestamp of 11:05 a.m., two days ago. Two days ago, that's all. But she hadn't gotten it then. Everything had gone wrong. It must have been delayed by lack of service, perhaps by some cruel circumstance, a solar flare. It wouldn't be the first time that happened. So when John had told her he was nearly there, what he must have really meant was not that he was close to home, but that he knew he was close to finding the deer.

She wouldn't have been worried yet. She would have been close to opening a can of tomato soup. The hands holding the phone shake; she looks at them as though they are separate from her body, and she doesn't bother trying to control them.

When did she last try to call John? When had she given up on reaching him that way? If she understands the time, maybe she can reorient herself in this unfamiliar place. She navigates to the call log. She had called him thirty-seven times, the last one yesterday morning at 4:00. She selects the outgoing call log and freezes.

There, at 1:38 p.m. two days ago, a call had been made. John had tried to call 911. It has the red X beside it in the log, indicating it had failed to go through. The call before that, at 1:36, showed that he had tried to call her, too. Anna stares blankly at it. *Oh.*

She slips to the kitchen floor still holding the cell phone. Its charger pulls from the socket and clatters down beside her. Rough sobs overwhelm her and bruise her ribs with their force; she can't breathe, and the border collie pads to her in alarm and rubs against her, whining and licking her face.

John had still been alive when the poacher left. He had been hurt, but alive. He had been waiting for her. How long had it taken for him to die alone among the silent trees, knowing that no one would come for him? Was it before the coyotes came?

Anna wakes some time later on the tile, propped against the cabinets, cramped and aching, cold but for where the dog lies against her side. *What time is it?* She squints to see the clock that ticks from the kitchen wall. *When will John come in?*

6

A nna decides not to have a funeral. Neither she nor John had ever purchased life insurance; their mortgage had been paid off several years before, and they had had no children. Besides the cost of a funeral, there is the difficulty of arranging one. Anna can't bring herself to do it. The calls and the decisions. The sympathy, the questions, the morbid curiosity. What food to serve. What kind of flowers to buy. It's worse even than planning a wedding—there isn't any chance for happiness at the end.

And where to even start? Anna can't convince herself that it matters. John wouldn't have cared anything about flowers, would have rejected the ceremony of death and resented the invasion of their home and privacy. A funeral would be a formality at best attended by Anna, a handful of meddlesome neighbors, perhaps, and John's local customers, people who could just as easily be strangers.

Anna had been closest to John and needs no more closure than what she has gotten. She can't justify making such an effort for the benefit of people who had only been at the periphery of their lives.

No, there's no good reason for a funeral.

Anna is alone for the first time. The ankle, which had not been badly injured as Anna thought, heals. The days pass in silence and all have the same shape. Without John, she has no reason to use her voice. It starts to sound strange to her when she does.

She speaks rarely to the animals in passing, and the sound of it almost always surprises her. She enters their world, one in which language depends mostly on movement or posture and sound isn't often needed for understanding. Anna, the cat, the border collie, the horse, the mule, and the chickens live together in peaceful, if bewildering, routine. Every day, the same.

Anna has no real reason to cook meals, either. She twice forgets and makes something that John would have liked, but ends up throwing the food out when she realizes what she has done, feels guilty, and loses her appetite. She is often angry with herself. She lives on cereal until the milk sours. Then she lives on the family-sized bag of potato chips that once had been lost on the top shelf of the pantry. Over two weeks, she loses fifteen pounds, but this shrinking doesn't bother her. She is drawn in, unattached to her body or its hunger.

The cat eventually runs out of food. She pours the last few kernels from the crinkles of the bag into the bowl, but it isn't nearly enough to get through the day. The cat gulps and crunches, then rubs its lithe figure against her leg, asking for more. Anna shuffles through what is left in the pantry. There is no canned food left for it, either. No tuna, no chicken. There's nothing that would be healthy for a cat, even if a cat could be made to eat it.

She will have to go into town.

Anna hasn't driven for a long time, though she renews her driver's license by mail every time it comes close to expiring, and as far as the state of Vermont knows, she is physically capable and in good standing. Really she hasn't felt safe enough to drive, isn't alert enough, reacts slowly. But there's no way around it. She leans against the counter indecisively for several minutes while the cat meows, running through scenarios in her head—slipping on ice and running off the road, swerving too late to avoid a loose cow or moose, flipping over and over, ground and sky rushing past the windows until she lands in the ditch, helpless and bleeding— She jerks the keys from their hook.

The garage smells of grease and clutter. It exhales dry chill and staleness like a freezer.

The farm truck has snow chains on the tires; she unlocks it and gets in. In the dusty interior, she runs her hand over the smooth steering wheel, over the cracked dash, feels the handle of the gearshift. What is driving like? She almost has it. If she doesn't overthink herself into inaction, she can do it. She turns the key and the truck shudders and dies. She tries again, and it catches and holds. It has over half a tank of gas.

She inches out into the driveway and puts the truck in park. The garage door closes behind her with finality while the truck idles. She touches again the gearshift, steering wheel, gauges, as if she is handling artifacts in a museum. She tries the blinker both ways. She turns the lights on and off, then back on. She swipes the windshield wipers once across the windshield, though the windshield fluid is frozen, and the rubber edges screech and only smear the dust.

The road lies ahead of her by about fifty yards. She eases the truck into drive and carefully lifts her foot. The truck coasts too quickly to the end of the driveway and skids to a stop partway into the road. Her knees scream with the effort of braking. Anna grits her teeth and puts one hand on her right knee to massage it. She has a long way yet to go.

Belbridge is about ten miles away—three by dirt road and the rest paved and winding. It is a proud, if poor, town. Its residents boast to outsiders that the famous Governor Aiken had Belbridge specifically in mind when he named the Northeast Kingdom—that the town's independent inclinations, the rugged beauty of its land, and the plentifulness of its game animals evoked royal associations. Belbridge hosted many of the governor's fishing trips. The snowshoe, bait, and sporting goods store he frequented still stands.

Anna has always felt invisible in town, overlooked. People spoke to John instead of her.

She takes a deep breath, flips the blinker on, and turns away from the house. The truck noses forward onto the street. She straightens it and lets it crawl forward until she gets the feel of it. She pushes the gas, but nothing happens at first; she pushes harder and her breath catches as the truck jumps forward. The wheel shakes in her hands. John had intended for years to fix the loose steering.

The level of alertness Anna has to keep up to drive exhausts her. At every thick clump of trees, she expects a deer to run across. She worries that hikers or horseback riders will appear without warning ahead of her, that she will hit them, ruin all of their lives. Maybe a timber hauler has lost some logs in the road up ahead, and her truck will barrel into them; she will be stranded. Maybe a milk truck has stalled. Such things have been known to happen.

At the stop sign before the pavement, she puts the truck in park again and rests. Her hands ache from gripping the wheel; her back and shoulders ache from the way she crouches forward; her knees ache with pushing the gas pedal and then the brakes over and over. She sighs and leans back.

A honk startles her, and she looks into the rearview mirror to see a car waiting. She turns on the blinker, waves apologetically to the driver behind her, and turns onto the highway.

At Belbridge Grocery, she finds a space away from other cars. She listens to the engine click while it cools. Sitting alone and tired in the truck reminds her of her last day at work, years ago. She and John had known she was sick, but not what was wrong. She never looked sick on the outside. She had arrived home from the office a few minutes before he had, and he had found her sleeping in her car in the garage, the overhead door closed, her car still running. No, she had told him, she hadn't been depressed, nothing like that. Only very tired. The garage had been cool and quiet when she closed the overhead door, and she had simply fallen asleep. He had been so shaken after that.

Had he not come home in time, she may have died. The incident had at least shortened the list of possible diagnoses: multiple sclerosis, chronic fatigue, an autoimmune or neurological disorder. Anna sits in the cab of the truck watching people go in and out of Belbridge Grocery until enough cold air seeps in to drive her out.

The store seems too bright and open. The labels on the shelves, seen together, are garish. The piped-in music is too loud and fast. It occurs to Anna that she may as well stock up so that she can limit her trips, so besides cat food, dog food, and carrots for the horses and chickens, she picks up items that won't spoil—cans of soup, canned pasta, canned milk, peanut butter, John's favorite wine. She fills her basket, though she hasn't felt real hunger for a long time. It makes her feel better somehow to know that her pantry will be full. It feels normal.

The cashier recognizes her.

"Here without your other half today?" she asks.

Anna studies her name tag but can't read the name. "Yes, I'm afraid so," she says.

"I hope John is well." The scanner beeps steadily in the background.

"He's busy in his shop. Lots of orders," Anna says. That she can lie so easily surprises her. But the grocery store is not the place to talk about a dead husband, or how quickly one's entire world can change.

"Well, I hope he likes soup," the cashier says, holding up a can and smiling. "This is enough to last through the apocalypse."

Anna's words come as if unburied from a great depth. "It warms you up in the winter," she says.

"I prefer mulled mead, myself," the cashier tells her.

A man Anna doesn't recognize gets into line behind her. Anna pays for her groceries and stands out of the way while she digs her key out of her coat pocket.

"How are you today, Mackie?" the cashier asks.

"Fair to middlin'," he says.

"Is that right?"

"You seen any strangers in here?" he asks.

"No, not lately. But I've been off for the last couple of days. Why?"

"Poachers again," the man says. "Cut my fence and took a whitetail. They cut off its head, took some backstraps, and left most of it to rot."

"Harder to get caught that way," the cashier suggests. "The meat's easier to hide."

They both notice Anna staring at them at the same time.

"Ma'am?" the man says. "Are you all right?"

"Where do you live?" Anna asks. "If you don't mind my asking."

"West of town a few miles," the man says.

Out toward our place. "What can we do about them, do you think?" Anna asks. "The poachers?"

"You got poachers at your place this year, too?"

Anna hesitates. "We've seen signs," she says. "We're worried we might."

"Well, there's not much you can do. Even if you catch them red-handed, they're hard to convict," he tells her. "You should put up some trail cameras. Check your fences and gates and make sure they're all still up and working. If one poacher sees that someone else has plowed through your fence, he'll be less shy about going in himself."

"Thank you," Anna says.

"Yes, ma'am. And make sure you post *No Trespassing* signs everywhere. That way you'd have a leg to stand on in court."

"*No Trespassing.* Got it," Anna says.

"Ma'am?" the man says.

"Yes?"

"Be careful. These guys are out in the woods getting drunk and shooting at whatever moves. Lots of them have buck fever."

Buck fever, Anna thinks to herself. She should look that up later.

The man is saying, "Most are just idiot kids, but some of them will do anything not to get caught. It wasn't more than a few years ago that a poacher killed a park ranger by beating him to death with one of those big flashlights." He looks at her with his brow wrinkled in concern. "What I mean is, don't get too close. Let them do what they're going to do, then call the police after they leave."

"I will," Anna says.

As she leaves, the talk turns, as it often does, to weather.

She ought to do more while she is in town—buy the *No Trespassing* signs that the man suggested, replace John's lost rifle—but by the time she has loaded the groceries into the passenger side of the truck, Anna has run out of energy.

The truck starts more easily than it did before, but she has to back out of the space, and turning her head to check for parking lot traffic hurts her neck. She puts the truck in reverse, and after a couple of near-misses, angles out of the spot despite the car that has to stop behind her. Its driver gestures at her, but she is out; she waves and mouths *I'm sorry*, then puts the truck into drive with relief.

The way home seems much longer and colder than the way into town. Clouds have matted together again; the sky hovers close and gray, stifling her. The road has grown busier, and she doesn't feel comfortable driving at the speed of the traffic. The cars stack up behind her on the curves and fly by her on the straight with breathtaking acceleration, then swerve in front of her with just enough clearance to avoid clipping the truck's bumper. Anna feels herself starting to panic. A mile or two before she gets back to the dirt road, there's a wider shoulder, and she allows herself to park there for half an hour until her hands stop shaking and her heart rate slows.

By the time she pulls into her garage, not bothering to back into it the way John used to, exhaustion has overtaken her body. She hasn't felt such a widespread aching since the last time she was bucked off a horse, in her twenties. If not for the danger of the food freezing and bursting its containers, she would leave it in the truck until morning. She unloads it instead an armload at a time, carrying it all to the porch first, and then taking it from the porch into the kitchen.

The cat eats its kibble as if it is starving. It's so eager in its hunger, though its hunger was short-lived. Anna decides she should probably heat up some soup for herself.

Chicken and rice. She waits for the watery stuff to cook, for the gelatin of chicken fat to melt, watching the tiny cardboard cubes of meat float in the pan as she stirs. Once the soup steams, she pours it into a bowl and sits down at the table. She eats a few bites, letting the liquid sit on her tongue for several seconds before swallowing. It warms her, makes her feel cared for.

The cat finishes crunching its dinner and leaves; the kitchen falls into silence. The border collie snores from somewhere in the next room. Anna can hear the breeze in the tops of the trees that ring the yard. She hadn't meant to eat the entire bowl of soup, but it is gone, leaving a line of yellow grease that clings to the sides of the porcelain.

For a while, Anna sits at the table waiting, as she so often had when it was almost time for John to come in from his work. It had felt as though her day couldn't move forward otherwise. She misses the rush of cold from the opening door, the sound of his soles hitting the floor as he stomped the snow from his boots.

She clears her dishes and drops the empty soup can into the trash bin in the pantry. The receipt from the grocery store has fallen onto the floor beside it, and she picks it up. She hadn't even paid attention to the total. John's work had been their only source of income. How much money does she have left in checking? How long will their savings account last? She has no idea; he had always done the finances, told her when to pay each bill. She frowns. The logistics of her survival haven't occurred to her before with so much else on her mind. She folds the grocery receipt carefully and puts it into the pile of bills on the counter that will soon come due, intending to make a budget soon.

She calls the shop phone to hear John's voice on the outgoing voicemail message, as she has gotten into the habit of doing two or three times a day, and always before trying to sleep. But instead of his mild tenor, a machinated female voice tells her that the mailbox is full.

After looking at the rates listed in the paper, Anna decides not to run an obituary, either. There doesn't seem to be a point in spending the money if there's no memorial or funeral to announce. She can just as easily tell people the news one at a time. Surely John's friends know what sort of person he was, what his many talents and accomplishments were, and don't need a paragraph to prove it. Don't need to remind each other of something no one who had appreciated John could possibly forget.

Mild-mannered John. He had seemed so amiable that people who didn't know better tried to take advantage of him, but they soon ran into that unwavering core of strength that Anna had come to rely on. He gave much, but he had never compromised. John, who besides being devoted to Anna, had adored stray pets and the children of strangers, who always stopped when he saw a baby and tried to make it laugh. She had seldom seen him lose his temper, and never for his own sake—because he was wronged—but because someone or something else had been wronged. It was for her that they had moved to this cold, lonely region where she might feel safe from the uncertain, often cruel world that had seemed always just outside the window before.

Here, they had finally been able to build a home exactly as they had wanted it, or close to it. Here, her sickness and all of her faults had become manageable. She had regained some control of her life.

John, who had been more social than she was, had given up a fuller existence, perhaps, to provide her with one of relatively little stress, one in which she could heal from her unpredict-able limitations and a lifetime of hurts and worries she couldn't count. It was John who had shown her that care for something could so often be equated with sacrifice. John who had pushed without complaint through the snow in the darkness to make sure the animals' water hadn't frozen. John who couldn't let a deer bleed to death slowly and painfully. John hadn't ever been able to stand seeing the innocent suffer, and he had seen her as an innocent.

Over the years, the thing they had learned to value most had been their peaceful wilderness home, of which they were both a part. John had helped her through illness, through sor-row and loss, through all the unintentional disappointments of a well-meaning marriage, gracefully and with good humor. And she had loved him.

An obituary wouldn't really be important to anyone but her—she is the one who would cut it from the newsprint and keep it—but she doesn't need it.

7

Anna opens the door of the saddle shop. The dust lifts into the air where she stands and floats in the morning light. She sneezes. The way the shop has changed during its short time without John in it surprises her. The air smells dank; a mustiness has settled over the clean oiled scent of the leather. The corners hold cobwebs.

Anna can see the red light on the shop phone blinking from its corner. She makes her way to it, the border collie zigzagging in front of her so that she nearly trips. She lifts the phone off of its cradle and dials into voicemail.

The messages sound like they come from far away.

"This is Colin," the first says, "checking on the progress of the saddle I ordered in October. Could you please give me a call back?"

"Hello, my name is Ondrea Castille. I was looking at your saddles online and wanted to speak to you about possibly placing an order. I have a horse with mutton withers and nothing seems to fit her. Can you help?"

"Yes, you have my saddle in for repairs. Fixing the seat and re-stitching around the skirt. I was wondering if I could pick it up soon? This seems to be taking a long time." Anna winces at the irritation that hovers under the polite words.

There are eleven new messages total, four from clients checking the status of their orders, and seven from people who want to place orders.

There are several saddles in differing states of disrepair or construction scattered around the sugarhouse. Anna had intended to delete the messages, clear the mailbox, and retreat back to her kitchen, but the voices nag at her more than she expected them to. Does she owe them an explanation? A refund? John would never ignore his customers, she is certain. He would be ashamed that they had received no answers. He would try to make it right, keep them happy. The dog, out of habit, has settled on its saddle blanket bed near the cold woodstove, as though it plans to be there for hours. Anna feels bad about that, too. Despite the shop's chill, John's presence lingers in it as though he has only just stepped out. He had loved this place. The dog wags its tail as Anna works on lighting the firewood that had been piled inside the stove by John in readiness for his next day's work.

Anyone should be able to light a fire when the wood has been prepared for them. Anna holds the lighter irresolutely, studying how John had stacked the wood, as a sort of scaffold with the largest logs on the bottom and the smaller logs perpendicular over those; the top layer is kindling. She tries to memorize its architecture. *This must be the best way to build a fire.* Shouldn't anyone who lives in the Kingdom find starting a fire as natural as breathing?

She lights the kindling and it catches and flares bright orange, but smokes and burns out within seconds. "Huh," she says. The dog doesn't even raise its head. John used to make this look so easy. In frustration, Anna spends several minutes trying to light kindling and some of the smaller pieces of firewood, holding the lighter on underneath them until her thumb hurts from pressing down the igniter wheel. At best, she gets a weak flame that struggles and then dies. It can't burn; it is malnourished and fickle.

Of course, fire is alive, it needs something; it needs air. Something to feed it. Anna lights the edge of a bit of kindling and, instead of closing the front of the stove when the kindling catches this time, she leaves it wide open. She steps back as the paper turns black, then coughs when the space near the stove fills with smoke. The fire has gone out again.

She has almost decided to give up and accept the cold when the wind whistling in the chimney pipe reminds her that the stove has a flue that allows air in. She studies the diagram molded into the metal of the cast-iron stove under the flue lever. One side means open, one side means closed. She isn't sure which is which, but she moves the lever to the opposite side of where it was.

After much trial and error, long after the dog has shifted to a quieter corner of the shop, Anna can feel the warmth begin to radiate from the fire she has built. She looks at the clock; it has taken her just under two hours to light a fire that keeps. And she has no idea how to put it back out if needed. So she will stay, she tells herself, until it burns out.

The heat emanates into the air around the stove, and she stands close to it until her calves get too hot, enjoying the improvement in temperature.

Though hungry again, she doesn't want to eat. She takes her time walking around the sugarhouse looking at the saddles. She finds the one that must be the repair order in the voicemail and looks at the yellow tag John had attached. It shows the customer's name, phone number, and address—a local. John didn't make this saddle; its latigo keeper has the stamp of one of the bigger brands. He had finished replacing the suede seat and had stitched a looping pattern into it, but the skirt still needs stitching, and the saddle needs to be cleaned— "knock the dust off," as John would say.

Anna walks to the row of leather-stitching machines and removes the cover from the one John most often used. It still has thread in it. She had watched John work with this machine many times, running the leather under the thick needle with slow, deliberate movement, but she has never used it herself. She sits in front of it, turns it on, and lifts the foot. How different could it be from sewing a spring jacket or mending a blanket for a horse, anyway?

But there is no way to maneuver a heavy Western saddle in order to stitch it the way she would a piece of cloth or canvas. Even if the table wasn't in the way of her turning the saddle under the foot under the machine, she doesn't have the strength to turn it. It weighs somewhere between thirty and thirty-five pounds. Surely John hadn't used the machine to do repairs like this one. Or he had had some trick at his disposal which she doesn't.

Anna sets the saddle on the floor and looks around the sewing table. On the shelves behind the machines, next to the bins of awls and rows of scrap leather, she spots a spool of thick white thread with a needle stuck through it. Of course—the holes had been made in the leather of this saddle long ago—she can stitch the skirt by hand, using the holes that are already there. It will be tedious work, but she can do it.

She threads the needle and sits with her eyes closed, trying to concentrate. She hadn't paid enough attention to John. He had done repairs like this, sewing, his hands going in and out with a regular sway, a waltz, one-two-three, one-two-three. That's it: the needle ought to be in the middle of the entire length of thread, the thread shouldn't be folded over. She had found that strange before, having only done home sewing herself. But this type of sewing differs; it's like a knot is tied front to back with each stitch. Yes, now she can picture it.

After finding the hole on the near side of the skirt, Anna runs the needle through it, enjoying the hiss of the smooth thread through the opening. Now that she has begun, finishing is a matter of weaving. She uses an awl from one of the metal cups of tools to push the thread from the back through, crossing it with the thread from the front. She pulls each stitch tight. After several minutes, she has created a neat row that runs along the edge of the skirt and under the fender of the stirrup. *So far, so good*. There is much to go, but it's a start.

She loses track of time as she works, stopping only to feed the animals. Sometimes she gets the thread tangled up in itself and has to work it back through and fix it. Unsnarling it can be difficult with the poor circulation in her hands. She runs out of thread once and has to tie off the stitches and open another spool. By the time she finishes, it's dark out. Tired, Anna steps back to look at the completed skirt, her hair stuck to her clammy face, fingers bruised from near-misses with the needle. No, it isn't perfect, but it is probably good enough. It will pass.

Since she has stopped concentrating on the sewing, feeling returns sharply to her fingers. They are cold and cramped. The fire has gone out. Cracked orange coals glow in the ashes. She throws another log in, and the stove is miraculously still hot enough for the wood to catch on its own. *I can do this*, she tells herself.

She brushes the saddle off, oils it, and buffs it with a soft towel. With her throat tight, she picks up the shop phone and calls the number on the yellow tag, hoping it isn't too late yet; it feels much later than it actually is.

The phone rings several times before someone answers. "Hello?"

"Yes," Anna says, her voice thin and tinny. "This is Anna with Northeast Kingdom Saddle Company. I'm calling for Walt."

"Speaking."

"I'm so sorry for the delay." She clears her throat to stall; she should have thought of what to say before she dialed. "My husband John . . . has been ill," she says. "But he's just finished your saddle repairs if you'd like to pick it up."

"Just in time," the voice says. "My horse has been eating his head off for the last few weeks and forgetting all his training. Could I pick it up tonight? I'd like to work him tomorrow."

They make the arrangements and she hangs up. The total, according to John's yellow tag, comes to four hundred dollars:

three hundred for the beautiful new suede seat, one hundred for the stitching. It seems a good wage for the work the two of them have done.

While she waits for the customer to arrive, Anna reads the yellow tags on the other saddles. Three of them are stock saddles—saddles John made in his spare time to sell for a slightly lower price than the custom ones when a client didn't want to wait. There are three well-worn demo saddles of different tree widths. The other five are custom orders. John had written the details out with care; the first says: "Size fifteen inch, seven inch gullet, wide tree, flared bars. No horn. Oak leaves tooling. Natural leather with chocolate seat." Each has a completion date penciled in. So far, only one is late, but the rest are coming due within two weeks.

At a knock at the door, Anna calls, "Come in." It hadn't occurred to her to straighten up the shop before the customer appeared, but at least the shop is warm.

A balding older man bundled in a tan coat steps inside and spots his saddle immediately on its stand by the sewing table.

"Anna, I think you said? I'm Walt," he says, and nods toward the saddle. "That one mine?"

"Yes," Anna says, lightheaded. "It's all done."

He walks around it in silence. Then he looks up. "It looks a lot different," he says. "My wife didn't think it was worth the money to get it fixed. Now it's good as new. Finally, an argument I get to win." He laughs, and Anna smiles politely.

"Yes," Anna says. "John does good work. And once again, I apologize for the delay. I'll give you a twenty-five dollar discount to make up for it."

After the man leaves, Anna rests by the stove, turning the $375 check over and over in her hands.

8

A
nna comes in from the shop tired but reassured. Here is a way to keep going. She eats a late meal at the kitchen table with the dog and the cat at her feet for company, and the house seems less empty than before. But not long after she finishes dinner, she is reminded of her danger, her isolation. The coyotes call in moans and yips that carry on for a quarter of an hour, slicing through the night's stillness and echoing off the trees. It seems like they will never stop. The sound is both close and wide, as though they have surrounded the house.

Anna can't see anything outside the dark window but her own reflection on the glass. She wraps up in a blanket and perches on the edge of the couch while the border collie sits stiffly by the door, listening. She snaps at it for whining and pawing where the weather stripping has peeled and the outside air flows in a cold stream into the house, carrying the noise with it.

After those wild tongues have quieted, the snow starts in glittering crystals and falls in thick silence all night. Anna wants to call the shop phone to hear John's voice again, now that she can, but something about the idea of the phone ringing alone in the darkness of the shop bothers her. She sleeps fitfully.

Under the pale morning sun, which is really only a bright circle behind the cloud cover, the ground looks fresh and white. Two or three inches of new snow smooth Anna's older foot-prints, and she slips a little as she makes her way to the garage, her breath a warm mist behind her scarf.

She has planned every detail of her commute this time. She

took acetaminophen with her breakfast to ward off the arthritic pains. She boosted her mind as best she knew how, mixing coconut oil, blueberries, and walnuts into her oatmeal and allowing herself a larger cup of coffee than usual. The extra caffeine makes her buzzy. Her heart jumps and flips with the stimulation, and her stomach hollows as it warms, but she feels alert and ready. More capable than usual. She must be having a good day.

She guesses that the least busy time to drive will be around 9:30 a.m.—well after office work has started and businesses have opened, but well before lunch. If she completes any errands before 10:45, she can be back home and off the road before traffic hits. No more creeping along watching other cars gathering in a line in her rearview mirror. Far less stress.

Her body still holds the memory of what it is like to drive the truck. This time, its rough idle and the loose weight of its steering don't surprise her. She backs smoothly to the end of the driveway and onto the dirt road, though she can feel the snow trying to pull the truck crooked, and her knee aches from braking before she even leaves her property line. But the pain is tolerable. She makes herself relax before allowing the truck to coast forward toward town.

The credit union, only a block off of Main Street, comforts her with its pile carpet and polished wood. Though the building is small, it leaves an impression of longevity, competence. The heater murmurs, white noise, almost too hot. She and John have banked there the whole time they have lived just outside the boundaries of Belbridge, and not much about it ever changes. It is hardly ever busy. Only one of the two tellers has a customer.

She walks to the counter with the check, signed on the back by herself as an authorized agent of the Northeast Kingdom Saddle Company. The teller deposits it without question, gives her a receipt, and asks if she needs anything else.

Anna hesitates. "Actually, yes," she says. "How would I find out the balance of my account? And how much I spend every month?"

"I can give you statements for the last couple of months if you like," the teller says. "Of course, if you use online banking, you'll have access to everything all the time."

"Online banking?" Anna asks. "How do I do that?" She can picture herself at the shop computer, toasty from the fire licking the inside of the stove, doing the accounts while the dog sleeps at her feet; she could take care of her obligations that way without involving anyone else.

The teller gives her a sheet of instructions, her account number, and a temporary password. Anna folds it and puts it into her coat pocket.

The interaction has only taken fifteen minutes. It has gone well. Anna glows with capability. She had been living in a bubble that has popped; she can touch the world again—there is no film between it and her, as there was before. The sidewalks and storefronts look sharp and appealing. *What else do I need?* Anna asks herself. Her feet feel good in her warm shoes and heavy winter socks. She has plenty of time, and her sickness has taught her that any good moments can be followed by as many bad ones. It is an irregular condition—unpredictable. Her heart has stopped its palpitations and thrums steadily when she checks her pulse. Good days must be taken advantage of.

She buys more feed for the cat, dog, and chickens. While she's at the grocery store she replenishes the few supplies she has used since her last trip; she even buys postage stamps and batteries to store against future need. Everything she can think of. With any luck, she won't have to leave home again anytime soon.

Her stomach starts to hurt, but she ignores it. Just a little bit longer, and she can go home and rest.

The sporting goods store is beside the grocer's. A large blackboard sign on the sidewalk proclaims, "Snowshoes for sale, today only!" Bells clink against the door as Anna opens it. Perhaps snowshoes would help her to walk less clumsily between the house, shop, and garage. Her old pair has long since worn out, rotted through the strings, loose like old tennis rackets. It had felt strange, she remembers, walking on top of the white ground without sinking, too high up. Indigenous peoples had developed snowshoes; each culture had its own design. Anna appreciates a tool that is meant to be used alongside the land-scape, not against it.

But the row of rifles on the far wall draws her eye. They look impersonal, competent. She shuts her mind against the image that flashes before her of John on his stomach in the clearing, the clothing torn and scattered, the red and brown. It's only a glimpse, a bare second. She fills her mind with clean snow, white trees instead. She counts to five, breathing with the numbers. The rifles in front of her come back into focus.

Here is something she needs. Even if she can bring herself to return to the clearing, the one full of snow, and search, even if the rifle is still there, it will have gotten soaked in wet and cold, expanded and contracted with the weather, and likely wouldn't be reliable or safe to fire anymore, right? And what about the coyotes, so close? They hadn't caused problems before, but this would be a hungry winter. It already had been. She would be far less vulnerable if she had a way to defend herself against threats. Even threats that are only rumors or imagination.

The store's owner sees her pause across the counter and greets her.

"Can I help you?" He peers at her with either curiosity or suspicion; she can't tell which.

"I want to buy a small hunting rifle for my grandson," she says, and a picture pops into her head of a grandson she'll never have, ten years old, blond-haired and serious, in a red plaid hunting cap. How easy it is to say what people will most believe if you can make yourself, only for a moment, believe it, too. "What do you recommend?"

"How old is he?" the man asks.

"Ah." Is ten too young? She pauses, and the picture changes. "Sixteen. He's coming to visit next month."

"Any idea what caliber you might be interested in?" he asks. In Belbridge, it's the sort of question anyone would know how to answer.

"A .22," she says firmly. "Something that doesn't have too much of a kick."

"Small game? All right. Let's see." He turns to look at the display. "One of our most popular rifles, especially for beginners, is the 10/22 Ruger." He lifts a black rifle off the rack and sets it on the counter. They study it for a moment in silence. It looks dark and heavy, with a finish that absorbs the light overhead and shows no highlights in the curves. Anna fears touching it, that her ignorance will be obvious if she does.

"It's easy to use," the man says. "Customizable. Light recoil." He takes the clip out, shows it to her, then replaces it. Still Anna keeps back. The price tag, tied on with red string, is underneath the gun, and she can't see it. "If you don't like the synthetic stock, I have the compact model in hardwood. Some people find the wood a little more attractive." He gestures to it on the rack. "It's used, but it's in good condition."

Anna looks where he points. It has a similar appearance to that of the old gun—less industrial, not as efficient as the black rifle on the counter.

"Which is more affordable?" she asks.

"The compact, if your grandson won't mind that it's used. We sell used guns for a considerable discount off the retail price of the new ones."

"That sounds perfect," she says. "I think I'd like to buy that one, then."

He helps her to fill out the forms. She browses the shop while the background check runs. There are flannel shirts on clearance that look like John's favorite kind. She flicks the shirts on the rack back and forth, touching all of them, trying not to think.

The man calls her over as he takes the rifle down and boxes it. "Your grandson will enjoy this gun," he says. "It's a classic."

"I'm sure he will," Anna says. "Can I get a couple of boxes of ammunition for it, too?"

Anna tries to stifle her surprise at the total, which comes to more than half of the check she had deposited only a little while before. At least she has enough in the account now to cover it, she thinks.

The background check had taken half an hour, and early midday traffic flows past the store. Anna angles the gun in its box across the floorboard of the passenger side of the truck and considers the multitude of other concerns the possession of it raises. Even their old gun, she hadn't ever used, and she had seen John use it so seldom. Though she can picture him shooting it, she can't picture how. She will have to learn from scratch on her own how to load this one, clean it, aim and fire it. She will have to teach herself how to make it seem normal.

The thought of that terrifies her. But there is no one to protect her now. No one else to care for her livestock and keep her home safe. Her jaw hurts. She is grinding her teeth the way she often does in her sleep.

Having the gun in the truck causes her to experience a mild adrenaline. She can't help looking at it every few seconds, harmless and blank in its cardboard box, as she drives. The box hides the potential for harm. She is too distracted by it to pay much attention to the road; likewise, she pays little attention to her twisting stomach and swollen knees.

She arrives home far more quickly than she expected to and pulls into the garage with relief. The drive has blurred; she can't recall getting there but she has made it. She feels both jittery and exhausted. She will have to eat something solid enough to counteract the caffeine from the coffee, which has started to make her nauseous. She leaves her purchases in the truck and wades through the snow to the house.

For the first time in days, she cooks eggs. Though the chickens don't lay many in the winter, when they do, they lay beautiful smooth brown ovals with orange yolks as big and bright as the hunter's moon. Her mouth waters as they cook. Anna is surprised when she realizes she is hungry.

She eats without waiting for the eggs to cool down. If anyone else were around, she would feel ashamed at how greedily she spoons them into her mouth, hardly swallowing one bite before taking another. But no one is watching.

After eating, she unloads the groceries and animal feed, storing them in their proper places in the house. The gun she takes with her to the sugarhouse, carrying the box awkwardly across her chest. Though Vermont is a state of hunters, and a gun is not an unusual possession, she's self-conscious. She walks quickly, head down, hoping no cars drive by, that her few neighbors won't see her and guess what she carries. She doesn't know enough about it herself yet to explain it to someone else. And she doesn't know her neighbors all that well, or want to know them. She has long been of the opinion it would be best to have no neighbors at all. Years of dealing with their trespasses and their pettiness (Anna can hear them like a litany: "Your rooster crows too early. Your horse is leaning on my fence. Your porch light is too bright. Your leaves are falling into my yard.") had made both John and Anna weary of them, drawn them more and more into their own sanctuary.

Intent on carrying the awkward burden of the gun without tripping, Anna nearly misses the track that she crosses in the snow. She drops the box onto the ground and kneels to see it better. The track is far too small to belong to an awakened black bear, her first fear, a beast that would lumber through this cold, white world as though in a dream. She wonders if it is the track of a mountain lion; although they are said to be extinct in Vermont, someone in Belbridge had sworn to seeing one a couple of years before. It had made the front page of the *Gazette*, though it hadn't ever been proven. Or maybe it's a Canadian lynx that has wandered south in search of prey. She doesn't know much about them and has never seen one herself, but it has happened before; animals, after all, don't know that countries have boundaries.

Anna brushes her gloved fingers around the edges of the print to get a sense of it, though she is careful not to disturb its shape. There are claws, too, at the ends of the toes, like little splinters chipping out from the edges. Big cats don't leave claw marks. Like house cats, they keep their claws retracted most of the time, and do not walk with them out.

If not feline, then, the track must be canine. But of what sort? She hopes it isn't a dog, left to its own devices or dumped out to fend for itself by irresponsible people. Anna frowns. Coyotes leave smaller prints than this one, and wolves haven't been sighted anywhere in Vermont for decades, thanks to the clear-cutting of trees in favor of farmland a century ago, and the state's historical offer to purchase wolf pelts from residents for twenty dollars each. She finally decides it must be the track of a large domestic dog breed. Larger than typical. A Saint Bernard, an Irish wolfhound, a mastiff maybe.

She sighs. That means she will have to keep a closer eye on the chicken pen. This time, the dog has gone straight through her yard, not seeming to stop; that doesn't mean that it will always do so.

Anna isn't afraid of dogs, though she has been bitten before, particularly in the early days when she and John had lived around more people. In their first neighborhood, a development in another state with tract houses boasting two acres each, people let their dogs wander so often that the animals had gotten used to roaming unsupervised and formed packs. Huskies, heelers, terriers, Chihuahuas, and Rottweilers all ran together in a disparate bunch, attacking smaller livestock and infuriating the dogs still kept behind fences. She had chased dogs off their small acreage every morning; if there were enough of them, they tested her, growled and lunged at her in her own yard. One day a couple of dogs had killed thirteen of their laying hens and left another three near death, then had run back to their separate houses; John had had to wring the necks of the birds that were lying torn open and alive. She and John had purchased their first mule in those days in the hope that it would hurt those dogs, or at least keep them at bay. The dogs had injured the mule instead, there had been so many of them.

This one, whatever its breed, will at any rate be a single dog, which will make it less emboldened. If she makes herself large enough, loud enough, frightening enough, confusing enough, she will be able to convince it to leave her alone when she comes across it. She will have to be more aware from now on when she goes outside.

She stands, brushes the clumps of snow off her wet jeans, and retrieves the cardboard box that contains the rifle.

Once inside the shop, she sets the box on one of the work-tables and opens it. It seems less incongruous here than it would in the house. Alone, she can finally bring herself to touch it—the smooth hardwood stock, scratched slightly at one end and soft with handling from other owners, the metal barrel so cold it feels damp.

She takes it out and places it on the table, intending to teach herself to get used to its being nearby. To learn to be comfortable, natural around it. She means to desensitize herself to it, the way she would desensitize a horse if it feared a tarp or blanket, by keeping the frightening thing close. But she still senses it behind her, its silence and its potential, after she sits down in the shabby chair in front of John's desk. The yellow foam cushion sticks out from the seat at the edges, uncomfortably uneven. Anna presses the power button on John's computer and waits for the screen to brighten.

9

At first, seeing the amount in her checking and savings accounts lifts Anna's spirits. She had assumed she had nothing, but this is far better than nothing. It seems like a lot of money, so many trips to the grocery and feed stores, one hundred or two hundred dollars at a time. Everything will be fine for a while.

But studying the account's monthly drafts in more detail reveals how close she and John came every month to overspending. John had never told her they were living paycheck to paycheck, had never acted like they were. Now that Anna can access their statements, she can see the whole shape of their expensive day-to-day lives like a map. Though John's saddles had sold for a good price, he had limits to how many he could craft in a month, and because of the rising cost of materials he seemed, from what Anna can tell, to have only drawn in about 30 percent profit, at best.

Besides food, income and property taxes, and health, car, and home insurance, they'd been paying for John's professional memberships and business costs, Anna's medications and supplements, the farrier and veterinarian, power, gasoline, internet access, and trash removal, among other, more varied expenses. There are bills in the kitchen now, a stack of them waiting to be paid; she had forgotten about those. Supporting one person instead of two won't make much of a difference to the size of John's former budget—particularly with no steady income to offset the money going out.

Anna fidgets in the seat, nervous energy that helps her to contain her mounting desperation. She turns to look at the saddles scattered around the sugarhouse. She can list the stock saddles for sale and make only a little less money for each than John would have gotten for a custom one. The thought of losing them, the last, unworn, perfect examples of the beautiful work John completed, depresses her. But what help is there for it? She has no skills herself, no stamina. She can't drive into town every day. She can ride a gentle enough horse, type a document, stamp leather. What demand is there for that?

She could sell some of the shop equipment—the extra sewing machines, for example. Some of the shelves and tables and tools and stands. She wonders how much John's livelihood would be worth. For how long could she afford to extend her lifestyle that way?

Anna rests her head in her hands, fighting the urge to give in to hopelessness.

She rouses herself and once again studies the incomplete saddles, the orders in progress. They are arrested in different stages of construction. All five need varied amounts of work, some much more than others. The meticulously written yellow tags tell exactly what they are intended to become. Of the older orders, one only needs sheepskin attached to the bottom, skirts attached, tooling completed, and the horn wrapped. On the most recent order, John had covered the tree, attached the rigging, and crafted the ground seat and jockeys, but that is all he had gotten the chance to do; it's unfinished, a skeleton, bare and rough as the new wooden frame of a house. John had begun to cut the other pieces for it; that was one of his first steps for any saddle, cutting the pieces the right way on the grain of the same hide. Those he finished are lying in a stack behind it on the table.

Anna had seen John do this work for decades, over half her life. She had come to think of him as an artist, untouchable in the quality of his work, even immaculate when he was at his bench. But he would have shown her how to do it, too. Why hadn't she ever asked?

Maybe she can finish the saddle that is farthest along. She outlines the steps in her head: Cut the fleece, glue it to the skirts, stitch it. Attach the skirts to the tree. Finish the tooling (the yellow tag says "oak leaves"). These are all steps of which she is capable. The seat is thick and padded, the stirrups wide and flat. There isn't any horn—it's a Western-style endurance saddle. Many of the locals participate in endurance riding, pacing their horses over twenty-five, fifty, a hundred miles. Riders can only complete the entire distance if veterinarians deem their horses to be in good condition throughout the race. Anna wants to try it herself, but though Keeper would enjoy the challenge, subjecting her own body to such abuse would be foolhardy.

The shop phone rings. Anna walks to it. It rings three times, four times. She cringes with the sound. She picks it up just before voicemail connects.

"Hello?"

"Is this Northeast Kingdom Saddles?"

"Yes," she says. "This is Anna."

"I called last week," the person says, "about placing a custom order, and I haven't heard back yet."

"I'm so sorry," replies Anna, the words sticking to her throat. "My husband has been unable to work. We're not taking custom orders right now."

"What?"

"I'm very sorry," Anna says again.

The voice gets louder, insistent. "Okay, I'm sorry for your husband, but there must be something you can do. It's important. I was really hoping you'd have an option for my mustang. I can't find anything to fit her."

Anna needs the money. "I can send you a demo saddle," she says. "It's pretty well used. It's $1,250 to try it. If you like it, just keep it. If not, send it back, and I'll give you a full refund." There's silence on the other end. "You'll only be out the shipping," Anna adds hopefully.

"Well," the voice says, "I would really have preferred something new." The line goes blank for several seconds and Anna wonders if the person has disconnected. Just as she is about to hang up, the woman on the other side says, "I guess, at this point, I'm pretty much willing to try anything."

Anna gives instructions for payment, writes down the woman's measurements, and tells her how to take a wither tracing of the horse so that she'll know which saddle to send.

"I'll get the saddle in the mail as soon as you get that tracing to me," Anna tells her.

The caller thanks her. "By the way," she says, "you might want to think about putting a message on your website or something about not doing custom orders. That way people will know."

The website! Anna had forgotten all about it. Of course. She thanks the caller and hangs up, heart still pounding.

She finds the yellow tags on a shelf beside a package of printer paper and adds one to each of the demo saddles so she won't forget that one of them is reserved. Her notes, unlike John's, are dashed off in a quick hand: *Send one demo saddle when wither tracing received from O in FL.*

The website is set to open as the home page with any new browser window. Anna knows where to find the saddle shop's information on it, and sometimes she takes new photographs for it, but she has no idea how to edit it. John hadn't known either; he'd hired a web designer that he found in the phonebook. When John needed an update, the web designer had done it for him. Anna has no idea who that is or how to reach them.

She opens the home page and sits looking at it. It has a gallery of some of John's most expensive and elaborate saddles; the center picture changes every few seconds to show another one. Beneath that, there are testimonials: customers with photographs of their saddles on their horses, the people all strangers looking into the lens of a camera, ready to vouch for John's work. Their willingness to do so awes her.

Anna clicks through all of the pages and then clicks in frustration on the backgrounds of the pages themselves. She scrolls up and down. There it is—a link in tiny blue letters at the bottom of the page: *Contact Webmaster.*

She clicks it and a new window pops up almost immediately. It's an email window with the "to" address automatically filled in. She types, "Hello, could you please update my website to say that construction of custom saddles has been suspended until further notice?" She reads what she typed over to herself and, after some thought, adds, "Repairs will still be done. Thank you— Northeast Kingdom Saddle Co." She hits send.

The response comes within half an hour: "John, hope you're well. I've updated your site per your request. You still have three updates left this month if you need them. Please let me know if I can be of further assistance."

Anna refreshes the web page, and the message appears across the top in a red banner. That should cut down on the phone calls and emails for a while. At least until she figures out what to do. She closes the window with the website and considers what to do now.

John had kept the saddle shearlings in dustproof plastic bins under one of the work tables. Anna pulls one out and digs her fingers into the fleece. The rich, musty odor that rises from it tickles her nose, makes her want to either cough or sneeze. She lays it on the work table, skin side up, and arranges the saddle skirts from the first custom order along it. With deliberate movement, she traces around their shapes with a dull pencil. She finds the good scissors—the ones that John wouldn't let be used for any other task—and begins to cut, enjoying the feel of the sharp edges through the soft hide.

She leaves the cut fleece and skirts pressed under heavy old department store catalogs to keep them aligned while the glue sets. Soon, she will try to learn how to use the leather sewing machine to go around the edges with an even white stitch, and then the fleece will stay on the saddle for years, decades maybe, until it wears out.

It has worked, this occupation in the sugarhouse. She has stopped being aware of the gun on the table, has been working around it without unease. She nearly leaves the shop without taking it with her, but remembers it as she tamps down the flue on the woodstove, on which the cast iron has started to cool. She closes the gun back into its box.

She blows on her hands—they always seem to be cold. She props the rifle in its box against her leg as she struggles to lock the sugarhouse door. The barrel slides a little out of the partially closed cardboard flap; its cold round end rests against Anna's thigh. She feels it even through the denim. But she ignores it until she hears the deadbolt slide into place.

10

John's ghost is not a presence, but an absence. Something the house expects, but never realizes. Pictures Anna has forgotten for years draw her in, black frames on the dresser, the two of them on their wedding day, young and holding the future in their hands like flowers. They have lived their lives now, and their story has not so much been one of romance, but of partnership. She lives on alongside the ghost.

Anna decides to take the mule Charlie out to check the fences. She hasn't ridden him since he spooked and left her with the horse and John in the forest. His scratches have healed, though a couple left scars in fine white lines across his haunches; they aren't noticeable unless you look for them.

She has started handling the mule and horse only on days of gentler weather, walking them to the small paddock behind the barn and turning them loose so they can get some exercise. Keeper paws and digs into the snow and mud and then gallops, flinging the mud with enthusiasm from his hooves onto the barn and the fences, but Charlie either paces along the rails snorting or stands with his head down, still. He acts jumpy and sullen around her, dragging behind when she leads him, or tensing at the noise of her coat rubbing against itself as she walks and leaping ahead, jostling her. He has lost a bit of weight, enough to sharpen the angle of his hip. His face has hardened, and his eyes no longer hold the calm depth they once possessed. Anna can't tell whether he is more afraid or angry, but a mule in either condition can be dangerous. Can be explosive. She handles him warily, fearing this new unpredictability.

How easy it is to feed him, water him, take him outside or inside, and say she cares for him. She has been focusing only on getting those mechanical tasks done. Now she has to admit to herself she has been neglecting him, this animal that had been such a friend to her husband, by not helping his body to release its trauma. She is lucky he hasn't colicked, started wood chewing, or gotten ulcers with the stress. That he hasn't hurt himself, her, or Keeper in his miserable attitude. A mule isn't a creature that forgets any kind of betrayal, real or perceived. Time isn't going to fix him. He needs to get outside of himself.

She lingers in front of the mule's stall. Charlie doesn't look at her but behind her, another habit he has recently developed. She holds his head so that she can look into his eyes, but he ducks, avoiding her contact. She doesn't force him, but lets him evade her touch, seeking to show him that he isn't trapped, though she follows his movement with her hand just inches away from him. She doesn't want him to learn to escape her altogether.

She tries not to fear the implications of how differently he behaves. She has thus far refused to ask herself if animals can grieve. Not now, when her own grief is enough. The border collie seems to notice nothing unusual, and likes being kept mostly in the house these days; the cat sleeps as contentedly as ever, and doesn't meow and search the empty rooms as Anna had worried it might. That would have been too much. But the mule . . . nearly every day, the mule reminds her that nothing is right.

She speaks to him gently as she tacks him up, in no hurry. She does not reprimand him as forcefully as she normally would when he acts cinchy, swinging around with teeth bared as she tightens the girth. She merely blocks his head with her arm and continues what she is doing, acting as though she hasn't been intimidated, that his threat is no big deal. She tries to keep from trembling. He had never threatened to bite her before and doesn't try it again. He licks his lips but stays alert, watching her out of his near eye.

The morning is cold but clear. Rare yellow light filters through the bare branches of the trees, which are filled with the noise of the winter birds, chickadees, juncos, nuthatches, and sparrows—chirps, peeps, and scratches. Today it's nearly as loud as in springtime.

Despite the brighter weather, Charlie feels dull and heavy underneath her. Anna wants to check the western boundary of the property first, the side of the land opposite of where Charlie had twice lost John, so that she can build the mule's confidence. Edged by large boulders and, along much of the boundary, a sheer granite rise of about eight feet, it is unlikely that poachers would come that way. She and John hadn't even fenced much of it, using the granite wall as a natural method of containment.

Rock is considered to be one of the Kingdom's riches. There are old granite quarries a few miles away in every direction, cratering the topography irrevocably. A nearby town had been morally divided when half its residents wanted to reopen an abandoned quarry as a boost to the local economy, and the other half fought just as desperately to protect the habitats of deer and salamanders, as well as their own quiet. The townspeople, once close-knit, had started vandalizing each other's homes, each side believing the other to be wrong. That's what it comes down to, Anna decides. Making money or preserving the environment. Someday, there will be plenty of money but no use for it.

She rides Charlie at a slow walk down the driveway and turns left just before the fence that separates her yard from the shoulder of the road. He balks when she turns him, and she can feel him start to deaden, but she is ready and kicks him hard, surprising him forward. She turns him in tight figure eights around the trees, keeping him moving, not letting him think. He pins his ears and grunts, but obeys her cues. She wonders if he can feel her legs shivering against him. What a big mule he is, and how little control she really has of him. *I'm going to get bucked off, and no one is ever even going to look for me.*

After several minutes of moving in fast circles, he grows more responsive, and she opens her hands and asks if he will go ahead. He says he will, straightens, and she guides him once more along the fence line. He walks steadily along it, finding his own way through the snow, and Anna concentrates on making her muscles loosen. She can't expect the mule to relax if she can't. He will be able to feel the rigidity of her body, the brace in her back and shoulders. She closes her eyes and sighs, feeling the mule's back round and slide underneath her seat in response. She opens her eyes. His ears have flicked forward. He's interested now in where they are going.

They skirt the perimeter of the front fence without incident and turn up the west side of the land. Charlie gazes around him with increasing but unworried awareness, and Anna drops the reins in front of the saddle and leans forward to rub her cold hands along his warm neck. She often does this when riding Charlie in the winter—the warmth is pleasant—and he doesn't react to her change in position. They have gone on that way for several minutes when they come upon a deer standing between gray trunks a few yards ahead. Charlie raises his head and stops to watch it, and she lets him.

She sits quietly. Under her legs, which have grown steady, she feels Charlie's breath deepen, push out his ribs. The deer is a monument as still as the trees; the two animals study each other. It's a young buck, narrow-bodied, with velvety antlers. Anna can easily see the kinship between mule and deer. Both prey animals, sensitive and intelligent. Both born to run. She doesn't know how long they stay there watching each other through the trees. This is not something that could happen if you hiked or drove or biked. Because of the mule, the deer can't read the human threat and is unafraid. Anna is invisible to it.

Charlie snorts softly and shakes his head, jingling the snaps and buckles of his tack. Anna pats him, an affectionate slap on the broad neck. She looks back up at a sound like a whisper. The deer has disappeared, fading into the trees as though it had only been a part of the forest itself, no different than a boulder or birch.

The mule seems brighter now, walking in swinging strides, and Anna is glad she took him out. The crisp air fills and refreshes her. It's good for them both. Only a mule can pick its way with the certainty Charlie does through the rocks and uneven footing of the western boundary. Anna lets her stirrups drop from her feet and stretches her legs. With Charlie going well, she is free to check the trunks of the trees they pass, looking for the dime-sized holes that mean Asian long-horned beetles have invaded. She views it as her duty to look out for them; they would decimate the forests. But so far, by some unknown grace, they haven't crossed over from neighboring states, and she sees no signs of them.

A brook forms most of the southern boundary of the property. She and John had fenced about ten feet in front of it to prevent the horses from muddying it and damaging the banks when they were sometimes given the run of the pasturage in the summer. Anna turns the mule and rides along the fence, the sound of the half-frozen brook loud in the chilly morning, but peaceful—it drowns out the noise of the traffic far away. The light is still and dappled.

Several trees have fallen since Anna last rode there, but none of them have hit the fence, and they are low and bare enough for Charlie to step over. He takes them in stride. Anna bends to peer alongside one of the logs at the same large paw prints she had seen by the sugarhouse. The tracks go in a straight line under the fence (the dog's belly fur had brushed the snow like a broom when it had crouched to get below the rail) and up to the edge of the creek.

Anna assumes it crossed there, and wonders again what exactly it could be. She's too far away to tell whether the tracks come out again on the other side. The dog would have to be a type that is large and slow. Long-strided. A Great Pyrenees, perhaps. Plenty of people with livestock have those as guardians. That's a working breed, and one impervious to cold and damp; such a dog would also be hard to spot against the snow.

Charlie stops at the tracks, paws, and scents, raising his upper lip to get a better smell. He tenses up again, but does not resist Anna's guidance further, except that he begins to prance instead of walk. "Easy," Anna says, but the mule's focus has shifted far outward to the deep woods. He freezes, turns, and stares back into the trees across the creek several times, but moves forward alongside the fence again each time Anna asks. Maybe she has asked too much of him too quickly. They should have turned back at the halfway point before he had a chance to get either bored or tired. She is relieved when they finally turn the corner onto the eastern fence line.

After a few hundred feet, Charlie settles back into his steady forward walk, and Anna relaxes and lets his reins back out. He stretches his neck down and yawns in response. A hawk floats overhead, dropping cries that drift on the breeze like dandelion seeds. A road borders the eastern side of the property, but only three or four houses have ever been built along it, and acres of woods separate those; cars pass infrequently at best. One comes toward her with a gravelly, crescendoing sort of static, and she says, "Whoa, Charlie."

He halts, and they wait. The car soon comes into view in front of the trees. She raises a hand and sits still while it passes. The driver only glances at her; she doesn't recognize him, but that means nothing. Over the years, neighbors move away and others move in; she only knows one of the families very well now, the one owning the property on the other side of the stream, and she hasn't spoken to them for months. There hasn't been any reason to. As soon as the car is out of sight, she nudges Charlie, and they move on. They're nearly finished.

Only a few minutes ahead, where the trees thin, she comes upon a scene that dismays her. She brings Charlie up short, then trots him straight for it, dismounting almost before he stops. First she comes to the trampled snow, gritty and almost black nearest the road. The rails of the fence have been removed from the posts and thrown into the borrow ditch. She can tell by the wide tire marks that a truck slid from the road through the gap in the fence. Its exhaust pipe had cut into the snow where the incline increased onto the property. It appeared to have gotten stuck just inside the boundary, and not long before, either—a day or two, maybe hours. One of the back tire prints is far deeper than the others and has gone into mud; dark clods of earth have been flung toward the road. Boot prints surround the posts in semicircles.

How many men had it taken to tear down her fence? She stoops to look at the prints. She only discerns one type of tread, flat rectangles like molars. There may only be one. Or possibly, one man took down the rails and then pushed the mired truck while the other had steered it. Maybe there were even three or four men. There is really no way to tell.

Anna walks back to Charlie and stands beside him indecisively. Her new rifle is far away, leaning safely against the shelves in the hall closet. She didn't think to bring her cell phone with her.

She leads Charlie next to part of the fence that still stands and uses it to climb back up onto his back. She feels clumsy and cold. Inadequate. She picks up her reins, and the mule raises his head, waiting for her to tell him what to do. But she doesn't know what to tell him. She wants to run, to forget she has seen something that isn't right, but this is her property, and only she can protect it. She doesn't move, can't make herself choose, so the mule steps off on his own in the direction that is the quickest way home, the one Anna fears may be the most dangerous. Charlie usually has better instincts than she does, so she decides to trust him. Nonetheless, it feels to Anna as if they are being pulled ahead by some dark fate, and it is not possible to turn away from it. They move inexorably into the shadows. The forest has grown eerie, silent. The mule follows the lines of the truck straight into the middle of it.

11

Anna pulls Charlie up when the laughter of the men reaches her. They are not trying to be quiet or careful; they sound loud, untidy, unsteady. They speak carelessly. They have been drinking. As she listens, a truck door slams, and Charlie startles, but he doesn't run. He stands quivering, his head high, breathing hard. *Not again*, she wills.

The men have set up hunting camp in the wide, level, oval-shaped clearing she used to use as a jumping arena. Though it has been a long time since she's ridden in it, its layout is familiar to her. With difficulty, she edges the nervous mule off to the side, into thicker trees. He tosses his head and sidesteps underneath her. She holds him in firmly, bracing her hands against the saddle's pommel to keep him from getting out from under her.

The men have parked their truck, a newer black extended cab, inside the clearing just past where she sits, near where the old jump poles and standards are stacked. The radio is on. The tailgate is down, and she can see the body of a deer, its tongue out and swollen pink, dark reddish brown pooled in a semicircle around its black and white muzzle.

It looks like they're starting to pack up to leave. One man, a heavyset figure in coveralls, walks toward a pile of supplies. Two rifles lean against a couple of large blue coolers. Beer cans litter the ground near the truck; one has spilled pale gold in the snow, melting it in a low crescent. Didn't she just hear two people talking? But she can only see one. She must have been mistaken. Was it the radio she had heard? Well, she'd rather face one unknown man than two.

The stocky man smokes a cigarette now and walks around the supplies, checking them. Impatient, Charlie paws at the frozen ground. Twigs crack under his hoof. Anna hisses at him and snaps the reins to get his attention.

It's too late. Anna looks up to see the man in the clearing aiming a rifle at them. She freezes. He won't shoot them, will he? Surely not. No.

She isn't wearing orange. The thought strikes her just in time. She isn't wearing orange, and the man will think that Charlie is a deer or moose. Sick with sudden adrenaline, she whips the mule with the reins, and he leaps ahead just before the shot rings out. It's so loud that time in the clearing stops. Anna expects to hear the bullet hit a tree, to hear a splinter or hammer, but it thuds as though it has gone into ground. A second shot, and Charlie's shoulder drops underneath her and her body starts to fall to the side. But the mule catches himself with a roaring sound that she has never heard before. It is made up of all the loss and hurt and anger that he has ever felt.

They are in the clearing, Charlie running all out with his ears flat and his teeth bared. They bear down on the man, who is lifting the rifle again, eyes wide. He shakes his head no. She sees him yelling but can't hear what he says. She pulls the reins with all her strength on either side, trying to do a one-rein stop, but Charlie is too strong. She tries a pulley—holds the rein on one side braced against the mule's thick neck and yanks as hard as she can with the other. She half fears that it will flip him over, but it has no effect at all. Charlie has either forgotten she's there, or he doesn't care. The trees blur around her. She digs her fingers into Charlie's short mane and holds on as he hits the man with all his weight. The man's face is pale, acne-scarred, and he hasn't shaved; his mouth is open and pink-gray; she sees every vivid detail of him.

As the man goes down, another shot explodes next to Anna's ear. The world goes silent except for a high-pitched hum. Charlie rears. She falls forward onto his neck and hugs it as hard as she can to stay on. She closes her eyes, buries her face against his rough mane as sound returns.

The mule plunges underneath her and the man screams, a sound as clear and desperate as an animal's, but it becomes a wet gurgle, and then it stops. Then there is only the noise of Charlie roaring and the thud of his feet hitting. Anna, sobbing, holds on as long as she can. It seems to go on forever.

Her arms ache and she has to let go. She drops the stirrups and is thrown clear on the near side of the mule. She crawls on trembling hands and knees to where the jumps are stacked and crouches behind them, struggling to get air into her lungs. Charlie still paws at the man in the clearing, snorting and blowing with rage and exhaustion. His hooves thump on flesh. She covers her ears and closes her eyes.

The clearing grows silent again gradually. At a strange whimpering sound, like the cry of a wounded rabbit, Anna looks up; with surprise, she realizes that it is coming from her. The mule must have heard it, too. He whickers uncertainly. She hears him take a couple of steps, muffled by the bed of pine needles.

Anna forces herself to quiet. She has her back to the clearing, but soon Charlie is walking toward her heavily, unevenly, breathing hard, dragging one toe, from the sound of it. He comes around the end of the stack of jump standards and stands beside her with a lowered head.

She has heard of mules that kill livestock or attack bears or mountain lions, but never a man-killer. The pain in his eyes makes her pity him, and she reaches shakily to stroke his nose, but there is softness in his eyes, too, a look that's familiar. He acts meek, submissive, hurt. His ribs move in and out, in and out too quickly with his ragged breath. Blood has run from a large graze on his shoulder and dried in sticky brown lines down his leg to his hoof. The wound gapes open to show muscle when he puts weight on that side. His legs and belly are spattered with blood, too, but that blood probably doesn't belong to him. Anna doesn't want to look at it anymore and gets up. Charlie leans his head against her and sighs, and she waits warily with her hand between his ears rubbing his lowered forehead, comforting him.

After a while, she gathers his reins and pulls them, telling him to step forward. His wounded shoulder has begun to grow stiff; he groans, but limps toward her without any objection. She leads him away from the clearing into the scattered trees, trying not to look back. They have a long way to go to get back to the barn.

The forest is quiet except for their labored walking. The shadows of the trunks grow long and stretch away from them. The snow that melted in the radiation of the afternoon sun starts to re-freeze into a crust, but the mud underneath stays slippery. Anna hobbles, sore from her fall, her head aching from the effort not to picture what is behind them, and Charlie limps, shivering, helpless behind her.

Anna's mind has emptied. She can see nothing ahead except that she must get home. She concentrates on helping Charlie find the best footing as dusk falls around them. If she doesn't know where to go, she watches him and walks where his ears point.

She has some sense that her life has changed again in ways she doesn't understand. She worries about Charlie—at first, that he might forget who she is in the dying, disorienting light, that something might set him off again, and he'll come after her. But he acts so dog-like that soon she forgets her fear of him and fo-cuses instead on the wound, how it opens and closes with each step. A little bleeding has started again with his movement; the blood trickles in slow, smooth red drops into the snow. She un-winds her scarf and holds it over the hurt, pressing it as they walk. He limps beside her with complete trust.

It has grown dark by the time they make it to the house, but Anna gets the impression that Charlie welcomes nightfall, feels safe surrounded by it; it's a night like a velvet blanket. Darkness makes everything one shade, simple, clean. It takes away the contrast of light and shadow. There is no conflict now. She leads him into the barn and turns on the lights. They jump to life with a buzz and glare as she puts Charlie into his stall, yellow bulbs illuminating his wound and the filth around his legs and belly.

As tired as she is, after she drags the saddle off of the mule, she tries to clean him up. The barn has its own small water heater, and though it had seemed an unnecessary luxury when John had installed it, she is grateful for it now. The steam from the bucket of hot water warms her as she carries it, and she inhales deeply.

Anna sponges the water over Charlie, trying to get only as much as necessary on him in the cold air. The dried blood comes off more easily than she had feared it would. She sponges around Charlie's wound, too, trying to keep the dirty water from running into it. The flesh around it has swelled and the edges are starting to take on a pink hue. It is just the sort of injury that might get infected. She cleans it as well as she can without hurting him, though he swings his head around with alarm several times when she presses too hard. Her efforts leave red water in pools in the bare places of Charlie's stall. She spreads fresh straw over the floor to cover them and dumps the wastewater from the bucket into the sink. It spirals into the drain. She runs fresh, cold, clear water behind it.

John had written the number for the after-hours veterinarian years ago on a pad on the kitchen fridge. In the two hours it takes the vet to arrive after she calls, Anna has changed into warm, dry clothing and gulped a cupful of hot coffee with four cubes of sugar. She feels tired but prepared by the time the white SUV pulls into the driveway.

The vet, a brisk upper-middle-aged woman in dark jeans, follows her into the barn while Anna thinks of how to explain what happened. She barely believes it herself when she says it out loud.

"This is Charlie," she says at the mule's stall. "We were out riding and he got shot by a hunter."

The vet looks away from Charlie and glances at Anna. "Poachers?" she asks.

"Yes."

"Are you injured?"

"No," Anna says. *Just dead on my feet.*

"Have you called the game warden?"

"Not yet," Anna says. "But they're probably long gone, anyway." She hates how her voice shakes and tries to control it. "They shot at Charlie, and he took off. I couldn't stop him for what seemed like a very long time."

The vet goes into the mule's stall and feels around the wound. Anna holds his head in case he tries to bite the woman, who is a stranger to him. But he stays calm. "They probably thought he was a game animal. How long ago did this happen?"

"I don't know," Anna says. "Maybe around two this afternoon. It took us hours to get home."

"You're lucky you weren't both killed," the vet says. "Has he had his tetanus shot?"

"Yes, in May, I think." Anna's voice sounds too young, still wavering. She's older than the vet, but seeks comfort from her. It bothers her. "Sometime in spring, anyway. He should be fine."

"Okay," the vet says. "It looks like the bullet just grazed right through the meat of his shoulder here. That's good news. There's enough skin here for me to stitch it, and we're not too late to stitch it yet. It might leave a scar."

Anna nods.

"I'll go get my equipment," the vet says. "I'm going to sedate him first. Once he's sleepy, we'll give that wound a good cleaning and fix it right up. Go ahead and move him to the wash rack for me."

Anna leads Charlie between the sides of the welded pipe chute and closes its back gate. The mule can't go forward or backward, so he shifts from side to side, waiting. She stands alone beside him. Both of them shiver. The vet returns with several syringes. "Sedative, antibiotics, Banamine for the pain he'll feel later," she explains. "And a tetanus booster, just to be safe."

Charlie's strong heart pumps the sedative through his body within minutes, and Anna and the vet watch his head slowly lower until his nose almost touches the ground. The motion of the vet's needle pulling the thread in and out, joining the torn flaps of skin together, hypnotizes Anna.

When the vet finishes, Anna returns the mule to his stall to recover from the procedure. She has instructions to hand walk him every day in order to manage the inevitable stiffness. The stitches will come out in two weeks. Anna pays the vet's bill without question, without even looking to see how much it has all cost.

"Wear orange next time," the vet says.

12

Anna lies in bed studying the shadowed ceiling. It is empty and layered with dust. It is a barren landscape bordered by cobwebs and dark corners. She can't close her eyes without seeing the man's face, its open mouth, the purple throat. He had been afraid. She couldn't save him. Didn't even try, not really, not enough.

The house sets her on edge every time it creaks and settles. She comforts herself by pretending that John is watching television downstairs, as he used to do sometimes when he couldn't sleep. It makes the house seem less vulnerable, less isolated in its clearing in the deep woods. It isn't safe to be so far from town, but town isn't safe, either. All those people. She covers her ears with the sheet, the way she had done as a child afraid of the dark.

She awakens near dawn feeling sore and cold, having kicked off the quilt sometime during the night. She sits up and rubs the tension from the muscles of her jaw. She knows she didn't sleep well because she remembers sleeping, how she had held herself just under the surface of unconsciousness and waited for time to pass. The night had gone on forever.

She doesn't make coffee but microwaves what is left from the day before. It tastes bitter and stale, and it scalds her tongue into something swollen and alien between her teeth. But that doesn't matter. Anna doesn't know how to make the day move forward, where to even start, there is so much to do. She has to protect Charlie, who has killed a man, and herself, who had allowed it.

She might not have much time. *The vet knows*, she tells herself. At least, the vet knows that *something* happened. But she doesn't know quite what. There's no real reason for the vet to think more of it, is there? Anyway, there isn't any help for that. Anna searches through some of John's tools, considering what to do. She'll pack what she needs into her saddle bags. She takes a hammer, nails, and work gloves from the small green toolbox stored in the hall closet.

The toolbox, so neatly kept, everything in its place, smells of oil and metal. She misses John. Her entire body hurts. It isn't the kind of ache that comes from being thrown off a horse, though there is that, too. It's something different that lurks underneath the sore muscles, something much worse. She pauses, then reaches for the rifle, too.

In the barn, both Keeper and Charlie greet her, nodding their heads over their stall doors. Anna checks Charlie first; his wound shows no sign of reopening, no hint of infection, and his eyes are bright and alert. He has not regained that hard, wary look that he wore for so long. He bumps her affectionately with his nose. He shows a good appetite when she gives him his breakfast, though he must be in some pain. The stitches march in a relentless uneven line across his shoulder.

She listens to the horse and mule chew while she grooms Keeper. The homey sound has always cheered her. If her animals are happy, healthy, eating all their feed, not everything can be bad. She saddles Keeper in his stall and steps back to let him finish. He knows she plans to take him out, and he eats quickly. After he licks the bottom of the trough to make sure he has gotten every last oat, he turns toward her, and she bridles him and leads him out.

Charlie watches with interest as they leave. Anna closes the door to the sound of the mule rattling his feeder to get stray grain out of the corners.

The unusual warmer weather has held, and Keeper moves

with care over ground more mud than snow. Anna can feel the eagerness in his small round body. He keeps his head up, ears forward. His thick mane bounces in time to his steps.

Despite the slick going, once he reaches the trees the sure-footed horse breaks into a brisk tolt, and Anna lets him, reveling in the wind and speed, the sense of the elms and pines flashing past. And her body, temporarily made smooth and aerodynamic, athletic instead of dull and clumsy. In fact, the faster they arrive, the faster they can get this done, the better. She guides Keeper in the general direction of the jumping arena, farther northeast than what she thinks of as John's clearing, but she doesn't bother to pick up the reins to steer the horse around the trees; he doesn't need her help. So she sits, barely moving in the saddle, as his smooth gait blurs everything but what lies ahead of them.

The forest opens into the big clearing that forms the old arena. Anna brings Keeper to a walk and keeps him just within the trees at the perimeter. She makes herself look only at the ground. When they are likely to be going alongside where the man lies, she closes her eyes, trusting the horse to keep moving ahead. After counting to thirty, she opens them again. She doesn't see the man; they have gone past him. They are near the black truck. Keeper looks at it curiously, but he grew used to seeing vehicles long ago, and he doesn't spook at it.

So much still to do. Staying in cover, she directs the horse around the truck toward the place she and Charlie had been when the gun went off. She half expects to see a bullet hole in the ground behind where they had been standing, lumped earth. It had thudded when it hit the dirt, as if in slow motion.

As they approach, Keeper tenses, then throws his head up nearly to Anna's chin and runs backwards. He spins around to bolt.

Anna, who is able to stay in the saddle because the horse is small and she is used to him, reacts on instinct. Holding on to his mane with one hand, she shortens the other rein and pulls his head around to her boot. It takes less than a second to do it. Keeper can't run in a circle that tight. He can only turn and turn, fighting for his head, as Anna holds on and wonders if he will lose his balance and fall or run into a tree trunk. Her nerves settle in her stomach.

After several seconds, she feels his hind legs step across each other, and he gives up and stops. She keeps the hold on his head as the tension slowly leaves his body. He quits bracing against her and stands still, neck still bent around to her boot. She rubs his forehead and evens her reins. He looks ahead again but doesn't move; his ears flick back toward her. He takes quick breaths.

Anna dismounts with the intention of leading him toward whatever spooked him and letting him examine it while she is on the ground. But upon turning him, she freezes.

There is another brown veil of blood along the ground (too familiar now, it is getting to be too familiar), and another body. Another man, thinner and younger than the first. Sandy brown hair, twigs. He has fallen on his back, eyes open, an empty, cloudy gray. One hand is across his stomach, holding his insides in; the other had scratched jagged lines in the wet black dirt as his fingers had opened and closed.

Anna backs away, confused. She turns and looks in alarm around her, the woods and the clearing, listening. Her heartbeat sounds like pulses of static behind her ears. Other than that, everything is quiet. A cottony, soft kind of quiet that fills everything.

Keeper knows Anna is frightened, too. She turns to see him studying her, trying to gauge whether they are in real danger. He knows that it means something if a person shows fear. He holds his head as high as he can and watches her with eyes that show the white sclera, the way he does if she gets angry with him. He backs to the end of the reins.

"Whoa," she says, trying to keep her voice steady. "It's okay." She lets him back up a few more steps, walking with him, then pulls him back toward her little by little. Wishing she had brought a treat, she opens her palm toward him. Curiosity gets the better of the horse, and he steps forward and lowers his head to sniff it. She feels as though the body watches them, but she ignores it.

Anna pats the horse's neck. She smooths his unruly mane. She acts like she has all the time anyone could ever want. She pretends everything is perfect.

Almost the first lesson she had learned when she started riding as an awkward little kid had been not to let a horse know when you were afraid. But she has always been afraid, even of the horses themselves, how large and powerful and unpredictable they are. She has simply loved them too much to stop being near them. As a child, especially, they had fascinated her.

She remembers trotting on a tall bay Thoroughbred, the fences rising and falling, trying to hold herself in the too-big English saddle with skinny, shaking legs, buckles of the leathers leaving yellow bruises through her jeans on her calves, while her instructor held the lunge line and the horse went around and around. How high up and dizzy she had been, how stiff her body bracing against the reins, using them for balance, so her instructor had tied her hands together. "Don't ever sacrifice the horse's mouth for your seat," the woman had said.

Anna had caught her breath when she lifted her hands and realized she'd be helpless.

"Are you afraid?" the woman had asked.

The dirt was a long way down. Anna thought about lying, but had been taught to be honest, had said, "Yes." But the instructor had wanted her to lie. Anna understood it immediately when the woman shook her head slightly, disappointed; *yes* had been the wrong answer. "Never, ever let a horse know you're afraid," the woman had chided her. "As soon as you do, you lose control. Then you get hurt. Understand? You have to pretend to be brave. The horse has to believe you're fearless."

She had stepped away from the horse. "Are you afraid?" she had called again. Anna's parents were watching from the rail. Anna flushed, feeling like a coward. "No," she said. She had finished the lesson with her empty hands joined at the wrists with baling twine and the reins flapping useless on the horse's neck; she had kept her heels down, back straight, eyes ahead. She hadn't ever forgotten what she had learned. About the reins nor about fear.

Later, while untacking the horse, Anna had heard the instructor tell her parents about a new student she'd gotten that week, how that student was a natural, "born to ride," she'd boasted. Anna had understood then that she was *not* a natural. She'd have to work to be good at what she loved. She would have to pretend.

Patting Keeper, humming to him because she doesn't trust her voice not to waver, Anna moves down his side and removes the rifle from the scabbard.

Still acting like the presence of the body isn't especially alarming, she nonetheless leads the horse in a wide arc around it, the rifle pointed to the ground at her side.

Once she is behind the body, she can see faint footprints in the mud and snow leading up to it. She can see Charlie's tracks, too, where they had stopped to watch the arena, then the deep gouges in the mud where he had jumped into a gallop.

She leads Keeper along the dead man's footprints, following them back. He had apparently been in the trees and must have seen her ride in, though he hadn't given himself away. After about twenty feet, she comes to a spot where he had relieved himself against a maple. There are flecks of yellow still at the edges of snow, and she can smell it. He must have been approaching her, then, must have been almost right behind her, when his friend had spotted the mule and shot. One man, shot by the other. Two hard deaths. But she is responsible for them both.

Anna backs the horse until they return to where the truck had driven into the arena. The tracks of the truck pool with snowmelt. She mounts Keeper and rides him a couple of feet outside the far edge of the tire tracks where the mud is firmer. It's a strange time for a warm spell, right as winter should be hitting with all its ruthless strength. Keeper's hooves make sucking sounds in the ground.

The fence appears in front of them, open and neglected, wet rails on the ground. She dismounts and drops Keeper's reins. The ditch slopes a little too steeply for her knees, and she winces as she grabs the end of one rail and drags it up to the posts. The wood splinters into her gloves and leaves wet brown smears on her coat. Once she has it laid out straight across the opening, she lifts the end of the rail into the socket in the post. At ten feet long, the rail weighs more than she would like. She leaves it propped on one post and stands panting. Keeper watches her work. This is going to take a while. Anna lifts the other end and pops it into the socket with satisfaction. Then she wiggles it until each post has an even amount of rail in the socket.

She has to rest for five or ten minutes between each rail, but finally they are replaced, and she steps back to appraise what she has done. It looks as good as before, except for the torn dirt around the posts and the ruts in the ditch. Lines in the mud and snow show where she dragged the cumbersome rails, slipping and falling once under the weight of one of them. But it is done.

Anna climbs over the fence, back onto the property, and walks to Keeper. The rifle, which has been leaning against one of the near posts as she worked, she replaces in the scabbard. She gets the hammer and nails from the saddlebags. She drives one nail above and one nail below each rail at an angle into the post. Then she goes back and puts nails on either side of the rails, too. No one will be able to remove those rails so easily again.

She gazes down the line of fencing, which seems to go down the road forever. She can't see more breaks, even to the front corner, which she hadn't made it far enough to check with Charlie. She walks a little way in each direction to make sure. Then she walks across the road and looks back—the trees are so thick that no one should be able to see even part of the black truck. There doesn't seem to be any better place to put it, and it isn't something she is willing to move, anyway.

As soon as her tasks are complete, Anna swings back up onto Keeper and turns him toward home, going at an angle this time, swinging wide of the truck in the arena and of John's clearing both, going between them. She used to get turned around, sometimes lost, in these woods, but today home is a beacon she can feel pulling from acres away. She will need pain medicine when she gets back, and maybe a long, hot bath.

The next day, Anna loads John's cordless drill and a box of three-inch wood screws into the old farm truck. She puts two screws into each rail, all the way along the fence, down the road to the stream. She tightens them until they suck down into the wood, and then until the drill bit wears away the imprint in the tops of the screws and begins to slip. She makes sure.

13

There are two weeks left of hunting season. Anna tells herself that soon, everything will get better, closer to normal. Once the season ends, there will be fewer strangers around town, fewer people willing to disregard the boundaries which old neighbors are more likely to respect, only locals left to deal with. Cold closets the Northeast Kingdom. It snows steadily for several days, covering the tracks of the black truck. Anna drives once down the road at the eastern boundary to see how it looks; the fence and ditch stand as irrevocably as they have for years, as though nothing has ever disturbed them. Even the churned ground around the posts is covered over with white. She doesn't try to see farther in, doesn't want to. The arena will be under snow, too, smooth and deep. She can picture it, an empty field of moonlight where the dark trees part, the black truck waiting beside it like a shadow. She tells herself that the men who left it are as harmless now as if they had never existed, and tries to forget the wide eyes and blotchy skin, the feel of the body underneath her, the unyielding fury of the mule. The forest surrounds all of it, keeping it in.

Anna lies in bed most nights with the warm light of the lamp encircling her as she listens to the soft flakes brushing the windows like sighs as they fall. Her dreams are disordered and full of strangers, and she does not belong among them. She usually doesn't sleep. She gets up several times a night to peer around the curtains into the blackness, trying to decipher shapes in the flat dark, then checking all the windows and door latches to make sure that the house is safe. The reflection of her own face across the surface of the window glass always startles her. The coyotes at night sound like people arguing, crying, screaming. But they leave a void behind them when they quiet.

The mule's wound heals a little at a time, and as it does, he becomes even gentler, more patient with her than he was before. Anna doesn't ride him or the horse again for more than a few minutes at a time, only when frustration harries her out of the shop and she has to get away from the leather and tools and her own ignorance, exchanging them for short hacks in the trees on the western side of the land, where she hopes to see the living buck she saw there once before. She ignores what is in the unfathomable east. That direction seems cloaked in bad weather.

She has been working more often than not. John's filing cabinet is full of notes, patterns, instructions, even books from when he apprenticed, and she spends hours poring over them, practicing on scraps of hide she finds around the sugarhouse. Several saddle repairs have come in. Anna turns away those that seem too difficult, telling customers that John's health has gotten too poor, that his hands aren't steady enough for some work anymore, but she keeps the others. Each repair teaches her something new. She takes her time. There have been a few complaints that her work was clumsily done, or that repairs are taking much longer than usual to complete. Those who hint at dissatisfaction receive a healthy discount and leave mollified.

After much trial and error, Anna also manages to finish the first of John's pending custom saddles. The hardest part is the stitching. The leather sewing machine works on the same principles as any other—press the pedal, guide the material underneath the foot, lay the stitches out in a neat line or along a curve, regular and even. But once the spool of thread that John left on the machine runs out, Anna can never get it right again. She spends all of one day threading and rethreading the machine; the thread just tangles and ends up in a hopeless snarl. Snags twist along the test piece of leather she used. She eventually pulls too hard on the knotted thread coming from the needle, and something in the machine snaps. It might be something that doesn't matter, but she has gotten too frustrated and gives up on it. She tosses the cover over the machine and leaves it where it sits.

Instead, she punches holes in the leather with an awl and sews it by hand. It is a tedious task that hurts her knuckles, and she takes to wearing her old tight arthritis gloves, as well as the small silver thimble her mother gave her as a teenager, which has been in Anna's nightstand drawer for years, forgotten. The gloves move like a second skin on her hands and bulk between her fingers, but they hold her together. The thimble saves her fingertips countless times and carries associations of high school, especially. She'd helped to make her own dress for homecoming. How strange, how her life had spread before her then.

Anna moves the border collie's bed from its place beside the stove nearer to her feet, underneath the work table. She sometimes presses her cold feet under the sleeping dog, which has learned to go back to sleep and not to mind it.

Though she is pleased with how quickly she has picked up basic leatherworking, Anna's unaccustomed lack of rest wears on her, and she finds dealing with customers to be difficult. She's slipping. Sometimes she says the wrong names, tries to give them the wrong orders. Speaking to them, she pretends to be someone friendly, interested, outgoing. It's like driving a familiar route. When a customer leaves, Anna knows where she has gone, but not how she arrived there. Alone in the shop, she finds herself more and more often sitting stalled in the middle of a task, daydreaming. How thoroughly John had shielded her. How well she had used him to protect herself.

Anna could buckle under the sickness again without much warning. She starts every morning with a headache, which the coffee almost keeps at bay. Her hands shake if she waits too long between meals; she has to steady one hand with the other when she eats, or soup sloshes from her spoon back into the bowl. But she grows used to that. What alarms her is that hours disappear from her days, and she can't account for them, doesn't know where they have gone. She relies more and more on the list that she keeps on the fridge to make sure that the animals are fed and chores completed. She finds herself adding even more mundane tasks to it as time goes on.

Anna begins to have mornings in which she forgets to rinse the shampoo out of her hair before she gets out of the bath, and has to wash it out in the cold kitchen sink instead, once she gets dressed and realizes what she has done. She is tired. She sometimes shaves one leg and not the other; she doesn't wonder why she still shaves at all. It's a habit. She has always done it. The cat has figured her out. Anna and John had been in the habit of giving it some wet food at breakfast to supplement its dry chow. The cat still begs every morning until Anna opens the can of meat-flavored mush for it. But lately, the cat begs all day long, and sometimes Anna opens the trash to throw away a can only to discover that an empty can is already there. She starts labeling the cans—*Mon.*, *Tues.*, *Wed.* Her system works, but the cat won't give up trying. It is a small annoyance, but it wears on her nerves. At least, in the shop, there is only a job to be done, and she can either do it or she can't. It's straightforward.

There is a knock at the sugarhouse door. Anna isn't expecting anyone. The border collie gets to its feet, shakes, and dutifully begins its staccato barking. Anna slides back from the panel of leather she is stamping and goes to the door. She hushes the collie. The rifle leans against the jamb, just out of sight.

She opens the door a crack. It's the veterinarian from before, when the mule was shot. The woman smiles and holds up a hand in greeting. Anna opens the door wider.

"I'm sorry," the woman tells her. "I checked at the house and barn first, but there wasn't any answer."

"No, it's okay," Anna says. "I help my husband in the shop sometimes. What can I do for you?"

"I'm here to remove Charlie's stitches," the vet says, holding up her kit. "We have an appointment . . . ?"

"Of course! How stupid of me. I completely forgot." Anna steps into the cold and closes the door behind her. "I'm sure he'll be glad to get them out," she says. "They've seemed itchy the past couple of days."

"How does he look?"

"Good," Anna tells her. "He seems to have healed well. He's been moving a lot better." As they walk toward the barn, their feet crunch in the new snow. "I meant to shovel this," Anna says.

"More snow'll cover it before you get halfway done, anyway," the vet replies. "Ours is the same right now." She clears her throat. "Hey, I wanted to ask, how are you doing with those poachers? Any more trouble? I've been worried about you guys out here."

"We haven't seen any more," Anna says. She hesitates, then adds, "I wish they'd just leave us alone. I'm not sure what to do about them." That is the truth.

"Don't do anything," the vet says. "Stay far away and worry about cleaning up the mess they leave later."

Anna pulls the barn door open and follows the woman inside. They are greeted by soft whickers from the animals; Anna has taken to bringing them carrots outside of feeding time. She likes that they are glad to see her.

"I mean it," the vet says. She stops in front of Charlie's stall and he looks at her with interest. "So what if they take a deer illegally. It's better than you risking your life. Or this guy's." She pats Charlie's neck and enters his stall.

"You've got a point there," Anna says.

The vet examines the wound, pressing around it. "It looks good," she says. "No tenderness, either. Maybe a slight scar, nothing too ugly."

She cuts down the line of stitches and pulls out the threads. Charlie flinches a couple of times, but his ears stay forward, and he never offers to bite. Strange that the same day that struck Anna with terror had fixed whatever was wrong with the mule. She doesn't even have to put a lead rope on him to take him to the turn-out paddock anymore. Charlie follows her like a dog, and Keeper follows him. As she walks between the barn and paddock, she can often feel the mule's breath warm on her shoulder.

"All done," the vet says. The two women are quiet for a moment, admiring the result. Aside from a line of raised flesh, the mule's shoulder looks whole. Dark mahogany hair has started to grow back. Anna marvels at the body's power to make right whatever has been put wrong within it.

"You do good work," Anna says.

"I do my best," the woman answers, "but I'd prefer not to get any more calls like this. Be careful out here in the middle of nowhere."

She steps out of the stall and closes it behind her. They walk toward the barn door.

"By the way," the vet says, "do you and your husband know how to use that rifle that you have propped beside the door in your shop?"

Anna stops. "You could see it?"

"Just barely. Maybe move it to the other side of the jamb next time. The side the door doesn't open on." She laughs.

"Ah. I've been practicing loading and unloading it," Anna tells her. "I haven't actually fired it. My husband isn't used to guns, either. We're both a little out of our element."

"If you're going to have a gun, you need to know how to use it," the vet says. "If you like, I could send my son around to show you how."

Anna considers declining, but the woman is right, so Anna thanks her.

Though she watches the vet back down the driveway with relief, she can't deny that she also feels regret. She likes the vet, her cheer and confidence. The loneliness and silence immediately move back into the space around her, oppressing her spirits.

It's no wonder. Besides that, my longest conversation lately has been with a mule.

She walks back toward the sugarhouse. The dog will need to be let out for a while, and she has the leather tooling to finish. It is almost dusk, and the clouds have sky between them. The shadows stretch away from the trunks in blue slabs.

A movement catches Anna's eye, and she looks up. There, at the edge of the trees, something watches just outside the darkness. It shifts its weight and tests the wind. Anna blinks, trying to focus on what can't really be there. Lanky gray and white body, loose in its own skin. Sharp angles of face and shoulder. Black nose, pink tongue. It is—has to be—a wolf. It turns and meets her eye. Then it melts backward into the trees.

14

The sickness is back. Anna lies in bed looking up; the too-bright morning light spilling through the window hurts her eyes; her body is stiff and painful, as though pins have been stuck through her joints into the mattress. She tries to swallow, but can't. Her swollen throat chokes her. The tendons in her neck knot and scrape when she turns her head. She feels dizzy and empty and thinks she might vomit. She has sweated through the sheets. She lifts a hand to her forehead. It radiates clammy heat. Her heart floats to the top of her chest and flutters there, ragged and gasping.

Anna lies still, taking shallow breaths, trying not to panic. She relaxes her toes and moves up her body mentally relaxing each muscle, the way she learned in her younger years during a junior college yoga class.

John had always taken care of her when this happened, from the time she was in her early thirties, when the diagnosis of the mysterious illness that had dogged all of her plans for her life had changed from anxiety, to depression, to chronic fatigue, to fibromyalgia, to Lyme disease. *The great imitator*, they called it. Once it becomes chronic, it never really leaves. It can be managed, it goes into remission. It reappears when the body experiences too much stress. A lifetime of being almost okay, then not being okay at all, over and over. The two states chasing each other in a circle, day and night.

She is helpless, weak, feverish. In such a haze, the events of the last few weeks oppress her unbearably, but it is missing John that breaks her. She clutches his pillow against her chest, and his scent, juniper and lemon, rises softly from it. Anna can't distance herself from the absence anymore, doesn't have the strength. Knowing that she really has to live without him, without all of the little sacrifices they each made that kept their lives entwined. A home is something you make with another person, though you know it will end one day. It has to somehow. But after all those years, they hadn't even said goodbye. It had always been easy to imagine John living without her, but now she is the one alone. What had the color of John's eyes been? Lying in bed, unable to move, Anna grieves.

Spent, she pulls herself to a sitting position by using the headboard for leverage. Her feet dangle over the side of the mattress. A wave of dizziness hits her, and Anna sits bent with her head in her hands, waiting for it to pass.

She has to get downstairs. She has to take care of the animals. Everything depends upon her.

She slides out of bed and lands on her knees on the wooden floor. Leaning against the wall, she makes her way down the hall to the bathroom. She looks at herself in the mirror. Her pale face with its red blotches of fever swims in and out of focus. Then the room tilts and she falls.

Anna awakens not knowing how long she has been out. It's disorienting not to have any idea of the time, or if it is even the same day. It is uncomfortable, lying on the cold tile. She holds the cabinets and pulls herself up. She feels feeble, but the dizziness seems to have passed. She focuses on herself in the mirror—the fever brightens her eyes into two points of light.

Anna half-crawls to the stairs. With both hands, she holds the rail and slowly makes her way down, placing each foot one at a time and testing its stability before moving on. She gets to the landing and rests, sitting against the wall. The sheetrock is cool and smooth on her back.

Finally, she makes it to the kitchen. She needs to eat something that will give her strength, and she needs water. The border collie runs from her to the door, whining to go out. Still leaning against the wall, she makes her way to the mudroom and unlatches the bolt. The cold air flows in around her, rippling her flannel night-gown around her legs. The wind is as raw as her throat. She waits at the door until the dog comes back in, shielding her eyes against the sparkling snow and letting the merciless air focus her.

The cat meows and begs as it trails Anna to the pantry. She selects a can of food off the shelf for it and a can of chicken for herself. Both of the cans have pull tabs that Anna struggles with, but she is able to open them and tries not to cry again as she sits on the cold tile beside the cat, eating chicken out of the can with a fork and struggling to swallow it while the cat gulps and growls over its pâté.

How to feed the horses? Has she thrown down enough hay for the week? Anna doesn't have the energy to return upstairs and dress. She puts John's trench coat on, buttons it all the way down, and struggles into her muddy paddock boots.

The barn seems miles away from the door, and the white yard rises up toward it, as if it is on a hill. The wind whips around her and numbs her, goose-bumping her flesh. It's too cold to inhale. She buries her face in her scarf and presses ahead, looking down at her feet. She doesn't step over the snow—she is too weak to lift her knees so high—but flounders through it, going more and more slowly the farther she gets.

She can't open the barn door at first, then almost falls through it. The mule brays at her, a weird, wavering, high-pitched call. Keeper strikes his stall with his hoof, and it cracks like a shot in the closed barn; Anna's frayed nerves make her jump every time it hits.

"Stop it," she says, but her voice is a whisper. "Stop it!" How it hurts her head to yell. The horse nods at her, surprised, his ears forward.

With relief, Anna discovers that there's enough hay tossed down to last for another three days. She throws a portion of it to the horse and mule, then goes into the feed room to mix their grain. She feeds them, checks their water, and leaves without speaking to them or rubbing them on their foreheads as is her habit. They will have to stand in dirty stalls for a few days, until this spell of sickness lessens. Anna doesn't have enough energy to feel bad about it.

The only animals left to feed are the chickens. In weather this cold and dreary, there should be no eggs to gather. When she gets to the pen, she sees most of them are bundled inside near the heat lamp. Anna doesn't have to fight any back from the gate as she normally might. She lifts the lid to check on them, and they tilt their heads and look at her wisely. Some of them cluck, contented warbles. She can't remember why she has them, why she has to care for them. She refills the heated waterers and dumps out scratch from the metal garbage can beside the coop. Three times as much as usual. It will have to do. She can skip checking them tomorrow that way.

The house is so far away from the chicken pen. It seems to move farther even as she approaches it. Her body numb with cold under the gown and coat, her feet turning to ice under the snow that has fallen into the tops of her boots, she struggles against the snow until she falls, then crawls on hands and knees the rest of the way to the house. She lifts herself into the mudroom, sits back, and closes the door with her foot, shivering. The chores have sapped all the remaining strength from her body, and all the warmth, too. She leans against the wall to stand back up and nearly falls again under the resulting dizziness.

Anna has never questioned the cruelty of the disease, or asked why it infected her, or why she was misdiagnosed until it was too late to cure. There isn't any point. She learned to take whatever each day offers. It has been a long time since her last attack. She had forgotten what it was like to be so useless.

Anna will have trouble making it up and down the stairs. The sickness might last for three days or three months. Maybe even longer. She will have to step out of her own life for a while and rest. She reminds herself that many other people do this alone.

Anna sets up the faux-wood folding TV tray beside the couch. She fills a tumbler with room-temperature distilled water. She gathers whatever nonperishable food she can easily eat, puts it in a box, and sets it on the floor.

It's 2:35 in the afternoon. She sets the alarm on her cell phone to go off in twenty hours. That's how long she has this time, Anna tells herself firmly. She has no time to wallow in misery. She needs to be well. Everything depends upon her, and no one else. She pulls the quilt that usually drapes over the back of the couch over her cold body, leans back against the throw pillows, and closes her eyes.

15

Anna wakes to the sound of her phone buzzing against the surface of the TV tray. She reaches toward the sound, finds it, and blinks at the bright screen. No one is calling; it's the alarm. Where is she? What has happened? She feels a relaxing emptiness, far from concerning, as it ought to be—she has been drained of everything, even the will to worry. She lies for a while enjoying the feeling of weighing less, her head cradled in the pillow, her body held gently by the soft cushions.

It has been two days. She must have left the house the day before to feed the horses. She recalls what it felt like to stumble through the snow in the raw cold as though the memory plays through a filter, through a white fog, as though it happened in girlhood instead of only the day before. She is hot and hollow; her skin prickles with dry sweat. She feels her unwashed hair lying limp against her face.

Anna slips out from under the quilt, taking care not to rush getting up. She is weak. And it isn't over, never really will be. The palpitations of her heart feel like the frightened flight of a hare, all starts and stops, but the headache has gone, and the pain in her joints is bearable again. It seems as though she's been in bed for a week. But the date on her phone proves it hasn't been anywhere near that long. She has been lucky.

She straightens and stretches, and, holding the arm of the couch for support, looks around the room, waiting for the dizziness to subside. The low-ceilinged den is dark, shabby, small, but comfortable. This is how animals must feel about their burrows when they go to ground after injury or during bad weather. She is reluctant to leave it, though she is starting to feel closed in. After she steadies, Anna takes her time going upstairs, leaning on the rail.

She takes real clothes out of the closet in her bedroom, though they don't actually have a lot more structure than her pajamas—a thick warm sweater, fleece knee-patch breeches. Holding them folded in one arm, she runs her other hand down the row of shirts that belonged to John. They are almost all the same style, with variations in shades of colors. He had been a man of habits. So easy to picture him wearing them. She can see him so clearly she almost expects him to walk into the room and take up all the space without warning, the way he used to.

The bathroom mirror shows her pale and drawn. Her chest aches as she sits on the side of the tub, watching the water run. She feels the veins running like threads from her arms to her heart. The amount of energy it takes to get undressed surprises her; she has so little stamina. She lingers in the steaming water for far too long. It feels good, and she has little motivation to leave. But she has to make the trek to the barn again, and feed the chickens, too.

Anna has dressed and is running a comb through her hair when the doorbell rings. She stops with her comb mid-air, dripping. She isn't expecting anyone. It can be nothing good, can it? If she is still and quiet, perhaps the person at the door will leave.

The bell rings again, and before the sound dies out, there's another ring. Then, an insistent knocking. Anna sneaks down the stairs, trying to look out the window, but the angle is wrong. She gets to the ground level and peers through the frosted glass of the door from several feet away. She sees a dark shape. A man. He knocks again.

"Is anyone there?" he calls. "Ma'am? Are you okay?"

She calls back, "Who is it?" But he doesn't hear her.

He knocks again. "Ma'am?"

Anna hugs the doorway into the mudroom. His shape is all shoulders, his face a blur of highlights and shadows. He looks through the glass. He knocks again. It must be important. Maybe the horse and mule have gotten out. Abruptly, she rushes forward and unbolts the locks. The strong, smooth sound of them steadies her. She holds the door open a couple of inches, just enough to see who is there.

A young man she doesn't recognize, one with brown hair and warm brown eyes, greets her. "Are you Anna?" he asks.

"Yes," she says. "What is it? Is anything the matter?"

"No, ma'am," he says. "Sorry to bother you. I'm Ben. My mother is Dr. Hulett. The vet?" He holds out his hand, and Anna opens the door wider to shake it.

"What brings you here, Ben?" she asks. Her last visit with the vet seems like months ago, though it has only been days.

"My mother asked me to stop by and check on you—but I'm not supposed to tell you that—and show you how to use your rifle," he says. "I'm sorry I didn't call first. Is this a bad time?"

"Check on me?" Anna says.

Ben offers an apologetic grin. "She told me about the poachers and asked if I'd see how you're doing," he says. "I hope that's okay."

Anna nods. Even leaning against the doorframe, she can feel herself collapsing little by little on her shaking legs. The chores still have to be done. "No, it's fine," she says. "I have to feed the horses first, if that's all right. And John isn't here right now, but you can still show me how to use the gun. Come in out of the cold." She stands aside and holds the door. "Thank you for coming all this way."

"Don't worry about it," he says. "I got off work early today, so it worked out fine." He steps inside and wipes his feet on the mat. Anna is embarrassed when he glances around the room. How dingy the little house must look to a stranger. Especially now.

The border collie, which had provided several sharp barks at the knocking, sniffs eagerly at Ben's boots, and he scratches it behind the ears, speaking kindly to it. Its tail makes a whump-whump sound against the wall. Anna leads Ben to the kitchen table, conscious of the impression she must be making—lonely old woman, not bothering to get fully dressed. Watermarks of melted snow on the tile. House cat rubbing against her as she tries to walk. Rumpled quilt on the couch in the den. He will think she and her husband are having a fight and sleeping in different rooms.

The kitchen feels cozier with another person in it, especially one with the brilliance of youth.

"Please have a seat," she tells him. "Where do you work?"

He chooses her chair, not John's. "At the grocery store in Belbridge for now, mornings and weekends. I'm putting myself through school."

"Oh? What program?"

"Pre-med." He smiles. "My mom fixes animals. I'm going to fix people."

"The world can't have too many good doctors," Anna says. *God only knows.* "Please make yourself at home. There's bottled water in the fridge. I'll be right back."

She walks back upstairs. The awareness of Ben watching her leave makes her try to stand straighter, look less frail, grip the banister less tightly. Once she moves out of sight, she collapses against the wall and rests.

In the bathroom mirror, Anna watches herself pull her still-damp hair into a thick ponytail. She should dry it before going outside. That would be the smart thing to do. But she has to hurry, doesn't want to keep Ben waiting downstairs. She puts a little blush on her cheeks to help with her coloring. It has been years since she's used it. She looks fresher immediately.

Ben looks up with an unreadable expression when she comes back into the kitchen.

"Would you mind helping me feed the horses before we look at the gun?" Anna asks him. "I don't know when John will be back, and I need to throw down some hay."

"Sure," he says.

How much easier it is to pretend that everything is normal with another person there to bolster the idea. Ben walks beside her to the barn, talking easily. He doesn't know anything is wrong; Ben does not feel John's absence. Ben has not let anyone die, does not know Anna's guilt. No one has ever made allowances for her being ill, since she doesn't look particularly ill on the outside, and sometimes that helps her to get through. She can act like the path to the barn isn't nearly impossible some days. Ben tells her stories about school, not worrying about what she does at all.

Once in the barn, he walks straight to Charlie. "This must be the mule that got shot," he says.

"Yes."

"He's healed well."

Anna agrees. "Your mother does a good job. If you're anything like her, you'll be a great doctor."

She shows Ben the hayloft and explains how he will have to swing the hay down. He climbs the ladder with the loose, graceful movements that the young take for granted.

"How many bales?" he asks.

All of them. But she doesn't want to raise his suspicions. So she says, "How about ten or twelve. That will last me for a while."

She stands out of the way near the stalls as the bales swoop over the edge of the loft and land with a soft thud in the aisle. During the pauses, she drags them out of the way, stacking them a couple deep. Even that exhausts her.

Ben comes down the ladder and brushes the hay off his jeans. "How's that?" he asks.

"Beautiful," she says. "Thank you. Can I pay you . . . ?"

"No, it was no trouble," he says. "Hey, I was thinking. We have a lot of vegetables and things that go bad at the market. We used to have an older guy that got them for his donkeys, but he died a few months ago, and now we just throw them away. Could you use them? They're cheap. Ten dollars for a big crate. Sometimes it's all pumpkins or watermelons or something seasonal. Sometimes a mix of things."

Anna doesn't know what to say. It's a nice gesture, but she doubts whether one horse and one mule can safely eat such a diet; she strictly regulates their food intake to avoid issues like colic, founder, and insulin resistance. Still, it could save money if she could do something with it. Give it to the chickens. Eat it herself.

"That's a kind offer," she says. "I'll ask John and get back to you."

"Let me know before Monday, and I can get you next week's," he tells her.

Anna leads the way to the sugarhouse, where she has left the rifle. Ben chats amicably beside her, comfortable in his skin in a way Anna envies. They both see the prints in the snow at the same time and stop.

Ben whistles. "Those are some big tracks." He kneels beside them. "Looks almost like a wolf or something."

Anna had forgotten about the wolf; it had appeared right before she got so sick, and seemed a part of a delirium. "I'm sure you know wolves are extinct here," Anna says. "The neighbor's Great Pyrenees must have gotten out again."

"Too bad about the wolves, too," he says. "I've always wanted to see one in the wild."

Anna has seen some in captivity, furtive and thin, trotting in manmade habitats with their tails lowered in defeat. The one she had seen in the trees, if she had really seen it, was regal and healthy. "I wouldn't mind having them around myself," she says. "I have far more trouble with loose dogs than I've ever had with wildlife like coyotes and bears." *Chickens, still alive with holes through their bodies. The mule at the old place, leg torn to the tendons and bleeding.*

"Dogs are too used to people to be afraid of them sometimes," Ben says. "Especially if no one's cared enough to train them."

They continue on in silence while Anna wonders if she had really seen the wolf. She can't be sure. If it was real, flesh and blood, it had been on her land, and its safety might rely on its being kept a secret. Wolves are not a protected species because they aren't supposed to be there in the first place, and the state has no interest in reintroducing them; people are still too afraid of them.

Although her neurological illness sometimes causes Anna to hallucinate, she can usually tell when it happens. But not all the time. She has been wrong often enough that she can't fully trust herself; she survives by not asking too many questions. The disease, how thoroughly it disconnects her, makes her distrust everything. Sometimes, nothing feels real. Sometimes everything does, and even the books she reads while waiting to fall asleep seem like her own life.

She opens the sugarhouse door and ushers Ben inside. As soon as they pass the threshold, he notices the rifle leaning against the wall and picks it up with the ease of someone who has spent years around guns, the same way Anna handles horses.

"You've got it here for protection, I see," he says, obviously stifling amusement. "But you don't know how to use it?"

Anna smiles. "I guess I figured that just showing it to someone would be enough. That would certainly work on me."

"Sometimes it is enough," Ben agrees, "but just in case . . . you have ammo?"

Anna gets one of the boxes from the shelf and sets it on the table.

Ben shows her how to operate the safety first, off and on, off and on, then has her do it herself. It's simple enough, though

Anna isn't sure she will remember which way is which. He shows her how to remove the magazine. They load it, reattach it, remove it, and unload it, then do it over again, over and over until Anna can do it without hesitation. And then beyond that, until tiredness slows her down again, and she begins to make mistakes. She fears it has taken her an unusually long time to grasp it.

To her relief, Ben doesn't push her further. "That's probably enough for today," he says. "I have a feeling I should get to my homework at some point this afternoon, too."

Anna thanks him. "Will you come back in a few days," she says, "and help me learn to shoot it?"

"I'd be happy to, but I don't know when yet. It depends on my work schedule. But I'll let you know. Actually give you notice this time," he says.

"I really do appreciate your help."

"No problem," Ben says. "Though I feel obligated to tell you that a .22 isn't exactly the most imposing weapon. Not much better than a stick, really," he jokes.

"I don't want to hurt anyone badly," Anna says. "Just scare them off."

"It should be fine for that, then. And it could definitely cause a world of pain at close range." He steps outside, then turns and offers his hand. She takes it, and he helps her down the steps. "I'll tell my mom you're okay," he says. "And you seem like you have everything under control. But just out of curiosity, do you know when your husband might be back?"

The question isn't rude, coming from such a pleasant countenance. "Soon," Anna tells him.

"I'll let her know. Call us if you need anything in the meantime."

She thanks him, and Ben walks her back to the house. She waves at him from the porch as he backs down the driveway. He waves in return before disappearing behind the trees, though the dull bass sound of music echoes from inside his truck for several seconds after he is out of sight. As soon as it dies out, she returns to the snow-covered yard and feeds the chickens, which coo at her contentedly from their boxes.

She takes the gun with her back to the house. She intends to keep it nearby. Let the neighbors think what they like if they see her carrying it. With the men in the black truck, the woods and even the yard have lost any remaining illusion of safety. Now that she knows how to do it, the rifle will be kept loaded.

16

Anna brings in far less money than John did, but it's enough to keep the animals fed and the electricity on. Her jobs in the saddle shop take less and less time as she gains experience. Her hands, once thin and soft under their age-spotted skin, grow strong and certain in their movements. She has caught up any of John's work that she is capable of doing. Perhaps she could build saddles from the tree up, after all, with enough practice.

At least two repair orders a week come in from all over the region, some of them dropped off by locals, some shipped to her. She buys a vintage leatherworking book with yellowed paper at the used bookstore in Belbridge and advertises to repair harness, too; this starts to make more money than the saddle repair. The Belgian draft horses used to collect maple sap from buckets during the season can be hard on their equipment, and harness is expensive to replace. Some of it has been mended so often that little of the original material remains.

The delivery drivers know Anna by sight and have learned to leave larger, heavier packages in front of the door of the shop. The trucks come around the same time every day, and Anna watches for them. If a delivery is left, the border collie barks a certain way, and Anna moves the boxes inside as soon as she can to lower the risk of theft or weather damage. She props the shop door open and pushes the more cumbersome boxes in while the warm air from the stove rushes past her into the yard and the border collie dashes in semicircles behind her, yipping at her efforts.

Anna keeps the gun with her as far as seems reasonable, though she still doesn't know how to shoot it. Ben has picked up an extra job in the sporting goods store for the holidays and apologetically delays the next lesson. Anna doesn't really mind. She has gotten used to the heft of it; she could probably figure out how to use it in a pinch, with adrenaline to drive her. How hard could it be? Safety off, pull the trigger. Bang. The only other thing she doesn't know how to do is aim. The rifle's weight has started to comfort instead of alarm her. Before she sleeps, she slips it into the dust under her bed, just within reach.

Anna never rides Keeper or Charlie on the eastern side of the property or walks in that direction herself. Every time she plans to do it, something comes up—it's too cold, she has too much to do, Keeper acts too spooky, she's too tired. She behaves as though her useable land has been cut in half. She takes the truck out every few days and slowly drives up and down the road next to the property line instead. The rails of the fence run from post to post in an unbroken stripe. She never gets out of the truck or stops it. She drives to the end of her land, turns around, and comes back.

Anna receives a Christmas card from the feed store. *Christmas?* The calendar in the shop indicates that deer hunting season has ended the week before. The knowledge washes her in relief, a wave of warmth that radiates from her center, pleasant as the feeling that comes from drinking a large glass of wine. She starts sleeping in stretches of several hours at night. The hold the illness had taken on her body slips even more.

The cat, the horse and mule, the dog, the chickens are well— all seems at peace.

Ben appears with his delivery of discarded produce every Monday. She keeps a cup of coffee ready for him, and he gulps it while they visit briefly about the weather, the store, and sometimes his mother and the clients she treats. He can never stay more than a few minutes, but that just means Anna isn't inconvenienced by him, and she looks forward to the visits.

Ben doesn't ask about John again, but Anna can tell sometimes that he wants to; if he hints toward that end, Anna interrupts and implies that John is either in the shop or in town. She tries to work him into the conversation sometimes herself, as though she has just spoken to him, like he has just left the room and is still on her mind. "He's been so busy lately. He'll be sorry he missed you," she says. When she says it, she believes it.

Though the winter does not loosen its grip on the Northeast Kingdom, the darkness will soon start receding, the days will start to grow longer and brighter again. Everyone can feel it. On bad days, Anna's words float out of her and hover above the empty bundle of clothes in the clearing, moved by bitter wind. On good days, she feels John in the kitchen as though he is standing right behind her, deep in his own thoughts, snow melting off his boots. She is glad that she has good days at all.

Anna never knows what she will find when she opens the crate of produce Ben brings, but something nice usually appears at the top. Because of the consistency of the little surprises, she suspects Ben throws in a few unbruised apples or cartons of still-good berries or fresh bunches of spinach on purpose. Understanding such kindness to be a spell that can be broken, Anna doesn't mention it, and neither does he.

Whatever Anna can't eat herself or freeze, she shreds and feeds to the chickens. The produce that they aren't likely to eat, she throws behind the paddock fence into a kind of compost heap, out of reach of the horses. The winter cold preserves or wilts it, depending on the type of fruit or vegetable, and it pauses in whatever state of decay it had been in when Anna had thrown it out. It will decompose once spring comes and the Kingdom thaws.

Perhaps, too, when spring arrives, Anna can try at having a garden again. It has been years since she and John planted anything besides a few flowers next to the porch. Flowers that they had neglected to tend the last few years, letting the butterfly bush nearly take over the door at the height of summer, so it would grab at their clothing and scratch their arms. Every time the door opened, bees got in. John or Anna would capture them buzzing against the window glass, cup their hands around them, carry them out. Neither of them had ever gotten stung.

This week after sorting, the pile of produce to be dumped out looms over the pile for Anna to eat and the pile for the chickens. She tosses the compost items back into the cardboard box and carries them out, unable to see where she puts her feet because of the size of the box she holds across her middle.

The quiet of the late morning makes everything about her seem loud—her boots shuffling through the thick wet ground, her breath behind the knit scarf, the swish and creak of the box in her arms, the rub of the hood of her coat against her ears.

She makes her way around the back of the barn, studying the items in the box as she goes. They look like a cornucopia that has sat out too long. Soft, wrinkled tomatoes with worm holes, gnats, and moldy stems. Potatoes with white sprouts growing from their eyes—some have bruises of rot and have started to stink. Rainbow chard that, on second thought, she can perhaps save for herself by sautéing it, despite its mushy edges.

She walks out of the shadow of the barn and stops abruptly at the movement in front of her. A doe stands tense at the compost heap, scenting the air, ears flicking back and forth, dark amber eyes watching her. Anna and the doe wait for a long moment, neither moving. Then Anna backs up into the barn's shadow, still holding the box. She flattens herself against the wooden planks to watch.

The doe searches the shadows for several minutes, moves off haltingly a few strides, then returns to the pile, lifting its hooves gracefully over the uneven snow. It roots, then lifts its head, chewing. But it has become too nervous to stay, and after peering again into the shallow blue twilight that hides Anna, it turns and bounds off toward the woods. It watches her for a while from just inside the tree line. Then it disappears, dissolving into trees.

Anna's arms hurt from holding the box. It is too heavy for her. She sets it down and stretches. She makes her way to the compost heap. The doe has spread it out a little, or some other animal has. She is surprised at the number of tracks marking the earth all around it, mostly the two teardrop marks of deer, and if she looks closely, the tridents of birds, the padded toes of rodents. The compost heap sits like the spoke of a wheel, with animal tracks radiating out from it toward the trees in all directions, though some of the trails are better worn than others. She is kicking the heap back together when a track that is far larger than those of the deer catches her eye. A familiar thrill of fear and excitement tingles up her spine. A moose has been there. One even bigger than the mule Charlie, from the looks of it.

Anna no longer takes the time to sort Ben's deliveries. As soon as he leaves, she carries the box to the compost heap and overturns it, then retreats to watch. The fruit rolls down to the edges, which, it turns out, keeps the animals from digging through the pile so much and making such a mess; they tend to eat the sweetest pieces first.

17

January and February are the worst months. The snow comes down slowly but doesn't let up until it is past Anna's ankles, then her knees. Keeping the pipes in the house from freezing is a struggle. The sky stays gray. Anna goes out once to look at her southern boundary; she likes seeing how the stream changes with the seasons. Though it usually clamors and flows dark and white even through most of winter, it has frozen hard at the edges. In the middle, under a thin sheet of ice, the water rushes soundlessly. It is a dark mirror, too treacherous to try crossing. She finds places farther upstream where animals have broken through to drink.

Anna spends more and more time inside the house on these short, cold days. Leatherworking orders had slowed immediately after Christmas, and they won't pick up again until spring. She turns up the electric heater, buys more firewood, and keeps an eye on her account, pulling fifty dollars at a time out of savings to cover bills. Though she misses the occupation, she is sometimes glad not to be spending as much time in the sugarhouse, not to have to go back and forth in the bitter wind so often, not to have so many obligations. She can get some rest.

Sometimes, she feels like she is the lone queen of a winter kingdom. She has no king, no royal children, few subjects. She lives in a wooden house on a white tundra, harsh country that draws its immaculate beauty from its isolation.

The warmth inside the house is a luxury. It seems miraculous that anything can survive outdoors. Seeking an escape from their seasonal hunger, the mice move farther into the walls and gnaw. Anna gets out of bed and hits the plaster with her fist when they grow too loud. Over a hundred years of mice, countless generations of teeth, seasons of famine and of plenty, ebb and flow of prey and predator, and the house still stands.

On the hardest days, her home seems to her to sit at the center of an expanse of cruelty. When fronts come in, the merciless wind breaks tree branches with the sharp noise of cannon fire. The windows groan in their frames. Even in the short walk between her home and the barn, her thin body grows stiff and dull, and she has to gasp to get air. She blows clouds of her warmth into the sky and walks into them. It hurts her chest to move. She quotes Robert Frost's poem "A Servant to Servants," set in the Vermont highlands, to herself like a mantra: "By good rights I ought not to have so much / Put on me, but there seems no other way." *Of course, someone named Frost would understand this place.*

The almanac says that the winter will be difficult—both colder and wetter than most. Anna takes to leaving the television on while she is awake. The degree of light that comes in the windows barely changes from morning to night. Sometimes the TV is left on even into the very early morning hours, and she sits restless and bored before infomercials trying to sell junk that would fall apart in your hands. But she can't abide the quiet. Without some kind of noise, the silence of the house yawns over her with barometric heaviness, an overwhelming lack of sound that makes her feel as though a storm is gathering, but will never break.

With a mug of tea and brandy, Anna unwinds every evening and watches the news without worrying about it, it seems so far away. She curls tightly under the quilt that she has draped across her knees; the border collie has finally been allowed onto the couch and lies tucked beside her, its head on her lap. It has learned also to get into her bed after she falls asleep. At first, it had inevitably woken her with its panting or its movement, and she would kick it out of the bedroom, follow behind its slinking form, and shut the door. But she soon comes to appreciate its presence beside her, the fact that it is warm and alive, that it snores and grunts and kicks and burrows in the comforter while it dreams, and makes her less alone. If she wakes up during the night, its form rests solidly against hers. Even when it isn't touching her, she can feel the warmth coming from it. Sometimes on a whim she hugs the dog against her so tightly that it squirms in complaint. But it still doesn't leave once she releases it, only looks at her with the same wise, forgiving eyes nearly every dog seems naturally to possess.

The forest doesn't have enough food left for all of the beasts that inhabit it, and the animals become lean and rough. Anna's compost heap becomes a gathering place. She can't count the deer that are there, whitetails and mule deer, bucks and does. Even the scraggly coyotes, foxes, fisher-cats, and skunks begin to come in for rotten scraps or the chance to catch an errant mouse or muskrat.

It doesn't take long for the coyotes to grow too bold. They sneak into the yard under the cover of darkness the first time they catch a hint of that attractive mix of sugar and decay, but soon begin foraging there openly during the day. Their yelps and snarls rip the freezing air all morning and afternoon, grating on the nerves of the horse and mule in the barn. Even with kinder weather, Anna would have feared letting Charlie and Keeper into their paddock while wildlife made desperate by hunger scuffled nearby, though she does not fear those animals herself.

Anna decides to go into Belbridge, though she doesn't need food yet. At the beginning of the spell of bad weather, Ben had offered to bring her groceries to her with his delivery of expired produce. She gave him a list, and now he brings the same items for her every week. He asks her occasionally if she wants some variety, but she tells him that older people like their habits, and he doesn't question that. For all they both know, it is true. Anna always tells Ben to buy slightly more than what she really needs; she is, after all, supposed to be feeding two people with it. She has a large pantry. And she really doesn't mind having the same menu over and over. She appreciates not needing to plan her meals one by one. It keeps her from having to add more to her lists of remembering.

No, she doesn't need to leave her home, but she wants to leave this time, drive away from the little pale house and abandon it behind her to mark where someone has been, like a buoy in an angry sea. She is weary of it and weary of being inside. She needs to get away from those small dim rooms, see something new. To know that her dreary, frozen world can be escapable.

Though Anna still dislikes driving—it makes her as jittery and nervous as ever—the truck itself no longer intimidates her. It is a sort of beige workhorse, uncreative but honest, and ultimately helpful. Its bulk encloses her, keeps her from the weather. She has grown used to its loose steering and less-than-responsive brakes, learns to keep her wrists relaxed (though she can never make herself relax her grip), learns to step on the heavy pedals early enough to keep from running the stop sign, even in ice. She has developed the habit of saying out loud to herself each landmark she passes: forked tree, street sign, mailbox, water tank, filling station. It has become like a nursery rhyme; she can imagine the route to Belbridge clearly when she recites landmarks from the shelter of her kitchen. She makes sure she can get through the list of landmarks before she ever picks up her keys.

Post-its spread across the dash of the truck in a flurry of hot pink and green. Their adhesive doesn't stick to the dust-covered, greasy plastic, so Anna has duct-taped them into position. They hold directions to the places she usually goes and list what she usually buys there. If she does lose her place, she checks the notes.

Though the truck's old heater chugs away at full blast, the temperature outside is so cold that the air only warms Anna's neck and dries out her eyes. She arrives at the grocery store with numb hands and feet. The sliding doors welcome her inside with a rush of heat, and she steps through with gladness, though her cheeks flush red and tingle with the sudden change in environment. She takes off her gloves and blinks at the bright lights of the store, the colorful displays of goods that stretch away from her, row after row. It isn't a large store, but Belbridge is lucky to have it.

"Anna!"

The friendliness in the familiar voice cheers her. "Ben! I didn't know you were working today."

"I'm filling in for someone with a sick kid," he says. "What are you doing here?"

What am *I doing here?* she asks herself. What is a reason that doesn't sound pathetic or depressing? "I wanted to make something different tonight," she tells him. Her mind grasps for something. Anything. "Pancakes."

"Sounds good!" Ben says. "Should I add some mix to your grocery list from now on?"

"Maybe," she says. "We'll talk about it."

Ben smiles. A woman has arrived at the register with the backlit number and is watching them impatiently. "Don't forget the syrup," Ben says to Anna.

"I won't."

He straightens his smock and walks around the end of the counter, says something to the woman about the impending snow. *He's a good kid*, Anna thinks. *Would my child have been that way?* and she contemplates him with fleeting regret before turning.

She makes her way up and down the aisles in no hurry, picking up items and putting them back. The store plays soft rock music through its speakers. In the café at the back, four gray-haired men sit in a red booth, drinking complimentary coffee. The coffee smells good, but Anna has tried it there before—it isn't worth pouring a paper cup's full—it's a commercial brand, too thick and bitter, with a stale aftertaste that suggests the beans have been burned. She can feel the men watching her as she circles the endcaps, though their attention feels neither curious nor malicious. It's more like how you have to watch a television that is on even if it's on mute and nothing interesting is happening, just because the picture moves.

Their conversation, though animated, refers only to the weather. One doesn't remember a winter this cold; one says that of course there have been others. This is a difficult one, true, but nothing special, nothing a true Vermonter can't handle. Just seems worse coming after that strange warm spell.

"But it's been hard even for the wildlife," one of the men says.

"Frank's right," the other agrees, nodding. "I haven't seen hide nor hair of a deer in weeks."

"Come to think of it, I haven't either."

This surprises Anna, and she stops just inside the aisle she has turned onto; the men can't see her there, but she can hear them. She had seen plenty of deer only that morning. Scores of them cross her yard, going between the compost heap and the trees, every day.

"Maybe they're holed up somewhere, waiting it out," someone says.

"They'd have to come out and find food sometimes. There isn't anything for them to eat right now in the mountains."

That's true; life gets progressively thinner at the higher elevations. Trees get smaller and smaller, and then disappear altogether. Not much can survive conditions at the summits, especially during winter. Farther south there's a place called Mount Hunger. Anna has always shivered at the name, believing it must have come about because a great suffering had occurred there. The name is said to have been earned after a hunting party returned from the mountain without game, which doesn't sound all that traumatic. But she has wondered if there is more to it than that. How devastating must someone's hunger be for people to call a mountain after it?

Anna picks up a box and shakes it absentmindedly. Skinny, light, bright blue, yellow, and red—spaghetti noodles. That sounds good. She acts like she is reading the ingredients, like it takes several minutes for her to read three words—*semolina flour, water.*

"I heard a lot about poachers last season," one of the men is saying. "You don't think that poachers have . . . ?"

"Of course not," his friend protests. "The population going into the season was healthy. If anything, there may have been too many deer."

"Maybe that's the problem. There were too many for the grazing to support."

"Wild animals can take care of themselves," a gruff voice says. "They'll be back in spring."

"Along with the bugs and bears and mud."

"I'll still take those over this weather," one of the men says. "It's too cold to get anything done outside. What are you working on these days, Cal?" The conversation switches to home brewing, and Anna wanders away.

Driving home in the half-light, she considers the disappearing deer. She imagines does and bucks standing quietly together in caves, breathing their heat in clouds that dissipate over them like ghosts while they wait in their dark shelters. A thought strikes her with such force that she stops the truck right in the middle of its lane.

It's her! She laughs. Of course. The missing deer are because of her. She is at fault. She has been feeding them for weeks; she may as well have baited them. The animals must have abandoned everyone else's land for hers. That's why she hasn't noticed anything amiss.

Then she really is a queen, with deer and coyotes as her lords and vassals.

She takes her foot off the brakes and lets the truck glide forward while she considers what such a consequence means, then urges the truck into speed. If she can keep the deer in her forest, that close to her house, where she can watch them, she can protect them. Not just the deer, but all of the animals. Not just from poachers, but from everyone.

18

Anna doesn't remark the precise moment that spring begins to quicken the Northeast Kingdom. There are little changes that add up. The snow cover thins, showing brown earth in patches that grow larger every afternoon, tears in a white cloth. Before long, there is more brown than white; then, there is no white at all in the open spaces, and then very little white stays on only in the deepest shadows and hollows, and elsewhere, the pastures blush with green. Every season begins by being unfamiliar.

The clearing with the black truck lurks always just behind Anna's thoughts; she sees the man pleading with her when she sleeps, or he stands at the window when she glances out; when he creeps into her awareness, she forces herself to picture the snow melting where he had fallen to reveal a ground wiped clean, as though nothing has ever happened to disturb it. She tries to convince herself that her existence is made up of days that she has chosen.

Anna migrates the compost heap—the odor of which, due to the warmer weather, has started to reach the yard when the wind is right—nearer the trees by dumping each box of produce a little closer to them, a little farther from the barn. Doing so results in relative peace in the yard immediately surrounding her house and outbuildings, though sometimes if she pauses in her chores and listens, she can still hear coyotes bickering with each other over the best morsels. The coyotes come less frequently than before, now that spring has innervated their blood and set them to hunting and breeding. The grass hasn't grown much yet, and the deer come as often as ever.

Everything is easier when it isn't so cold. Anna releases the horse and mule into the paddock to spend their days and brings them in at night. Every morning they stand taut with quivering skin in the chilly air, then, as if in response to some invisible signal, run at breakneck speed along the perimeter of the fence, bucking and kicking up clods of earth, sliding to last-minute stops before they hit the rails. Skids in the mud ending at rounded points of hooves show how close they get to hitting them. But they are both athletic and not prone to clumsiness. Anna watches them transfixed for a while after releasing them; she enjoys the recklessness of their play and couldn't stop it even if she wanted to.

She doesn't drive out to check the boundary fence anymore. The warmer weather, which allows wildlife to move around more freely, to go farther into the mountains and deeper into the woods, brings with it a much lower risk of poaching, and there is no longer any need.

In mid-March, the *Gazette* begins to run articles about the missing deer. By early April, some related commentary is always on the front page. The town of Belbridge relies on the hunting season, and vanishing wildlife does not bode well for the next year's business. Now is the time for herds to start recovering from the hard weather and increase, but instead, the townsfolk note, they have gone—assumed to have migrated elsewhere for food and shelter, or to have starved over the winter. The *Gazette* observes that hunting season is the one time of year the town's hotels and cabins are full. The owner of the grocery store depends on the extra profits for the small holiday bonuses he gives to the manager and cashiers. The owner of the sporting goods store tells the *Gazette*'s one reporter that his shop would disappear in a year without the business of deer hunters to buoy it.

There are several editorials bemoaning how the tension in parts of Belbridge manifests in new irritabilities some of the residents display when dealing with each other. They are said to be less prone to waving off fender benders or errors on receipts, more likely to snap and argue. "This used to be a nice town," one woman complains. Even outsiders have apparently started to argue, but about how the missing deer might change the ecosystem. There have often been too many deer, not too few. How will predators and scavengers adjust? Can the surrounding forests stay healthy? Will dangerous parasites like ticks decrease? No one knows.

Anna absorbs these paragraphs with a mild interest; though she is responsible for the situation, its consequences don't seem likely to affect her. She reasons away any rare flinches of conscience by telling herself *I am doing something important.* She keeps herself busy. The saddle repairs and tack orders have picked back up with the change in seasons, and she stays for long hours in the sugarhouse, toughening her body once more against the awl and needle. She possesses the benefit of muscle memory this time, and it doesn't take her long to get back into the habit of the work.

She lifts the harness she intends to mend next, rubbing it between her thumb and forefinger. The tarnished buckles gleam with a dull light in the curves. Soft and dark-chocolate-colored with age, the leather smells of horses, salt, and loam. She is starting to appreciate the tack as much as she appreciates the animals themselves. It, too, has its own history and personality. Its own stories. Anna hums as she works.

There is a loud thud outside, followed by the mule's trumpeting bray, and Anna drops the harness and stands tangled in it, gazing around the shop in surprise. The dog sits up in its bed, ears upright, then goes to the door and barks in sharp, brittle raps like knocks on a window.

Anna stumbles free of the harness and looks out; she can't see anything. There's another thud and the sound of galloping hooves. She picks up the rifle and runs, the border collie racing low in front of her.

At the paddock she scrambles to a stop, aghast. Charlie screams and paces the fence in fury; Keeper cowers in the far corner. A black bear, hungry and groggy from its winter sleep, stands on its hind legs near the barn.

It yawns, blinks, and looks around the blur of forest and buildings with its small, near-sighted eyes. Its lips curl over its yellowed teeth, and its snout wriggles, wet black nose reading the currents of air. The remains of the compost heap behind it spread in a swath across the pasture. The bear must have dug in the refuse for some time before it noticed the horse and mule.

Before Anna can react, the border collie bolts beneath the rails of the paddock and between the hooves of the kicking mule. It darts past the outer edge of the fence and runs barking toward the bear, which grunts and begins to lower its heavy body in response.

"Come here!" Anna cries. The dog runs in circles, darting in to nip the bear's heels, then flashing out again. The bear lumbers on all four feet and growls, snapping its jaws.

"Come here!" Anna calls the dog again and again, begging, demanding it obey, but it won't come. It doesn't even twitch an ear at her. It is John's dog, really, after all. The bear takes swipes at it with paws matted by mud. Charlie strikes again and again at the fence with his hooves, knocking the rails loose.

Anna sprints around the end of the paddock just as the bear lands a blow that sends the border collie yelping and rolling. The hit thuds, as though the dog's soft belly has been struck with a wooden bat, and Anna nearly falls to her knees.

The dog lies struggling to rise at the edge of her view as Anna stops and lifts the rifle. It is foolish to shoot a bear with a .22, but she has to try to distract it somehow, and it is all she can think to do.

The bear looks at her, its small eyes glinting. If Anna were closer, she might see a tiny image of herself reflected against the sky in its pupils.

In slow motion, she presses the cold weight of the gun against her shoulder and leans her cheek against it; it is uncomfortable, strange. She closes one eye, the way she's seen in old Westerns; she lines the sight on the bear's forehead, trying to keep it near the bear's ear as the bear turns toward the prone figure of the dog.

Anna takes a deep breath out, a deep breath in, and holds it. Her body goes still. Though the dog whines and thrashes, and the mule still tears at the fence, she ignores them. The world falls silent around her, as though she stands in the center of all the bad that could happen. She feels the trigger with her index finger—its thin metal ring has been worn smooth by someone—and she squeezes.

Something is wrong. There is no explosion of sound, no thrust into her collarbone, nothing Anna had braced for. She presses the trigger again immediately, harder. It isn't working. The trigger sticks fast.

She squeezes again, holding the gun out from her body and looking at it. It's like something is behind the trigger, blocking it. *Shit shit shit.* With shaking hands, Anna clicks open the magazine, but everything looks fine as far as she can tell.

The bear has forgotten all about her and towers over the whimpering dog. Anna tries to fire again, wildly, toward the bear, but the gun won't go off. In desperation, she yells at the bear, "Hey! Hey, get out of here!" and waves the rifle like a flag, but it doesn't turn.

She looks around the ground for rocks—none. Only mud. Still yelling, she races behind the bear and hits it as hard as she can with the barrel of the gun. It bounces off the bear's shaggy back with a satisfying thump, and the bear turns to face her and stands there, baring its teeth. It swipes at her.

Anna backs away, holding the rifle between herself and the bear. She screams and waves her arms, scrapes up clods of mud at her feet and throws them, then steps toward the bear again with no fear in her posture, the way she would run at a horse that charged her, making herself seem bigger than she is. Still, the bear holds its ground.

Anna swings the rifle at its head as hard as she can. She manages to hit its open mouth.

The bear closes its jaw in silence and falls back to the ground, shaking its head, pawing at its nose. Anna stands panting, holding the rifle across her body, and waits.

After backing up several slow steps, the bear hesitates and looks from her, to the dog, to the mule that still brays and throws itself at the splintering fence. Anna takes off her coat and waves it, letting the breeze fill and lift it so that it spreads, rippling and crackling. Then she snaps it back. "Git! Get out of here!"

The bear turns and takes a step away. It squints back at Anna. Then it breaks into a lope, runs toward the woods, and disappears between the trees. Beneath the whimpering of the border collie and the snorting of the mule, there is the sound of the bear crashing through the brush, all power and no grace. Anna listens until she can't hear it anymore, until the sound seems far enough away. She drops the gun.

Lightheaded, she approaches the border collie. It flounders in the grass like a broken bird.

19

The vet's office picks up on the fifth ring. Anna counts them as she waits. Between each insistent clanging, there is the buzz of low static that seems to take an eternity. It is the noise at the background of the line, the noise of empty space. The receptionist tells her to bring the border collie in right away. Dr. Hulett happens to be on the regular day shift, and will see her as soon as she arrives. The office sounds busy in the background—dogs barking, people in conversation, a bird whistling a clumsy tune and squawk-talking.

Anna opens the garage door, turns the truck on, and leaves it idling with the passenger-side door open.

She doesn't want to touch the dog, much less move it. It lies at her feet on its side, panting and wheezing and whimpering while blood drips in bright beads from its nose and mouth. When Anna had asked how she should pick it up, the receptionist had said, "Carefully." There isn't enough care in the world for this. Anna kneels beside the border collie and begins to work her hands underneath its warm body. It yelps once and turns with an open mouth as if to bite her, but groans and falls back. Anna says, "I'm sorry," and keeps going.

She carries the border collie to the truck trying not to jar it, ignoring the strain of her arms and back, but it whines with every concussion of her steps. It stays where she lays it in the passenger seat, looks at her with its light amber eyes full of hurt, but doesn't move.

The shocks of the old truck seem to have gotten worse. As Anna bullies it down the dirt road, it creaks and shudders as though it will shake apart. With every bounce she winces and glances at the dog, though it only stares at the dash in resigned silence. She puts one hand on its head and it looks up with great effort and tries to lick her. She wants to take this as a good sign, though it really doesn't mean anything; John once told her that even dogs that were being vivisected had licked the hands of the people who had cut them open on the table, who had watched their hearts beat down like watches unwinding. This effort didn't save them, didn't mean forgiveness, didn't mean that they stopped dying.

By running through all of the intersections, Anna speeds through Belbridge faster than she had expected to and arrives at the vet's office within twenty minutes. She runs inside and cries for help; the faces that turn toward her over the bright clusters of jackets are pale and surprised. The tech looks at her suspiciously but follows her outside. Anna opens the truck door. The tech whistles through his teeth and gives her a look that makes her shrink.

"Bear attack," Anna says. "Please hurry."

The tech cradles the cringing dog in his arms and carries it right through the office and into the hallway while Anna holds the doors. She tries to follow him into the examination room that waits ready with its cold metal table and jars of swabs, but the receptionist steps in front of her.

"Let them get her settled and take a look at her," she says kindly. "You can wait in here."

Anna stands frustrated for a moment, closing and unclosing her hands. She turns to look around the waiting room; most of the people there try not to look back at her, uncomfortable with her distress. They pet their healthy dogs, which are there only for vaccinations or routine surgeries. They stick their fingers through the cages of their pet carriers for their cats to rub. She selects a chair in the middle of two unoccupied seats, fills out the paperwork the receptionist hands her, and settles in to wait. There's a stack of torn and grimy magazines nearby. She picks one up and turns the pages, but can't concentrate well enough to read.

The door opens, and the vet tech says her name. She walks down the hallway with trembling knees. The border collie lies on a table with tubes in her front leg and a clear plastic cone over her nose. Dr. Hulett greets her by squeezing her arm.

"I'm afraid she's got a broken spine, Anna," she says.

The dog on the table is too small, can't possibly be hers. She reaches for the prone figure, touches its side, feels its insensibility to her, and draws back.

"Oh," she says. "Is there anything you can do?"

"I'm sorry. There's too much internal damage." Dr. Hulett shakes her head. "Anna, she's dying. All I can really do is help her to go more peacefully."

Anna bites her lip, fighting tears. "Euthanize her?"

"I think that would be the right thing to do," the vet says, "but you have to make that decision yourself. I can't make it for you. Do you understand?"

Anna nods. "Yes. Please. I don't want her to keep suffering."

"Do you want me to leave the room so that you can say good-bye?"

"No, that's okay," Anna says. She moves around the table and cups the border collie's sharp face with her hand, rubs between its ears. She can clearly picture the eyes' golden flecks, though the lids are closed. The dog doesn't respond to her touch.

"She's not feeling any pain," the vet says. "We've got her on morphine. You can take your time."

Anna strokes the rough black and white fur that has always stayed knotted no matter how much she brushes it. She feels herself start to collapse, feels the lump rising in her throat, and swallows it. It hurts all the way down, like a pill that is too big.

"Anna," Dr. Hulett asks in a soft voice, "can you tell me how this happened?"

Anna can't keep looking at the dog. "A bear," she says. "She ran at it, and it hit her."

"On your property?"

"Yes."

"Any idea where it came from? Or why it was there?"

Anna shakes her head. She should have known better than to keep a compost heap in the open. So foolish, to get carried away in her grand, unrealistic plans. Pretending to be the savior of the deer! At the expense of common sense. Why would someone like her think she could save anyone?

And once a bear finds food, it will return again and again. It will become dangerous to people. You can't even keep birdseed outside past the beginning of April. You aren't supposed to feed your pets outside. Bears always find it. Always. Everyone knows that. There are public service announcements, signs. Leaving out food that attracts bears is against the law, even if you don't intend to leave it for them. They can't be relocated once that happens. They usually have to be killed. Anna feels she has been unforgivably irresponsible. And now look—her dog is suffering.

"I have to report a bear attack to the game warden," the vet says. "He might want to contact you with questions."

"That's okay." Anna endures a nauseating wave of exhaustion and draining adrenaline. She will have to hide the compost heap. Even more unpleasant than paying the fine would be that others might know her complicity in bringing a dangerous animal into their neighborhood, in killing her own dog. The vet watches her closely.

"I don't mean to pry, but are you still out there alone much?"

"Sometimes," she says, watching the border collie's sides rise and fall.

"Your husband?"

"He travels a lot. He'll be gone for a while longer." Anna grips the edge of the table tightly so that her hands won't shake.

She hasn't asked herself why it is so important to keep the secret of John's death. Perhaps it is because she needs to make a living on the reputation he created. And, beyond that, can the police take her away if they think she can't take care of herself? Put her in a home? What about the horse and mule? She doesn't know. They rely on her. It's true that she has made mistakes—the poachers, the bear. She has, she considers, endangered others. Is that forgivable? In spite of the dog that will die in front of her soon, she wants to hurry, she needs to get home and prepare. The dog doesn't matter anymore, not really, she tells herself; it's already gone; she is here, and has to survive.

Perhaps she keeps the secret for some other reason, too. She doesn't want to think about it.

"How much longer? Anna?" Dr. Hulett asks. Anna worries she might have asked it twice.

"I expect him any day," Anna says. "He couldn't come home soon enough for me." She meets the vet's eye, then looks back down at the border collie. "He'll be sad to hear about our dog. She's really his more than mine."

"You're doing the right thing by her," Dr. Hulett assures her. "She won't feel any more pain. She'll pass in her sleep."

Anna holds the dog's head between her palms one more time, rubs her thumb along the thin bridge from the dog's nose to its forehead, noticing, as she hasn't ever before, its long eyelashes.

"I'm ready," she says. She waits with one hand on the dog's collar, the other on the table in front of it, where she feels its warm breath go in and out, in and out.

The vet tech draws a clear solution into a syringe and hands it to Dr. Hulett.

"This is an overdose of anesthesia," the vet explains. "It will stop her heart. To her, it will only feel like a deep relaxation."

Anna nods. But no one can know how it feels for sure, can they?

Dr. Hulett inserts the syringe into the tube that is bandaged into the border collie's leg. She says, "It will take a minute or two to work."

They stand with their heads bowed, touching the dog, like they are in one of the prayer meetings Anna's parents used to frequent in her youth, when she was mysteriously ill, and the congregation had anointed her with oil. The border collie inhales and exhales peacefully, the only sound in the room. Then it stops.

There is no twitching, no convulsion, no frightened cry. It isn't like putting down a horse, which kicks for so long afterwards. It isn't like when a cat kills a rabbit and causes it to shriek. It is quiet, and it is soon over. Dr. Hulett and the tech start to remove the tube.

The receptionist doesn't mention Anna's red eyes, only hands her a tissue and says, "Would you like a plaster casting of her paws? There's no charge."

Anna almost says yes, but changes her mind. There's no need, she tells them. The ratty old blue collar is enough to keep. She doesn't say it, but she worries such a memento as the one they offer will cause her to remember more about the dog's death than its life. When really, its death is the smallest part of it.

All things considered, it has been the most peaceful transition from wholeness to nothing that she has ever seen.

20

The game warden has arrived. Fatigue keeps Anna inside a bubble that puts a film even over the bright sky just past the porch—her voice comes from some automatic place—their conversation seems like a scene she is watching on film. With his mud-colored uniform and solid figure made bulkier by a protective vest, the warden reminds her of Smokey Bear, and she fights a fleeting urge toward hysterics. It makes her nervous, the way he fills the doorway and calls her *ma'am*, the way he takes notes on a yellow pad with a pen he keeps shaking to loosen its ink, the way his radio perches, a dull black rectangle, on his shoulder. Every time it crackles, she jumps.

He is too concerned, too polite to make her comfortable. He explains that he has come to see her so quickly because bear attacks are a priority. Anna invites him inside and offers him coffee, which he accepts with thanks. They both drink it black.

Anna cradles her hot coffee mug as the steam rises. As they sit at the kitchen table, the warden informs her that her incident with the bear is the first this season, but the state office suspects they'll have a busy one due to the hard winter. There just isn't much left for the bears to eat when they awaken. In the habit of easy conversation, he tells her about black bears and their tendencies, past encounters he's had with them, gesturing as he speaks; he knocks his cup, and it sloshes out drops of liquid that pool around the bottom, but he doesn't seem to notice. Anna stifles a mild irritation at such carelessness. But she thinks, *Here is a man who enjoys his work, and he is probably good at it.*

Still, she struggles to connect with his words; she feels so sluggish. It takes him several minutes to notice her lack of responsiveness. He glances at her, draws up short, and looks again at his pad.

"I'm sorry," Anna tells him. "I'm just not quite awake. Is it okay if we get started?"

"Ah . . . yes, we should." He clears his throat. "The vet's office told us a bit about what happened yesterday, but we'll need it in your own words, too. First, to your knowledge, do you have anything near your home that might attract bears?"

"No," Anna says. "Nothing but bad luck." *At least, not anymore.*

"No beehives, chicken coops, bird feeders, trash bins? You don't feed any pets outside?"

"No. I have chickens, but there's hotwire around them, and we haven't had much trouble since we installed that."

His half-dry pen scratches the pad like a fingernail. "I'm sorry to hear about the loss of your dog," he says. "Was the dog loose or on a leash when the attack occurred?"

"Loose. I heard a racket and ran out. The dog ran out with me. The bear was by the paddock upsetting my mule." She sips the coffee, still too hot; the warden nods. "The mule was charging the fence, and the bear was standing on its hind legs. I guess it was all too much for my idiot dog. She went right after it. It swiped at her and she rolled a few times."

"Did the bear continue to attack the dog after it was down? How did you retrieve the animal?"

"No. I chased the bear off," Anna says. *It sounds impressive when I say it, but it really wasn't.*

"Can I ask how?"

"I went up behind it and hit it with a stick," she tells him. She has rehearsed what to say; it's close enough to the truth. "On the back and on the jaw. I think what actually convinced it to leave was when I waved my coat at it, though."

"That's good," the warden says. "People often try to play dead for black bears, but that doesn't work for them. It works for grizzlies. Black bears, you should fight."

"It was all just instinct," Anna says.

The warden looks at his notes. "Well, the good news is that you were able to run it off. The bad news is that we don't know what attracted it in the first place. If it was drawn by something in particular, it will probably come back."

"If it came here for a reason, I'd sure like to know," Anna says. Then, in the interest of transparency: "Do you want to take a look around?"

"Yes, ma'am, that's what I need to do next. First, I'd like to see where the attack happened. Then I'll take a look around the vicinity, the house and outbuildings."

The green spring air seems, compared to the staleness of the house, wonderfully fresh. Anna leads the game warden to the paddock, then through it to the newly created pasture behind it, opening the gates for him as they go. Keeper whickers and raises his head from his grazing. Charlie watches them for a moment, decides they aren't of interest, and goes back to the young grass. Both are gleefully muddy; Anna had anticipated that they would roll when she released them into the pasture that morning. They usually did. And as was also their wont on spring mornings, they had galloped hell-bent from boundary to boundary when she had first turned them out, leaving clods of torn earth in their wake.

She hadn't been careless, though. She had led them both around the edges before turning them loose, as the field had different boundaries than what they had been used to in past years, but they were gentle and intelligent, and had no trouble remembering where the new electric fence was, even in the soft darkness of dawn.

The pasture stretches away from Anna and the warden, a mess of churned ground.

Electric fences are easy to put up, and no one can tell how long one has been there. The hardest part had been getting rid of the compost heap. Anna had shoveled and raked until her entire body ached, shoulders and back especially burning with pain. By lantern light, she had made sure only a large, bare patch of dirt remained. Since the horse and mule have run over it, it still looks strangely blank of vegetation, but it has been churned like the rest of the mud, and its lack of grass shouldn't be obvious to someone not looking for it. She had even carried the lantern a little way into the woods, picking up old rinds and seeds that had been scattered there.

In the broad light of day, she admires the result of her night's work.

"The attack was there, by the paddock," she says, pointing. "One of the rails is still loose from the mule striking at it." She waves toward the woods. "When the bear ran off, it went that way. The electric fence was down on that side; a branch fell on it a couple of days ago and snapped it. I had to fix it this morning to let the horses back out. If I had fixed it yesterday . . ." She lets the idea hang in the air between them.

"Yes, ma'am," the warden says, taking notes. "That's just how it goes sometimes."

"It is."

"Are the horse and mule friendly? Will it bother them if I walk around nearby?"

"Go ahead," Anna says. She retreats to the paddock and sits on the top rail.

The warden walks in zigzags through the mud, from the paddock to the wire fence and back again, studying the ground. Several times, he kneels to examine the remaining bear tracks more closely; he snaps pictures with a small point-and-shoot camera he takes from his pocket. He speaks to the horse and mule when he nears them, but besides a pause in their grazing, they don't acknowledge him; they are unconcerned. Anna holds her breath when he bends over the electric fence where she indicated the bear had gone through; he will find a carefully spliced wire, two ends looped around each other and twisted. The clean repair of a wire she herself had broken.

He steps over the wire and walks into the trees, carrying his yellow pad under his arm. Dressed as he is—in uniform— he blends in with the forest, but every now and then a cracking branch betrays his location. He casts back and forth in the woods, as Anna had only hours before. After a few minutes, he reappears at the edge of the pasture. He makes his way toward where Anna waits.

"Well," he says, "I'm not much of a tracker, but it looks like your bear ran straight southwest for at least fifty yards after it left. I found its tracks just inside the tree line. You must've given it a decent scare."

"God knows I tried," she says.

"I'll get a report in for this," the warden tells her. "I can't say whether the bear will come back or not, but I want you to give me a call if it does." He digs a business card out of his pocket; it's dirty at the edges.

"I will."

"Remember, if the bear does come back, it's illegal to use deadly force unless there's no other option. You should be extra careful the next few days." He clicks his pen closed. "And be aware, too, that it's illegal to leave anything out that might attract bears, even if you don't intend to do it. Once they associate humans with food, there's always a bad ending."

Anna nods. "I understand. Thank you."

"Yes, ma'am," the warden says. They walk back through the paddock and into the yard in silence. Then he adds, "Oh, by the way. Dr. Hulett mentioned you had some trouble with poachers this past season."

Anna's heart pounds in her throat. "Did she? What did she say?"

"Just that your mule had been shot in the crossfire. He looks fine now, though, doesn't he? Doesn't seem any worse for wear."

"She did a good job sewing him up," Anna agrees. "And yes, that's right. We came across them in the woods."

"On your own property?"

"Yes."

"Do you have signs posted?"

"Yes, on every side now," Anna says. She had nailed them up herself once the thaw set in. *No Trespassing. Violators Will Be Prosecuted.* Their neighbors will certainly think John and Anna unfriendly now, if they didn't before.

"Well, in the future, if you're horseback riding during hunting season, or even just turning your livestock out, make sure they're visible and easily identifiable. Wear bright colors, stay in at dusk and dawn. And if you come across poachers or anything that looks suspicious, get away from the area immediately and give me a call. Not just if you see them on your land, but in general, like if you're driving behind someone who's shooting from a car, something like that. Okay?"

"I will."

"Do you eat venison yourself?"

"No," Anna says. "I tried it once, at a friend's house, but it tasted almost spoiled to me. I didn't like it. And besides, deer have such large, gentle eyes. It's like eating a rabbit. I can't make myself do it."

They have arrived at the warden's truck; he opens the door and gets in. He puts on a pair of reflective sunglasses and turns to face her. She curves back in the two small mirrors of his lenses.

"I did see something unusual in those trees that I should mention, ma'am."

Anna says nothing. Her reflection leans toward him, out of proportion, arms crossed over her stomach. She looks frail and scared.

He says, "I noticed that there seem to be an awful lot of tracks from deer, considering that deer have gone missing everywhere else in town."

"Oh?" Anna swallows hard.

"This is purely speculation, but if a well-meaning person were to feed deer, say with food more attractive to them than their natural diets, that food would also attract bears, which besides putting that person in danger, would put that person at risk of legal proceedings. That person might also risk attracting more poachers to their land as the poachers try to find the deer. That person might also risk poor relationships with the neighbors who depend on hunting season to survive."

"I see," Anna says. A knot twists in her stomach.

"That person might also risk poaching charges themselves, should anything befall the deer that are coming to feed, particularly if anything happens to them by spotlight at night. It wouldn't be the first case of that nature we've seen."

"Those are all good considerations," Anna says.

"Yes, ma'am, I would say they are."

He seems to wait; Anna doesn't know for what. So she says, "Thank you for your help."

"Yes, ma'am," the game warden responds. "I'll be in touch if anything comes up. Be sure to call the office if that bear comes back."

Anna sinks into the safety of the porch as he backs out of the driveway and turns onto the road. Once he has gotten out of sight, she puts his card into her pocket and slides down to sit on the cool wooden step, her thoughts a disorienting blur of fear, relief, and exhaustion.

21

Anna's land regains its usual peace soon after the wildlife stop having a reason to linger there, and one morning the paper posts the announcement of a town potluck to celebrate the news that the deer have returned. Several times, Anna thinks there are animals' eyes flashing between the trees, watching from a place just below the surface of the forest, but the electric fence discourages most of them from entering the pasture and rooting at the spot the compost heap had been. She cancels the produce deliveries from Ben, explaining that she doesn't have a way to use so much food, after all. "Maybe next fall and winter," she tells him. The grass should green and grow taller soon, providing more nutrition for the grazing animals, at any rate. The hay supply in the barn has nearly been depleted, so this must be true. There is room to store just enough for two horses during a difficult season.

With the warmer weather, her joints pain her less, and she begins driving to Belbridge more often. Though she can get the hybrid car out without difficulty since the snow on the roads has melted, she has grown comfortable with the truck and keeps using it. She feels almost invincible in it. She associates reliability with its solid frame.

Anna forgets her grocery list once and accidentally buys more dog food. She doesn't know what to do with it. It seems wasteful to throw it out. The bag slouches forlornly on the floor of the pantry, where Anna half-hopes the mice will find it and take care of it for her. She throws a threadbare saddle blanket over it so that she won't see it.

She works several hours each day on tack repairs. Sometimes they challenge her, and she stomps around the sugarhouse cursing. John and his border collie would both have been surprised at the wrath evident in her usually soft-spoken demeanor. Sometimes the repairs take her no time at all. The latest assignment is an unstitched saddle horn; the thread that goes the circumference of the leather that covers the metal horn has rotted out. The round leather top flaps open like a toothless mouth; the leather is wrinkled and weak where it is still attached, and sticky residue left by duct tape gums its edges. She holds the saddle facing her with the gullet on her knee, working the needle in and out to insert the waxy thread into a seam. It is satisfying work, now that she has gotten the hang of it, and she loses herself in its rhythms. She can see the hours of work now in every careful detail of a saddle, no matter who created it. The art inherent in it reminds her of knitting or painting.

Focused on the sewing, Anna ignores the chime from the computer that means an email has been received. Moving without hurry, she finishes the stitches and leans back to admire them. They lie neat and bright at the edge of the circle of leather, following the curve perfectly. Her secret before returning the repairs, what really makes the saddles or bridles or harnesses look finished and dramatically different than the condition they arrived in, is scrubbing them with a good-quality glycerin soap and then polishing them with neat's-foot oil. Doing so makes the leather soft to touch and deep-hued. It is easy to do, too, if tedious, but it goes as far toward recommending her work as the repairs themselves.

On completing the cleaning of the finished saddle and brushing its old fleece, she throws the sponges back into their bucket and replaces the saddle on its stand, where it seems to gleam with an attitude akin to well-being. When she picks up the telephone to call the customer to retrieve it, she glances at the computer screen. She rarely uses email, but there is one at the top from John's favorite customer, Edison. She has met the man several times before—he runs a high-end riding stable in New Hampshire and has bought saddles regularly over the years.

Edison had traded the Icelandic horse, Keeper, to John for one of his saddles long ago. While Edison had pulled away, empty trailer rattling, new custom saddle in the back seat of his extended cab, Anna and John had watched the short, stout yearling with the unkempt mane pace and call frantically in its stall, pausing only to paw at the door. It kept this up for hours, until their nerves frayed thin and the other horses in the barn jumped at the most familiar sounds.

"I think you got the raw end of this deal," Anna had finally said, discouraged. She had wanted to like the colt.

John had sighed, and they had gone in for dinner. "Maybe it just needs to settle in," John said at the kitchen table, and she had nodded. Maybe. She had wondered if they could take it back.

The next morning, they had tiptoed to the barn and peeked in the door. All was quiet except for the older horses shuffling and chewing hay. Though the morning sun came through the slats and striped the floor, it still was too dim to see well, so John had flipped on the lights. They had walked in to find the yearling with both of its front legs over the door of the stall. The top edge of the door was at its girth. From what they could guess, the colt had reared up to try to jump over the door and had gotten stuck, its bodyweight too heavy and the angle too steep for it to thrust back and free itself.

When it saw them, far from spooking and hurting itself as they feared, it had whinnied as if with relief. The sentiment had been so obvious that they had laughed. They haltered the colt; then, Anna stroked its head and spoke gently to it while John maneuvered it so that he could lift its weight off the door, Anna guiding its front legs as well as she could to keep them from getting scraped. They stood back panting when the task was done, watching the colt anxiously. It had taken a few stiff, lurching steps ("His legs are asleep," said John, and Anna replied, "Well, who knows how long he was stuck there?"). It staggered forward clumsily, and they had stepped back in case it lost its balance and fell toward them.

But they had quickly realized that what it was doing was trying to approach them; its expression was both friendly and chagrined. The furry half-wild colt was following them like a dog, and when they stood still, it leaned its head against them and nuzzled their pockets, lipping their coats. It was thanking them.

"Well, I guess he's a keeper, after all," John had said.

Edison's email is short and familiar: *Hey, old man, I was sorry to hear you're not making saddles anymore. Are you feeling poorly or just spending your days fishing? Hope it's fishing. If you'll make an exception for me, the client will pay extra and you can take all the time you need. It's for a lady with chronic illness that boards at my place. She has bad arthritis in her hips but needs to ride for her health. She owns a classic-style Haflinger (short and stocky). The rider will be as hard to fit as the horse. She really needs the help. Do you have one more in you? Remember, don't go gentle into that good night, etc. Yours, Ed.*

Anna chews her thumbnail and rereads the email. She minimizes the window and turns away, then turns back to the computer and opens the email again. She admires Edison, though she doesn't know him well; he has always treated her with respect and good humor. His easy manner camouflages years of horse training and showing expertise. He has had to work extra hard to make it in a profession that does not treat him fairly, one mainly available to the privileged. He has a reputation for being kind to horses and tough on riders; those who survive his program seem fiercely loyal, and those who don't nonetheless speak of him with grudging awe.

Should she answer? She wants to. Besides that, ignoring Edison might inspire him to check on John more thoroughly.

The appeal for help nags her, too—the idea of a woman like herself riding her horse in pain. And Edison is a friend, so she doesn't worry as much about offending or disappointing him with slow work. She needs the money, she tells herself, to replenish the savings that she drained over the long winter. It would really be foolish to turn down such an offer.

Still, she doesn't know if she can build a saddle from start to finish. It will require significant time and effort. She studies the palms of her hands, her fingers, thin and strong now, nails clean white crescents, her wedding band loose and silver in the place it has been since her wedding day.

She closes her eyes and pictures John at work, trying to imagine the steps in order. She has his notebooks. She can see him laying the hide across the table with the same fastidiousness he possessed when he put clean sheets on their bed, pulling the material even and smoothing it with deft movements. She can picture him tracing the pattern lightly so that the hide runs the same way on each piece, cutting the leather with care, soaking it and molding it to fit just right around the tree. She can imagine everything except building the seat—that is the part that stops her, the part in the process that occupies a blank space. But maybe, if she has to, she can figure it out. She has figured so much out already.

Holding her breath, Anna hits reply. At the top of the screen, the cursor blinks. She types but then erases what she has written. The time ticks by in the bottom corner of the screen. *Come on,* she chides herself. This shouldn't take all day.

Ed, she writes. *Nothing's wrong but age. You'll understand all too soon! Haven't caught any big fish lately, though I did try a couple of weeks ago. I'm not getting out much anymore, but Anna knows how to do the measurements and could come out to look at*

your rider and her pony. She'll get you all set up. How's next week?
I don't mind making one more saddle for an old friend. If you fall
off any horses, make sure they're short ones. That's a rule I try to
live by. Best, John.

Anna sits back and reads it, testing it to see if it sounds
enough like John. She tries to read it in his voice but it isn't available to her anymore; she can't recall its timbre, its rise and fall.
With eyes closed, she listens to John's old voicemail recording
once, twice. It has been months since she's heard it. She drums
her fingers on the desk. She hits send.

Besides building the saddle, a big problem will be getting
there. Edison's place is about forty-five minutes away, just across
the New Hampshire border. The route is little used, so traffic
shouldn't be much of an issue, but she tends to get disoriented
in unfamiliar places. She could take the car, which has cruise
control and might be less taxing on her knees. She could allow
double the time and go half the speed, leaving herself a cushion
of reaction and rest.

The urge to try, to see if she can make something beautiful
on her own, to show herself that she can, enthralls her more and
more, and she feels a core of determination growing dense and
tight in her center, solid and stuck as an apricot pit. From that
center comes a heartbeat of the old Anna, the one whom the
sickness has buried until even she has forgotten about it. The one
who used to do difficult things because it was important to show
herself that she wasn't a coward.

The answer from Edison arrives within minutes. She will see
him in a week. The anticipation, almost pleasant, is also almost
painful.

In the meantime, she has an idea. Perhaps a foolish one. The
pawn shop in Belbridge sometimes sells old saddles for less than
a couple hundred dollars, usually the solid, heavy kind from the
'70s that have a wooden tree and no brand stamp. Sometimes,
they stock flat, worn jumping saddles that have lost all their

flocking. She will buy one or two and take them apart. Dissect them, see what had made them live. Then she'll rebuild them and resell them. That would be the quickest, cheapest way to learn.

She is unsure what sort of saddle this new client of Ed's might want, but common sense tells her that the seat will have to be different than a standard one if it needs to accommodate the woman's arthritis. It will need a narrow twist to make her small draft-type horse seem narrower to sit, and it will need a deep seat that holds in the rider, that smooths over errors in balance. It will be the kind of saddle that Anna would like to have herself.

She finds a pencil in the cup of writing utensils next to John's computer and begins to sketch.

22

nna leaves early. The road reflects the morning's milky light in its bends with a sheen that turns into smooth yellow pools through Anna's sunglasses. The small car makes her feel like she doesn't know her own strength. Surprised early on by its responsiveness, she spends some time before getting onto the main road practicing steering, accelerating, and stopping. Fearing she will measure the horse incorrectly, she has packed a collection of saddle trees in the trunk. They are arranged so carefully that they don't budge with her careening style of driving, though she listens to see if they will slide or topple. Driving the car is like going from riding a Percheron to riding an Arabian. Everything about it feels quick, light, and ready, if a little confined; the truck dulls and lags in comparison.

Once she has gotten used to the feel of the car, she almost enjoys the drive. It's a day of sun and towering white clouds with billowing highlights. The trees have budded with tender young leaves that are too green and sparkle with dew. The sun coming through the window warms the left side of Anna's face but leaves the right side cool. Tall trees with thin trunks swoop by in lines of shadows that look like flashing lights. It reminds her of being a child and riding her bicycle with her eyes closed during rare moments of daring.

At a country store on the state line, Anna refills her coffee and walks from aisle to aisle, studying the mix of motor oil, porcelain figurines, canned goods, postcards, maple syrup, refrigerator magnets, T-shirts, and candy bars on display. There is a sign for maple creemees at the register and, feeling indulgent, she orders one. On a bench outside that is sticky in places, Anna slurps her cone, licking the ice cream from her fingers as it melts and drips. The splintered slab seat feels rigid and cold, but it is pleasant to eat outside, huddled in her jacket with the sun on her back. She kicks her boots against the gravel underneath the bench. It has been ages since she felt so unstuck.

She has only twelve miles left to drive to Edison's stable, and she has made good time, so she doesn't rush. By the time she finishes the creemee, her coffee has cooled, and she sips it, watching sparrows search for crumbs nearby. When one of the birds finds something, a brief but cheerful commotion occurs among them as they bicker for it.

The interior of the car has warmed pleasantly. The light on the asphalt has brightened enough to hurt Anna's eyes, and she squints even behind her dark lenses. She checks the map that John has always kept in the dash, then pulls out onto the road.

The sign for Moose Hollow Farms hangs white and green between two cedar posts. Anna pulls from the two-lane country highway onto a narrow tarmac drive lined with birches. Just behind the trees, miles of white rail fences enclose well-kept pastures and riding arenas. There are sleek horses and professionally turned-out equestrians everywhere she looks. She parks at the lot in front of the main stable where Edison keeps his office. In the round pen nearby, a teenage girl lunges a liver chestnut warmblood.

Anna admires the horse's movement though it leans on the line and won't concentrate. Every time it passes Anna, it slows and looks at her with interest, and the girl flicks the whip toward it to keep it going. Each time, it plunges forward and shakes its head rebelliously. "He's got enough leg to jump over the moon," Anna calls.

The horse canters past again and snorts, warming up. "We'll see," the girl says. She seems hot and frustrated. Anna thinks she could handle the horse a little easier, let it play and then work on settling it; it's obviously young. But she keeps her opinion to herself.

At the sound of a door closing, Anna turns. Edison strides up to her, walking briskly, hand out. He radiates both welcome and competence. This is a person who takes up all the space in a room, who takes care of you. "Anna! Good to see you!"

He claps her on the shoulder as she shakes his hand; it is dry, brown, and strong, calloused from work. Warmer, too, than her own hands. "You, too, Ed," she says. "It's been a while."

"Too long. I was sorry to hear about John. Is he doing any better?"

"He just gets tired so easily," she says. She retrieves a pad of paper and her measuring tape and flexible curve, used for taking gullet measurements, from the car, and they turn and walk toward the stables.

"I'll have to come by and visit him soon. And how's that magnificent horse?"

He means Keeper. She smiles. "Happy the grass is growing again," she says.

"Not so happy he'll get stuck trying to get to it, I hope." He laughs. Long ago, when John had called him to tell him about Keeper's experience with the stall door as a yearling, Ed's laughter had bellowed out of the phone. John had had to hold the receiver away from his ear.

"Tell me about this client of yours," she says.

"There's a little bit to tell," Ed says. "She has some kind of neurological or autoimmune disorder, I wasn't clear on it when she explained it. Her doctor told her that the riding is good for her balance and muscles, she needs exercise, she needs to get outside, all that. She insists on riding this little Haflinger she saved from a kill pen down south. It's the right height but too wide for her, of course. And, as you know, fitting a saddle to a Haflinger is no easy task to begin with. We tried a hundred saddles. If any fit one, it didn't fit the other." He sighs. "I finally told her we were going to have to go custom. I was nervous about telling her she'd have to spend about three times on a saddle what she spent on her horse." He grins. "But she didn't bat an eye."

"She must love the horse," Anna says.

"Probably more than it deserves, but it's a gentle little mare. Built solid, fancy action. Though why someone would buy an unknown from a kill pen, pay for quarantine, and then pay to ship it all the way up here when there are perfectly reputable breeders all around is beyond me."

Anna knows, but she couldn't have explained the reason to someone as cut-and-dried as Edison. Sometimes a person wants to do some good. But at a given time, you can only do whatever good you know how, whatever kind of good you can reach from wherever you happen to be. She has often felt the same way herself, that desperation. To give life a reason, no matter how small, to continue, another connection to pull it forward—like a spider anchoring its web with pebbles because the ground is too far away.

The Haflinger stands quietly at the end of the stall row in the crossties, one hip dropped in relaxation. Anna likes it immediately. It has a kind, intelligent eye in a refined head; a broad white blaze runs from its wide forehead down the middle of its small nose. Its strawberry blonde coat and long buttercream mane and tail make it look as pretty as the plastic model horses she had played with as a girl. "She's lovely," Anna says.

"Thank you." A woman Anna guesses to be in her mid-thirties comes out of the tack room with a currycomb. She doesn't look ill, though she is thin. But how she looks might not at all indicate how she feels. She wears half chaps and full-seat breeches with an untucked, too-big Western shirt, but on her the combination of styles is charming instead of sloppy. Her dark hair has been pulled into a thick, low ponytail. "Her name is Honey."

"It's a good name for her."

"Are you the person who is here to save us from our saddle woes?"

"I'm certainly going to try," Anna tells her. She offers her hand. "I'm Anna. The saddlemaker's wife."

"Julie. How do we get started?"

"First I'm going to get some measurements from Honey and do a wither tracing so I'll have it to refer back to," she says. "I brought some saddle trees so we could go ahead and get an idea of what might work, since John couldn't be here. After that, we'll talk about what you need as a rider."

She snorts. "I know what I need. A saddle with a seat belt and armrests."

"What kind of problems do you have when you ride that make you say that?" Anna asks.

"Pain in my hips and legs, mostly. I tend to slouch, too, into a chair seat, with my legs too far forward to balance. I can't post a trot. And my toes stick out. I can't use spurs even if I want to because my heels are always in the horse's sides."

Anna can't help smiling.

"Did I say something funny?" Julie asks sharply. "Because I've found all this to be very frustrating. I was a good rider when I was younger, before I got so ill."

"I'm sorry. It's just that, you're probably still a good rider," Anna says. "Your problem sounds like it isn't your illness. It's that you're female."

"What?"

"The vast majority of riders in this country are women, as I'm sure you've noticed."

Julie nods. "Sure. 'A girl and her horse, a boy and his dog,' I guess."

"But almost every saddle you can buy off the shelf has been made for men. Riding in a men's saddle causes all of the problems you're having. Think about it. Their clothes don't fit us right;

we've got curves. It's the same way with saddles. Some women can ride in a men's saddle just fine. Most just learn to ignore the discomfort, take it for granted."

Julie looks at Ed, and he shrugs. "Makes sense, I guess."

"Sure it does. We have wider hips, different muscling in our thighs. Of course you can't get your leg straight. You need a wider seat for your seat bones, but a narrower twist for the angle of your leg." Anna hears the excitement in her own voice and worries she is getting carried away, but she can't stop. This is a problem she can solve. "Right now, you're having to struggle against your tack while trying to ride a round horse. That's why it's not working for you."

Julie shakes her head. "That's incredible. I've never even considered something like that."

"I have the same sort of problems myself," Anna admits. "Arthritis makes them worse. You shouldn't have to fight your tack to get into the right position. A few of the higher-end brands are starting to catch on to that, but they're all custom." She smiles. "In fact, John promised to make me a women's saddle someday, but he stayed too busy with outside orders to do it. So I've never ridden one myself. Yours will be our first. But we'll get it done right." She hopes as she says it that she isn't making an empty promise. Building a different seat means making her own pattern, discovering her own method, not using some of those John has left her.

"Well, then, I look forward to seeing if it works," Julie says. "I sure hope it does."

"Hell, now I'm curious, too," Ed says. "Tell the old man to keep me posted on his progress."

Anna nods. "Let's go ahead and measure Honey, and then you can give me your measurements, Julie. I can tell the horse is built downhill. Do you have a problem with the saddle sliding forward?"

"Yes, and it's hard to find a tree wide and short enough for her back, as you can imagine."

"Let's do the wither tracing, then we'll grab the trees from my car and see which will work best for her." Anna's own enthusiasm astonishes her; she should be paralyzed by misgivings. "In a few weeks, all that uncomfortable tack is going to seem like a bad dream. You guys can ride all day if you want. Enter some endurance rides, even. That's something I've wanted to do myself."

Julie smooths the Haflinger's mane and says, "Well, if this works, maybe we will."

23

The way home seems to take far longer than the journey to New Hampshire did. Anna, tired, feels herself drifting. She can't concentrate on the road; her head fills with the impossibility of the task she's agreed to do. Sometimes she pictures herself failing, but occasionally she lets herself succeed, make a beautiful saddle that does all it ought to do, and that is just as distracting as the failures. She stops at the country store again and gets more coffee. It has sat in the carafe thickening for some time by now and has grown dark and bitter. Against her better judgment, she douses it with sweet flavored creamer. The coffee helps, at first, but it ends up making her more jittery than alert and unsettles her stomach.

She forces herself to concentrate on the road, calling out objects, landmarks, and mileage signs as she passes, counting the stripes that blur together in between, when there are only trees and hills to look at. To forget the road or her way even for a moment would be dangerous. Not only for herself, but for others. The families in their minivans, the young professionals in their Subarus and Saabs.

The pale face of the man the mule killed keeps peering from the trees at the corners of her vision, but if she turns toward him, he disappears. It's only early afternoon. She should stop to rest, but what she wants more than anything is to get back to her lonely house in the woods and unwind. Her excitement, as it always does when felt too strongly for too long, has dulled to a vague apprehension.

With aching shoulders and her head pounding from eye strain, she drives for what seems like hours. The road unfolds more and more. It feels far later than what the green digital numbers of the car's dash say the time is. She sings to keep herself awake, old songs from her teenage years. Songs with a melody that she only knows half of the words to. She can feel the road buzzing underneath the tires, the way the speed smudges cubic yards of tar and rocks into a flat, smooth surface. It reminds her of when her mother used to push her in a shopping cart, how when she left the concrete sidewalk and hit the parking lot, the cart rattled over the asphalt, a sensation that tickled her ears, and how they'd laughed together, though her mother probably hadn't known why.

What would her mother think, if she could have understood how her daughter would turn out? Would anyone have children if they saw how they ended up? After all, every life is finite. Everyone who has been born will die. A birth is only a guaranteed death. That's the way of things, in all of history. So why do we do it? What makes us willing to live, to struggle?

She can still feel how small and empty the house in Colorado she and John shared those early years had become once loss was in it. How they had lain uncovered in the hot bed one summer, looking up toward the blank ceiling, the oppressive box-shaped room next door to the nursery they'd never use, waiting to sleep, each knowing the other was awake but silent. How John had finally said, in a voice that cracked and surprised her with its vulnerability, "Let's move. Why are we still here? Let's move." There was nothing in that old place to keep them there, he said, no friends, no more family, no one to treat her mysterious illness, or even to tell her what it was.

Outside every window, past the neatly arranged frame houses with their allotments of acreage, the landscape there had stretched away flat and brown to mountains that seemed cold and unreachable. Other people's dogs wandered John and

Anna's acreage and growled at them. And the neighbor who had attacked her after he'd spent the weekend drinking, who made her afraid to go outside, whose secret she kept out of shame, he was shut up in his big two-story across the street, made untouchable by wealth and connections.

So they had moved; John had opened his saddle shop, Anna had learned what her sickness was, and that she had many sicknesses, and why she had lost all that she had lost, and how to live around it. It wasn't so bad. Together she and John had built a life that they each fit into. They had polished over each other's disappointments. How could it have turned out any better than that?

At the honk of an approaching dairy truck, Anna jerks the steering wheel to get the car back into one lane. She has nearly made it to the turn that will take her onto her own road. It can't come quickly enough; her strength fails more by the second. She makes herself look ahead and focus.

Something is in the road along the next curve, in the middle of her lane. A large gray and white mass, its fur rippling in the spring breeze. A dog. Anna slows and steers closer to the borrow ditch to slip by. But as she does, she glances out at a familiar body, one that has been scraped raw by the hard rocks as it slid, tongue flopped out between the open teeth.

At first, because it is familiar, she thinks it's the border collie, but that is impossible, and then she understands that it is the wolf. She pumps frantically on the brakes, forgetting the car's light handling, and it skids several feet along the gravel shoulder, nearly off the bank.

Anna opens the car door and steps out to a disorienting silence. She has grown used to the motion and noise of the road. She stands upright with a strange sense of disconnection. The engine clicks as it cools. She leaves the door open, its muffled chime an anchor, and walks to the wolf. Its torn and stiffening form repulses her, but she reaches out without thought, wanting to feel its wildness, to bury her hands in its coat. She touches behind its neck, where a dog's scruff would be. Just the lightest graze of her flesh against the wolf, just to see if wolves are soft.

The body trembles, and Anna jumps back.

She retreats beside the car and watches the carcass—that's all it is now—for several minutes.

It doesn't move again. Anna returns to it, pausing every few feet. When she gets up next to it, she steels herself and tries to push it with her foot. The body is dense and still pliable; the toe of her boot disappears underneath its belly, but she doesn't have the strength to shift it that way or to lift it and see what caused it to move. It hadn't been a death convulsion. Surely the wolf died too long ago for that. Maybe she had only imagined the movement.

She withdraws her foot and the body settles again. There is another strange twitch; this time she can tell it comes from near the haunches. Feeling out of place, that she shouldn't be there, Anna pushes the blood-smeared bristle of the tail aside.

Two pups, still in their membranes, writhe underneath. They are almost shapeless, like any puppy; they are lumpy and have no angles yet; their eyes, sealed shut, bulge beneath their lids. Their toothless mouths open and close. They're suffocating.

Anna bends over them. What should she do? She and John had delivered plenty of animals over the years. People often dumped off their pregnant pets outside city limits—dogs and cats seemingly without number. Once they'd even tried to save a nest of naked and abandoned cottontail rabbits they found covered in ants. They had gotten into the habit of keeping rubber nipples, eyedroppers, and cans of goat milk around just in case.

Anna pinches the birth sac of the first pup between her fingernail and thumbnail, then puts her fingers into the slit and tears, opening it wide. She pushes the membrane off of the pup and rubs it with the bottom of her shirt, trying to get it to take a breath. "Come on. Come on," she says to herself, but she says it with the fervor of a prayer.

She worries she is rubbing too hard. But the pup gasps and starts to whine, a wavering cry like the whimper of a newborn child. She sets it aside and turns to the next one. She has to work on that one for much longer, until she almost gives up, and her hands are tired with the effort of drying its grimy fur. It stays unresponsive. Anna pries open its soft gums with her thumb and feels down into its throat. That seems to clear it, and the pup coughs.

Her dull pocket knife isn't sterilized, but it will have to do. She cuts the pups' umbilical cords as best she can with it, holding the ropes of flesh against the surface of the road for leverage as she saws back and forth, cringing at the jagged tissue the knife leaves. She gathers the squirming pups against her stomach and carries them to the car, putting them in the passenger-side floorboard on top of her jacket. That done, she returns to the wolf.

Without asking herself why, Anna slides her arms under the front of the wolf's body and begins to drag it. It is heavy with its trauma. She has to almost hug it before she can budge it. She pulls it over the shoulder and into the ditch, where it lies stretched out and looks even more obscene, even less like a wolf, than it did before.

With the body in such a position, Anna can see a black bubble under the tail where the mass of it has pulled out straight with the friction of being moved; she stares at it, feeling as though she is in some kind of fever dream, and discovers that a third pup has died in the birth canal.

The pups cry faintly in the car; they are hungry. With her years of living around livestock, Anna knows she needs colostrum to give them any kind of chance. She retrieves her empty coffee cup, speaking gently to the creatures that struggle blindly on the floorboard. Holding the cup under the wolf's teats, she squeezes and tries to get milk. But the teats are shrunken, and the wolf has none. Getting hit must have triggered an early labor.

Her body hadn't been ready for it. Anna gets back into the car and lets herself cry while the pups grunt next to her.

She turns into her driveway with the sun just at the tops of the trees, slanting the shadows, but she feels like she's been gone for days. She carries the pups, quiet now, inside and puts them into a laundry basket lined with towels. They are limp and don't resist.

Their resigned stillness hurts her, betrays how quickly they have grown used to a world in which they don't have enough. Maybe the hunger and cold are what they should have expected. All she has to offer them is goat milk, and she doesn't know if that will come anywhere close to making up for it.

24

The male pup lives for less than a day. Anna sits up all night the first night, feeding the female every three or four hours and trying to get the male to eat. He clamps his mouth closed, turning his head away, mulish. She can pry his gums open and get the eyedropper in, but he refuses to swallow the milk and chokes on it instead. It bubbles from his nose, white and useless. He weakens as the hours wear on, and his skin sags as he shrinks inside of it. Perhaps he has received some other injury in the accident, one that Anna can't see. Or maybe he just took his first breath too late.

She leaves the pups grunting in the laundry basket while she dresses. When she comes back, the male lies still, his sister curled against him to get the last of his warmth. He weighs less than a pound. Anna digs a hole behind the house for his tiny form. Softness from the snowmelt still lingers in the ground. She can't find any shoeboxes, so she buries him in a brown paper bag. She buries him two shovel lengths deep to keep anything from disturbing him. She stands over him for a long time, feeling there is something else to do.

"This is the story of the wolves," she says finally. "Long ago, your kind ruled this land. Everything in it was yours. Then the settlers came. They killed you because they were afraid of you. They felled the trees and turned your forests into farms. Without the trees to anchor it, the soil began to wear away, and the rivers ran with mud, and then dried up. Those of you who escaped the guns were killed when your home was ruined. But one day the people left the farms for cities. Some of them moved West. And the trees began to come back. And your kind will, too." She tells the pup, where he rests under the dirt, "Wait for them." He is proof of it. This isn't the end.

The female, unlike her brother, has suckled greedily from the first try, grabbing the eyedropper with surprising strength in her toothless mouth and pulling it. She swallows as much air as milk at first; her stomach distends into a hard ball, and she whines and squirms with discomfort. Anna selects a small bottle from the collection of orphaned-animal supplies and convinces the pup that its rubber nipple holds the same goodness as the eye-dropper. She learns to hold the pup on one leg, supported by her forearm, and to hold the bottle upright so that the pup gets only the milk and is more likely to keep it down.

The worst part is setting the alarm to wake her up throughout the night. The pup whimpers when it is awake, too, in between feedings. Anna lies in bed trying to rest with her hand in the pup's basket, stroking and soothing it. She fears the wear that such constant attention has upon her body; she may as well be sleepwalking through her days; she worries she'll fall ill again. She takes handfuls of supplements, trying to keep up her own strength. Sometimes after feeding the pup, she falls asleep in her chair and wakes to the warm animal drooling through her shirt onto her stomach.

During working hours, Anna takes the pup with her to the sugarhouse. She had called John's suppliers not long after her return from Moose Hollow Farms and ordered the materials to make Julie's saddle. She had over-ordered, just to be on the safe side. The suppliers, all small family-owned companies, had been surprised to speak to her, but were as willing to sell leather and suede to her as they had been to her husband. As it turned out, the Northeast Kingdom Saddle Company had some credit that John had never used, so Anna has used it. She can get the materials now and pay the vendors later, which leaves her bank account in tolerable shape.

While she waits for the materials to arrive, she researches saddle design and does sketches with a yellow pencil that has lost its eraser. She finds several companies online that boast specialization in women's saddles, but the reviews she finds are mixed: the saddles are too heavy or sit too far above the horse because of their thick padding; the twist is still too wide, forcing the thigh to sit too far open; the rider's leg is placed too far forward or back; the saddles are too long, placing the rider over the horse's loins and soring the horse. Anna has the comfort of possessing Julie's specific measurements and knowing they have been done correctly, so far as she could manage. If nothing else, she ought to get the rider position right. And she has evaluated the horse in person, found a tree that fit the golden Haflinger perfectly: a wide flex-tree with flared bars to allow room for the mare's elevated shoulder movement. She should at least get different complaints from Julie than those other women had made to other companies.

By the time the materials come in, the pup has gained three-quarters of a pound and Anna has settled on the design of the saddle she wants to build. Julie only cares that it is hornless and medium brown in color. She has given John the freedom to determine the details at his discretion, deferring to his experience.

Anna often imagines what it will be like to see the finished saddle sitting on its stand waiting to be delivered. Picturing it helps to keep it within reach. It will be an endurance saddle, mahogany with a tan suede seat, tan knee rolls, English leathers, and black leather-wrapped angled stirrups that will help Julie's leg fall straighter against the wide horse and eliminate her knee pain. It will have gold and silver rose conchos and—something Anna has never seen on an endurance saddle—floral tooling around the edges of the flaps. The seat itself she intends to build up and shape with memory foam. It is the saddle she has always wanted and would have asked John to build for her, if she had known in time exactly how much she wanted it.

She doesn't hold it against him, that he never built one just for her. Their two regular riding saddles are early examples of John's work; though they are of good quality and have always fit their particular horses well, they are plain and have no special features. John really had gotten too busy when the saddle-making business took off to make custom saddles for either of them. He hadn't had one, either.

Sometimes Anna has to remember that John is gone. He has split into different people. Sometimes she remembers the John who had confidently bent over the work table, glasses on his nose. Sometimes he is the John who had sat so often at the kitchen table, slurping coffee. With his death, he has gotten lost in white mist, and Anna is not reliable enough to keep him whole. Sometimes his face becomes the face of the man under the mule.

Anna clears the two large work tables and lays the tanned cowhides across them, making certain the grain goes the same way. They are thick but pliable, of good quality, processed by tanners in Pennsylvania. She has decided to try to use John's existing endurance saddle patterns for everything but the seat. If there's a little overlap between the pieces there, it will be covered and won't show.

The patterns are thin cardboard—cut originally out of manila folders—and keep sliding off the smooth leather in the drafts, so Anna leaves the pup in its basket and goes to the house for some canned goods. She returns with full arms. With the brightly labeled cans weighing the patterns down, she traces around them with old whalebone from the tool shelf, something John had shown her when he taught her tooling—it indents the leather, but doesn't scratch it, and it doesn't leave a mark like the pencil would.

Anna has just gotten everything laid out and sat down to feed the pup when a car door slams outside. She puts the pup back into its basket; it squeaks into its towels and bumbles forward on its trembling legs, nosing into the corner blindly, disappointed. Anna hurries to the window and peeks around the curtain. A game warden, the one she'd met before, has gotten out of his truck and stands on the porch of her house, ringing the doorbell. When she doesn't answer, he turns and looks around the yard. His gaze alights on the sugarhouse, at the end of its well-worn path, and he starts toward it.

"Wait here," Anna tells the pup. She leaves the shop, careful to look down at her feet instead of up toward the warden, then turns and locks the door. The man says, "Ma'am?" and she jumps as though he has startled her.

"Oh—hello!" she says. "You're the officer who came after my dog was attacked. Nice to see you again."

He touches the brim of his hat. "I know you weren't expecting me. I was in the area and wanted to follow up on your bear."

"In the area? What else could bring you all the way out here?" *Chasing poachers? Tracking animals that I taught to look for meals in people's yards? Confiscating exotic pets?*

"A rumor," he says. "Someone called in a wolf on the highway not far from here."

"I didn't think Vermont had wolves," Anna tells him. "I've never seen any around."

"It doesn't," he says. "It was a low-priority call, but we still have to check those out within a reasonable timeframe. The person who reported it said it had been hit by a car and was lying near the shoulder, but they didn't remember which mile marker."

"But you didn't find one?"

He shakes his head. "Nope. If there was anything, I'm sure it must have been a dog. People are always calling in huskies as wolves and bobcats as mountain lions. Those smaller animals look a lot bigger to people who are bored or excitable."

"That's good, I suppose," Anna says. "That you haven't found any. That's one less dangerous animal in the woods. The bears, elk, and moose are plenty for me. Not to mention the dogs running around everywhere, turning wild themselves."

"How have things been out here? Any more signs of your bear?"

"Nothing," Anna says. "But I've been checking my electric fence every day just in case it decides to come back through."

"That's good news," the game warden says with relief. "We'll assume it was just a fluke the first time, then."

"I sure hope so." They fall into silence. "I was actually about to head to the house and make some tea. Would you like some?" Anna says, walking farther from the sugarhouse.

"No, thank you," he says. "I have other calls I should make soon. A warden's work is never done, you know."

"No holidays for you?"

"Not until we reach our goal. Every Vermont game warden's dream."

"What's that?"

"One moose per square mile." He winks, and Anna lets herself smile.

"Out of curiosity," Anna says, "some people keep wolf hybrids as pets, right? Is that allowed here?"

"Not without a permit. And it depends on how far removed it is from being a purebred wolf. Why, are you thinking of getting one?"

Anna laughs. "I think I have enough to deal with without harboring predators," she says. "I just wondered if maybe a hybrid had gotten loose, and that was your highway wolf."

"It's possible," he says. "Though no one around here has a permit that I'm aware of."

"Could someone have one without a permit?"

"Not for long," he says. "Someone would turn them in, and we'd confiscate it."

They stand in silence listening to the birds in the trees. "Well," Anna says, offering her hand; he takes it. "I won't keep you, but thank you for coming by. I'll give you a call if I see anything unusual—bear or otherwise."

"I'd appreciate that," he tells her. "You have a nice day." He touches the brim of his hat again—a gesture that, in the country, means both hello and goodbye.

Anna waits at the window over her kitchen sink and watches him back out onto the road. So someone else had seen the wolf. Of course, she shouldn't be surprised; she hadn't been the only car on the road that day. She wonders if the body is still in the ditch where she left it, or if something or someone has carried it off.

Anna boils some water to make her excuse for leaving the sugarhouse true in case the game warden happens to come back, but by the time her tea has steeped, it has been quiet outside for several minutes. She carries the tea with her to the shop, walking with care to keep the hot liquid from sloshing out. The pup will think she has forgotten it, will perhaps be remembering that dark, lonely time of hunger and suffocation just days before, the cold world that took no pity.

The pup has fallen asleep in the basket, its soft sides rising and falling evenly. It makes little grunting noises that seem to have no meaning. In a rush of tenderness, Anna wonders if, despite its blindness and deafness, the pup can dream. It wakes when she picks it up and places it in her lap. She guides its head as it nuzzles for the nipple of the bottle; it scatters flecks of foamy goat's milk on Anna's jeans as it slurps. She speaks to it of nothing for a while, then recites her favorite poem, the Frost one: "Bless you, of course, you're keeping me from work, / But the thing of it is, I need to be kept. / . . . The worst that you can do / Is set me back a little more behind." She strokes behind its ears. "I sha'n't catch up in this world, anyway. / I'd rather you'd not go unless you must."

After it finishes eating, Anna replaces it in the basket, where it burrows into the towels, front legs splayed, hind legs tucked under. She's free for four hours now, and she turns her attention back to the saddle-making. She cuts the pieces out of the hide, taking her time. The naked tree itself sits unassuming on a stand, where she glances at it occasionally with a mixture of awe and dread. She has affixed a yellow tag to it, still using her own version of John's record-keeping system. She has found yellow tags everywhere, on shelves, in boxes, in drawers. A rare sign of disorder. She is amused that even John hadn't been perfectly organized.

John had sold far more Western saddles than any other style, though he could craft them all; Anna doesn't know if the process should differ much for an endurance saddle, so she follows the same steps, hoping she isn't leaving anything out. She selects the cantle and gullet wrap pieces from the stack of cut leather. They have a satisfying heft when she holds them. The leather gives off a cozy smell. She wets the two pieces in the shop sink.

A blue wool blanket with a white center stripe edged in black diamonds hangs against the near wall. Anna doesn't remember what the next step is called, or why it has to be done. She takes the blanket down and shakes the dust from it, then lays it on the table. She puts the wetted leather pieces into it and folds it over. Tomorrow they should be ready to thin and shape to the tree.

Anna gathers the pup's basket but leaves the rifle hidden underneath the space between the computer desk and the floor, where she has gotten into the habit of storing it lately since she can't carry both it and the basket at the same time. *Just imagine if anyone saw me, a gray-haired woman living alone in the woods, trying to carry a wolf and a gun with her everywhere.*

Three days later—a little earlier than Anna had anticipated—the pup opens its eyes and sees her for the first time.

25

One part wet canned food, one part milk. Anna hates the smell of it, sour and musk and fat. She hates the mushy brown clumps on the spoon and in the tin pan, how they drown in dirtied white, how the drops splatter and smear on the clean counter. The wolf pup, at two-and-a-half weeks, moves with a slow clumsiness but can hear her mixing its meal and crawls toward her feet when it realizes Anna is opening and pouring the cans. She has to be careful not to take a step sideways or backwards without looking. She has come close to trampling on it several times.

It has been eating this mixture of food for four days, ever since Anna realized her health would quickly give out if she kept waking through the night to bottle-feed it. If that happens, if fatigue pulls her under, she won't be able to care for the pup at all. Sickness threatens at the edges of her body, a dull ache in her head, weak muscles, shaking hands, ragged nerves. Under such a burden, she loses her patience, and daily tasks become more difficult.

It had probably been too early to ask the pup to eat on its own, but it had adapted after Anna left off bottle-feeding it one afternoon, then later dunked its nose into the bowl with more force than she had intended. After lapping the congealed stuff off its lips, the whimpering pup had crawled halfway into the mess for more, spilling the food as it went. Anna leaves it in the bathtub every night with a large round pan of the mixture. Though its fur is matted with filth every morning, it keeps growing and does not seem hungry. It fights Anna's fussing and scrubbing no matter how often she bathes it in the sink, where she rubs mild dish soap into its coat to get off the grime. The indifferent house cat sometimes licks the food off the pup, purring while the pup wriggles under its tongue; mostly, the cat doesn't condescend to notice it.

Knowing she can't chance Ben's inevitable curiosity about puppy food in her grocery cart, not having a real puppy to account for it, Anna has been buying it at the feed store in bulk. They knew John there better than they know her, and they ask after him. She tells them things that are true: he is unable to come to town—there is too much that keeps him at home. The proprietor nods and sends his best wishes.

Anna misses the visits from Ben, but with the wolf pup nearby, it's too risky. He might report her, or at least tell his mother about it, and then Dr. Hulett would have to report her. Anna makes excuses until he stops asking if he can drop by, though she makes a point of talking to him when she sees him in Belbridge.

Stifling a gag reflex, Anna sets the pan down. The pup stumbles into it in its haste, scraping it across the tile. It smacks and grunts as it eats, front paws in its food. Its dark coat frames icy blue eyes. As she pushes the pan aside to wipe up what has slopped out, Anna nudges the pup over, too. Still gulping and slurping, it growls at her.

Anna draws back, astonished. Maybe what she heard was actually a whine, garbled because of the food. The pup eats as though nothing has happened.

It must have been a mistake. Anna reaches toward the pup again. It freezes and guards the pan, the miniature growl rising in its throat insistently, like the buzz from a nest of wasps.

The audacity of it angers Anna, and she plucks the pup off the ground and jostles it despite its twisting to snap at her with its black gums, which have little points of milk teeth just starting to press through the surface. It is still small enough for her to do as she likes with it and will be for some time yet, and she tells it so crossly.

Is it possible for a pup so young to develop aggression? Or is a young wolf like a dog pup, simply testing vocalizations as it grows? She doesn't know. Her favorite part of raising a dog occurs when the puppy learns how to bark and surprises itself with its own noise. Anna doesn't know all the ways wolves might differ from dogs, but she chides herself for forgetting that what she has in her care is a wild beast, a dangerous one, not a pet. She must not forget it again; one day soon, the animal will be able to cause her real harm, even kill her if it wants. She certainly can't give it the benefit of the doubt anymore.

From that day on, any time the pup eats in her presence, Anna takes care to push it away from its food, to interrupt or move it, even to roll it onto its back the way a more dominant wolf might, until the pup learns to accept her interference in its meals with patience, if not good humor.

Its feet and legs grow more quickly than the rest of its body, and it starts climbing out of the basket when Anna takes it into the sugarhouse. One day when she is busy with Julie's saddle and paying it no attention, it chews through the cord of the printer, which pops and sparks and makes it yelp. Anna rushes to unplug the cord. The pup moans and worries its nose with its paws, the way the border collie used to do when stung by the hornets it had chased in the yard. Anna stops using that socket when the center of it turns black, though she never actually sees it smoke.

The pup also tugs the end of the casing blanket that hangs over the side of the table and drags it down, along with some additional wrapped leather pieces Anna had soaked. After staring aghast at the chewed hide, she has to throw the pieces away and cut them out all over again, taking extra care to get the grain right on the little bit of hide that remains, and the pup has frayed the corner of the blanket besides, so that threads go all directions, an unraveled nest of wool.

Anna wonders if she ought to move the pup to an empty stall in the barn and care for it there. But when she tries, the mule, Charlie, stands rigidly in his own stall, refusing to eat or drink, only staring in the direction of the wolf. The mule instinctively loathes the scent of it. Charlie had behaved aggressively toward the adult bear, and Anna doesn't feel safe leaving the pup there with him alone. So it stays with her in the shop, and she tries to keep it out of further trouble.

The saddle-making progresses well despite the distraction inherent in the care of a young wolf. Anna covers the cantle and pommel and attaches the rigging—centerfire, so that the girth can be placed farther behind the Haflinger's elbows, where it won't gall the skin as the stocky mare trots. She has started the first layer of the ground seat, too, but delays it again by tooling the flaps with roses and vines instead. She will have to do the seat soon. All else depends upon that, really. Saving it for as late in the process as possible is foolish—it would be better to know earlier if her project failed—yet, she can't seem to commit to it. She works on every other piece she can first.

Anna can't control her hands as well when she is tired, and as worn as she is with worry for the wolf, she often revisits those early feelings of frustration in her work, before she had known quite what to do. She pokes herself with the needle and draws blood, she presses too hard on the awl and causes crooked holes, she curses, she has to rewrap the pommel because she didn't pull the leather tight enough or smooth it well enough to lace the edges together with rawhide string the first time. Still, they are all problems that she has encountered before; she can get through them. Sometimes she talks to John to get herself through it. There are notes in his files from his apprentice days that sometimes help. Sometimes, she imagines that he does the work instead of her, and she only watches. On the good days, when she thinks of how little time she has worked alone in John's shop, the amount of skill she has acquired amazes her. On bad days, she turns on the shop radio, sings whatever lyrics she knows, and gets little done. She hasn't changed the station. It is still the one John liked best.

Anna has the volume up one day in early summer while she takes inventory of the parts and progress of Julie's saddle. She can't put the seat off any longer. She runs her fingertips along what is there—the barest rawhide base with the tree rigid underneath. What she has to do is build it up layer after layer, memory foam and leather, and then shape it with sandpaper into the form she needs—*wide seat, narrow twist*. Over the weeks, the four words have become like a holy chant.

Anna is singing a song that John had liked, though she doesn't care for it. She misses him. She understands that she is starting to lose him even more because she is forgetting his faults. Real people are never perfect, but John must have been. That isn't right, but she can't remember differently.

A knock on the glass of the shop door startles her, and the wolf pup stands and stares. Anna reassures it, speaking to it in a low tone that she hopes is calming. She doesn't recognize the man who peers in the window at her with his hands around his eyes to block the glare. But he sees her, so she has to answer. As soon as she switches off the radio, she regrets the silence. She turns the deadbolt. The rifle is shoved under the desk, gathering dust, and there is no time to drag it out.

She steps outside, pulling the door closed behind her. A woman is standing just behind the man; Anna hadn't been able to see her from the shop. The man's red sweater has pills on the sleeves but is clean. His beard, gray peppered with white and black, is messy but not long. The woman's knit shirt and quilted vest have been faded by much washing. Both wear dusty hiking boots with creases across the tops. The cigarette smoke residue wafting from them hurts Anna's throat, and she swallows a cough. "Can I help you?"

"Hello, yes," the man says. "You're the owner of this property?"

"One of them. My husband is in the middle of something right now and can't be disturbed."

"He's the saddlemaker?" the man asks. "I've met him before, several years ago, when I came to talk to him about your rooster."

"That was you?" Anna says. "He didn't tell me who had complained. Now roosters have been restricted in our neighborhood, haven't they?" She's babbling; she is, for some reason, nervous. "Poor Rusty—John couldn't stand to kill and eat him, so we gave him away. He did crow his head off. I hope you've been able to sleep more peacefully since then?"

Rusty had been a handsome Rhode Island Red, friendly as a house pet. They had given him to a client who needed a rooster for his hens. Anna had said the whole thing was petty, that they should ignore it and tell the neighbors to worry about themselves. They lived in the country. There were going to be roosters. But John hadn't wanted to cause any issues here, near their little clapboard house; they hadn't wanted to move anywhere else. They both had only wanted peace. Anna is talking too much.

"Yes, thank you," the woman says. "I've heard your husband does good work."

The woman looks past Anna, and she understands that the woman wants to see the inside of the shop, though Anna can't guess why. Everything about the couple feels intrusive. They are probably just nosey. "He does." She is being curt, but she can't help it.

"Does he ever have to travel to sales and conferences and things?" she asks. "It must get lonely out here when he's gone."

"He doesn't travel these days."

"I'm sorry," the man interrupts. "How about a real greeting? I'm Hank and this is my other half, Lauren."

Anna forces a smile and holds out her hand. He shakes it. "Remind me which house is yours?" she asks.

"The box house up the hill." He waves to indicate the direction.

"The yellow one? Your place looks so cheerful." Anna doesn't mean to sound surprised.

"Thank you," Lauren says. "We've lived there for years and years, and it's finally starting to look like how I want."

"Well, I've always thought it was lovely, with the garden and that big old barn."

"Thank you," Hank says. "Speaking of the barn, we're actually here because we've recently gotten some livestock. Sheep."

"Oh?" *Why would that matter to me?*

"We've already lost some of them to dogs, so we wanted to give a friendly warning to the neighbors about it. We'll have to start shooting loose dogs if they keep going after them. We won't have a choice."

"Oh. Well, I don't blame you," Anna says. "I hate loose dogs myself. They cause far more problems than coyotes ever did."

"Probably because they're not afraid like coyotes are," offers Lauren, with unexpected astuteness.

"Well, you have nothing to fear from me," Anna says. "I used to have a border collie. She wouldn't have hurt your sheep, though I'm sure she would have run them around if she had ever gotten the chance. But it doesn't matter anyway—a bear got her a few weeks ago." Anna tells them what she believes are the relevant details. They exchange a glance ripe with some kind of meaning or intention, but it's quick enough that Anna might have imagined it.

"What about the fellow you all have in there?" Hank says, gesturing to the sugarhouse.

"What do you mean?" she asks, confused. "John?"

"When I peeked in just now, I thought I saw a dog."

"Ah," Anna says. So, the man's intrusiveness doesn't shame

him. "That's only a foster puppy. A little husky mix. I don't expect to have it much longer. It's started on solid food."

"Good for you," Lauren tells her. "I always wanted to do something like that. Foster an animal."

"You should," Anna says. "Lots of rescue groups need fosters. I really need to get back to it, though. It's nearly the pup's dinner time."

After they say their goodbyes, Hank and Lauren walk back down the driveway several feet apart in silence. The experience, for some reason she can't name, leaves Anna rattled. And she is angry again, as she had been before, about the rooster she'd long since forgotten. It had been an insignificant thing for them to complain about, and it's still a stupid thing for her to waste her anger on. She sighs.

She opens the shop door to find the pup curled in the bin of fleeces. It has shredded the edges of two of them and has nestled in the softness of its destruction to sleep.

26

Ben arrives unexpectedly with a gift. "Hold on!" Anna calls from the kitchen. After casting frantically back and forth for long seconds, she pushes the growing wolf pup into the ground floor powder room with a bowl of water and a tin of some of the adult dog chow from the old bag in the pantry. Ben is gazing around the overgrown green yard when she opens the door. He is unfazed by the embrace of the butterfly bush. He hasn't wrapped his present, but holds the small box out to Anna with a grin. She is surprised at how glad she is to see him. She pours coffee, and they sit at the table with the box in between them, Anna listening anxiously for noises of mayhem from behind the powder room door; the pup had been sleepy when she had locked it in, and it is quiet.

"Since we haven't been able to get back to those shooting lessons yet," Ben is saying, "I thought this might help to keep you out of trouble."

"What is it?" Anna asks, turning the box over and looking at the graphics. Snapshots of woods filled with deer, hogs, bears. "It looks like one of those video cameras people put on their bike helmets." She has seen cyclists with them in Belbridge, which is, she has to admit, a scenic town with its old storefronts and barns, though she isn't sure she'd want to film it herself.

Ben laughs. "Not quite. It's a trail camera." He opens it and shows her the green and brown camouflage case with its lens. "Now you can watch over your forest without getting too close to danger. It's technically for hunters to use to keep track of game. This will show you anything moving through your land."

"You mean like poachers?" She takes it and weighs it in her hands. "Someone a while back told me I ought to get one of these. I don't remember who."

"That's right," he says. "Now you'll have something to show the game warden if you do have anything strange come up. If you see trespassers or bears or something on it, you'll know to steer clear for a while and call the law to handle it. Maybe we can keep Charlie from getting shot again. Or if we can't, we'll at least know who did it."

I know who did it. Anna sees the man again, falling underneath the mule. But she thanks Ben with sincerity; it really is nice of him to think of it. "How does it work?"

"I'll set it up for you," he says. "We just have to attach it to a tree or post. When it senses motion, it takes a picture and stores it. We can look at the pictures on the view screen or your computer. It's easy."

"What about at night?" Anna asks.

Ben points at a gray and white example picture on the box, a buck with glowing eyes. "It has night vision, too."

"I didn't know you could even get something like this. It must have cost you a fortune!"

"It was on close-out at the sporting goods store," he says. "They're going to stock a newer model. In fact, you might want to buy another so you can watch two different areas."

She offers to pay him back, but he refuses to let her. "It was such a good price that I would have bought it for myself, anyway," he jokes, "except I only have my roommates to keep track of. Do you know where you want to set it up?"

"I think I want it at the southern border by the stream," she says. "It's the hardest place around here to keep an eye on, and the farthest away."

They spend a few minutes testing the camera; one of them holds it while the other walks in front. Then Ben shows Anna how to look at the images on the viewfinder. The colors in the photos are a little dim, but the focus is clear. "If you take this memory card out," he says, and pops the cover open, "there'll be a slot in your computer that fits it. You can open the pictures from your computer that way. I brought two memory cards so that you could leave one in the camera while you unload the other."

"Can we put it up today?" Anna asks.

It's been a long time since she has ridden horseback with company. She lets Ben ride the dependable old mule, Charlie, while she rides Keeper, who tosses his head in frustration at her tight grip on the reins—though it is humid, the green air invigorates him, and he wants to move out. He arches his neck and lifts his feet high.

Ben and Anna ride in single file with Anna in front in case any monsters jump out of the trees at the horses. Ben hasn't gotten to ride often, he tells her, though he enjoys it. His voice floats up to her as their mounts duck under the branches and step over logs. The myriad lives among the trees chatter, chirp, and sing. The mosquitoes and gnats follow them in swarms, and Anna slaps them several times from her arms and from Keeper's neck, but Ben doesn't even seem to notice them.

"How's your mother doing?" Anna asks.

"She's good. You should give her a call sometime. Go out to lunch or something."

"You think she'd want to hang out with a boring old stick-in-the-mud like me?"

"Sure I do," Ben says. "She asks about you all the time. You're not that old. And you do train horses and wrestle bears, from what she can tell."

Anna laughs. "Well, when you put it that way."

Ben wants to know more about the bear attack, so Anna tells him how the bear had been near the paddock upsetting the mule and how the border collie had followed behind her and charged at it. "If the dog hadn't distracted it, I think it might have attacked me. I was so scared that I actually tried to shoot the bear with the rifle," she confesses. "But nothing happened when I fired."

"Are you sure it was loaded?"

"Yes."

"Did you turn off the safety?"

Anna pauses. "Hmm. I don't know. I didn't think of it."

"Well, it's probably better that you didn't," he says. "You might have gotten in legal trouble if you had shot it, and you would have just made the bear angrier. Though it's sad about your dog. I liked her, too. What bad luck."

In what seems like no time at all, they arrive at the area Anna wants to watch. It is densely wooded and busy with wildlife due to the stream. There are all sorts of tracks crossing the mud, from moose to fisher-cats. Between the cover and the water seems to Anna to be a prime spot to catch poachers who might travel on foot down the banks.

They ground tie the horse and mule; both stand with a hind leg resting, enjoying the rare sun that falls in ribbons through the shade. Ben affixes the camera to a tree trunk with its strap and angles it down while Anna wanders nearby, soundless on soft loam covered by layers of dead leaves and pine needles. The earthy scent hovers over where she walks. After checking it for ticks, she scrambles to the top of a large gray boulder that sits by itself, as resigned and as bowed as if it has been dropped there by a god. She surveys what she can see of her land while Ben finishes installing the trail camera.

"Ben!" she calls, pointing. "What is that?"

He jogs to the boulder and climbs up. They can both see something out of place. Something unnaturally colored, and a curve of metal, too perfectly shaped to be something you'd expect to appear by itself in the forest.

"Let's go see," he says.

They lead Keeper and Charlie toward it, swinging wide to avoid the mud. The thing is closer than it had seemed.

"A trash barrel?" Anna asks, surprised. It's a metal drum, but the top has been cut out, and something pale and round left on top and all over on the ground. She holds the horse and mule while Ben approaches the barrel and crouches, then scratches his head. He picks up a piece from the ground and brings it back to her.

"Doughnuts," he tells her. "Just some stale doughnuts and cinnamon rolls. And a lot of bird droppings."

"Doughnuts?" Anna takes it from him and examines it. Bright cherry frosting on a circle of pale fried dough. It is dried out but the glaze is still sticky, and Charlie reaches for it, stretching his neck and quivering his lips when she holds it away from him. "What can it mean? Is it poisoned?" She tosses it back toward the barrel.

"I don't know," Ben says. "I have no idea. I haven't ever seen anything like this before. Have you?"

Anna shakes her head. "Never."

"This is so strange. Like someone had a lot of old baked goods to get rid of and just decided to dump them here."

"Why here?" Anna asks. "On my land, in the middle of nowhere? What is there to hide?" She laughs. "What kind of nefarious bakery are we talking about here?"

Ben laughs too, but they look at each other with unease. What does it mean?

"Should we do something?" Ben asks.

"What can we do? If whoever did this comes back, maybe we'll get them on the camera and then we can demand an explanation."

"I could help you clean it up," Ben offers. "Though not today—

I have to get some stuff done this afternoon that I've been putting off."

"Don't worry about it. You've helped me so much already," Anna says. "I can clean it up in the next few days. I'll just come out here with a trash bag and pick it up a bit at a time. It'll be a good excuse for me to get some exercise."

"What about the barrel? That'll be heavy."

"I'll just leave it until I can figure out a way to drag it off," she says. "I don't think there's much harm an empty barrel can do out here."

Ben hesitates. "Let me take one more look around," he says. "It just doesn't feel right." He walks back and forth around the barrel, scouring the ground. He looks around at the trees, too, but sees nothing else unusual. At least nothing he tells her about.

"Well, you'll need to clean this up pretty quickly," he says, returning to where she waits. "I'm sure other animals will find it before long. Especially since you know a bear is around."

"The bear. I didn't even think of that," she says. "That's the last thing I need. Ben!" she cries. "We're being foolish. Don't you think that's exactly what this is? Something set up to catch bears?"

"I don't know. It could be," he admits, "though I didn't see any trail cameras watching it. Wouldn't poachers need to keep track of when the bear comes through so they'd know when to be there to shoot it?"

"Maybe we just didn't see it." *Or maybe they're here now, watching us.*

"Maybe. It's really the only thing that makes sense."

Anna says, "I think we should probably leave."

They lead the horse and mule away in silence, until they find a fallen log high enough to help Ben climb up onto Charlie's back. As soon as he has his stirrups, they head out at a brisk trot, putting distance between themselves and the place with the metal barrel.

The light dapples their way. Their saddles creak and they hold their reins loose, not having to guide Charlie or Keeper, who know the way home without being told.

"Anna?" Ben says. "You should go ahead and call the game warden when we get back. Call him this afternoon. And I think you should stay far away from there until he's had a look. Especially don't go there alone."

Anna will have to hide the wolf again, of course, and hide it well. By now, it has probably torn the wallpaper and towels in the powder room to shreds. But Ben is right.

"Okay," she says. "I'll give him a call." His card is on her dressing table, where she had emptied her pockets after the first time she met him.

27

Anna knows she should wait, should not risk going out on her own with possible poachers near. The game warden, who has likely been assigned a territory that is too large for one person, is supposed to be by within a few days, and that doesn't seem like too much to ask of her. She's not sure he believes that she really found a baiting station. And the bear bait on her property does seem ludicrous. Who would do such a thing in her woods? Who would have the nerve to set something that permanent there? The anger wells up in her every time she considers it. She itches to know who did it, who has made such a claim on what she herself owns.

Besides that, she has finished the saddle after having put so much thought and work into it hour after tedious hour, day after day, that she had constructed it even in her unsettled dreams. She both loves and hates it until it seems an extension of herself. She wants a reason to use it, to see if it rides the way she hopes it will. She has an overwhelming urge to find out if she has succeeded—she can't stand to look at it on the rack any longer.

The saddle's tree is too wide for Keeper, but Anna temporarily adjusts the fit by using a saddle pad with shims designed to keep it from sitting against his spine and withers. Though the saddle must have flaws somewhere, she refuses to look too hard for them. If they aren't obvious to her, she reasons, they won't be obvious to anyone else. The oiled chocolate-tinted cowhide, gold and silver conchos, floral tooling, and padded suede seat shine with the quality of their materials and the care of their craftsmanship. Each stitch lies evenly after another in tracks of bright white thread that don't overlap or trail down in fraying strings the way those of commercially built saddles sometimes do. Even the scent of it is perfect—leather and oil and the musty lanolin odor of the real wool fleece underneath. Every time Anna walks by the saddle on its stand, she has to stop and touch it, breathe it in.

The morning air is as cool and soft as water, and Keeper moves over the ground with the strength and grace of a greyhound, without concussion as his hooves hit the ground and he pushes gently off again. Anna, whose figure is close to being the same size and shape as Julie's, sits with her ankles under her knees and hips and her toes slightly up, in just the right position. It is a thrill to feel her seat so secure, to have none of the usual pain in her legs or back as she rides.

She feels like she could ride until she runs out of land, and for the first time in a long while, years even, she lets Keeper out into a gallop. As soon as he understands that she has told him to run, he shakes his head and leaps forward, taking the bit in his teeth, and Anna almost pulls it away from him again instinctively. But she catches herself and sits back in the saddle, lets him take it, pushes him into the bridle with her seat, rounding him. He races ahead with his neck arched like a warhorse's and mane rippling. The wind stings Anna's eyes and makes them water; she can't see except for a smear of green, blue, and brown. She can sense the trunks flying past, totems of tan and white. She smiles. She feels foolish doing it; she imagines what she must look like, old woman on a furry little horse, running through the forest and grinning as though she hasn't a care in the world. But she can't help it.

Keeper fights Anna when she pulls him up, but he soon softens and yields to her hands. He huffs and snorts as they walk toward where Ben installed the trail camera. She dismounts several feet away and leaves him ground tied. He drops his head to graze on the sparse grass that has grown where light filters between the trees.

Anna reaches the camera with a little difficulty, moving a log to stand on since she is shorter than Ben, and pops the front open to switch the used memory card with a blank one. But the slot is empty.

She looks at the replacement card lying in her palm, then looks down at her feet. Perhaps the one from the camera has fallen or she has dropped it. But of course, she hasn't. Hadn't she and Ben put a memory card in when they set it up? She is almost certain that they did. That they had had two of them. Hadn't she brought the card she is holding now in the saddlebag with her all the way from home?

It doesn't make sense, but Anna doesn't know what to do about it, so she puts the blank memory card in, turns the camera on again, and goes back to Keeper. The saddle looks good on him, and it hasn't slipped forward or back. It is nice to be in the quiet of the woods. She strokes the horse's neck and lifts his thick mane to let out some of the heat that has gathered underneath it. The mosquitoes and biting gnats float around them in thin clouds. A bumblebee buzzes around the wildflowers. She kills a fat red-bellied mosquito on Keeper's cheek and leaves a smear of blood. She kills one on her wrist and wonders if her blood has mixed with another being's inside of its body—perhaps a horse's, or a hawk's, or a dog's, or another person's.

Anna can't help looking toward the mysterious metal barrel where it waits with its stale pastries; it still stands, but it is far enough away that she can feel its presence there more than see it, and she will at least be smart enough not to go near that, at any rate.

It's hot. Anna swings up onto Keeper's back. She doesn't immediately turn him toward home, but rides first alongside the stream, hearing voices in the sound of the chattering water.

There are raccoon tracks in the mud, elk, coyotes, and maybe beaver. If a beaver has moved into the area, she will have to keep an eye on it; an overzealous one could dam the stream so much it floods and drowns the nearby trees. Keeper swishes his tail and shakes his head to get the bugs off his ears. She guides him at an angle off the boundary line until she estimates the house and yard to be straight north from their position. She lets him tolt with the hope that the breeze created by his movement will keep the mosquitoes from landing on them.

They have only traveled twenty or thirty yards when he spooks. It happens so quickly. Where her horse's shoulders had been, and his head had been before her, only air. Anna clutches at his mane as she is flung forward. He skitters sideways and turns, blowing hard, toward what has frightened him. *So much fear these last few months.* Anna is always riding spooks these days.

Anna does not lose her seat. She takes up the slack in her reins. Heart throbbing in her ears, she holds on to the pommel and looks toward where Keeper's ears point. It takes her several seconds to catch sight of what has frightened him while her horse shifts his weight impatiently beneath her. There is a black mass lying several feet away, mostly in shadow. Anna blinks hard but can't seem to focus on it. She hears cawing; crows are nearby. She glimpses them over the canopy of pines, negative space in a bright sky.

Anna wills herself to be calm. She rides Keeper toward the shape, walking him back and forth in a zigzag that approaches a little more closely to it with each pass. He is jumpy, but not acting foolish any longer. She stops him before the pressure gets to be too much for him; he stands tense, alert.

Anna can see what the mass is. It is the bear.

The sight of it stuns her. Although its death means that she is no longer in any danger from it, there is no relief; grief settles in her chest like a round stone, and she feels dizzy. The animal must have suffered. It lies as though posed.

The bear hasn't bled out much; the dirt around it is churned, as though it had paddled its feet as it died, but the soil holds only the smallest dark stains. The bear's life would have dripped so slowly into the earth, and the earth would have soaked it in. There could have been no good reason for someone to kill it; if anyone had a reason, it would have been Anna, but she has never blamed the bear for the harm it caused. No, she blames herself. Dead, the bear is not a fine or fierce or terrifying animal, but one that has been violated, deflated into skin and waste. The act senseless to the point of obscenity.

Then they are right about the baiting station. She wonders if the poachers will return for the rest of the carcass, or if they have already gotten all they wanted from it. It wasn't hide or meat they'd been after. The large body, in its unnatural position and with its matted fur, looks messy and abused, but relatively intact, though if she were to get closer, she might see too well what had been taken. Her stomach turns over at the thought of the strong forelegs without their padded, heavy paws. The reproductive organs removed with a cold blade. The gallbladder, its bile believed to heal the sick, cut out. The crescent-moon claws violently unshafted.

When she looks ahead, it is as though the trees have shifted to hide within their density something sinister. She shivers and squints into the shadows. Keeper tenses again because she has; her knees grip his ribs; his back is tight as a spring waiting to be released. She turns him so that she can look back the way they have just come; she can't see anything but forest. The horse snorts and prances in place, and she can't steady him because she is also afraid.

They run home then, Keeper flying over the ground like a ghost, so fast he is almost silent. Anna does not try to control him.

At the bright barn, Anna untacks him and turns him out to cool off. She places the saddle, the remarkable saddle, back on its stand in the sugarhouse, where she cleans Keeper's hair and sweat off of it and wipes off the dust until it looks like it has never before been near a horse.

28

The game warden arrives a day later, early in the afternoon. Anna has just finished lunch and is reading at the kitchen table with the wolf pup sleeping beside her feet. At the sound of a car door, she plucks the pup, leggy and awkward now, off the floor and searches for a safe place to contain it. It groans and stretches as she carries it. Much of the trim and cabinetry in the powder room had been gnawed to splinters during the pup's last confinement, and that is no longer a safe place to leave it unsupervised. Anna hasn't had time or energy yet to tidy it up.

The game warden knocks. Anna takes the pup to the cellar in a rush. Before the closed door, she pauses, listening, but there is nothing except the echo of emptiness in a large space. Cold air leaks from the gap at the threshold. She shivers as it flows around her feet. The pup, growing bigger every day, squirms uncomfortably in her arms. It twists and she nearly drops it. She sets it down.

There's another knock, louder. Anna opens the cellar door and pushes the pup onto the landing. Before she closes it into the darkness, it turns with its head cocked, testing the draft that comes up the stairs. Surely there isn't anything down there that the pup could hurt or that could cause it harm. Perhaps exploring a new place, one of crumbling wet stone walls and a packed earthen floor, will even occupy it enough to keep it quiet. If there are mice hiding in the darkness, it will certainly find them.

The game warden is turning to leave. Anna opens the front door a bit breathlessly to let him in. "I'm so sorry," she tells him.

"I was cleaning upstairs and almost didn't hear you knock."

"That's all right," he says. "I'm just glad you're at home. If you're right about what you saw, we need to get this taken care of right away." The yellow pad comes out. "You think you found a bear baiting station?"

"I hoped it wasn't, but I'm afraid it must be." She describes it to him again, the way she had over the phone—a metal barrel, the pile of stale baked goods. "Every time I say it, it sounds ridiculous."

"No, from what you've described, it sounds like you may be right," he says. "Pastries are commonly used to attract bears. Unfortunately, bear organs can bring a lot of money in the right circles. Can you take me to see the baiting station?"

"Yes," Anna says. "But there's something else. I had a trail camera near there, just to keep an eye on the stream. When I went back to check it, the memory card was gone. I think whoever set up the baiting station took it."

"Did you try to retrieve the card after you found the baiting station, or before?"

"After," Anna confesses.

The game warden sighs, then rubs his temples as though he has a headache. He looks Anna in the eye. "Ma'am, we're dealing with some dangerous people. Not teenagers getting drunk and shooting a deer from their truck, but organized poachers. They may threaten you or worse to keep you quiet. I would ask that you not approach the area again until someone from my office okays it. Is your husband in town? Or do you have a friend who could come and stay with you?"

"It gets even worse," she tells him. "The baiting station worked. They've killed the bear. My bear." She swallows. "The bear that got my dog."

He looks at her sharply. "How do you know? You've seen it?"

She nods. "Just yesterday. I can show you where."

"I think you'd better," he says.

* * *

The game warden has come prepared. Anna had intended to take him to the baiting station by horseback, but he has brought an ATV hitched to a small trailer. "To haul off the baiting station," he explains.

The ATV seems a real luxury at first. It goes as quickly as a horse, perhaps more quickly, and it is much more predictable. It doesn't shy even once. But after several minutes of riding in it, Anna misses the quiet of the woods. The machine leaves no chance of surprising and observing even a woodchuck. The trees seem as if they stand back, wary of the noise and unwelcoming.

Anna directs the game warden so that they will go by the prone bear first. She stays in the passenger seat while he gets out and walks all around the body, making notes and taking photographs. He squats to examine it, then returns, his expression grim.

"They took the gallbladder, of course," he says, "among other things."

"Its paws?"

He nods.

That seems worse, somehow. To leave it without its pads and claws. At the thought of someone cutting through the skin of the bear, once so powerful and wild, so close to where she lives, Anna shudders. It must have taken some time. It must have taken a frightening kind of heartlessness. "What are the odds of catching who did it, do you think?"

The game warden sighs and doesn't look at her. "Not good, to tell you the truth," he says. "It takes years to build a case, and you have to have rock-solid proof to get a conviction. I'm hoping we can tie this one to some other open cases. I doubt this is the first time this poacher has gotten a bear this way."

"Maybe the trail camera will have something."

"Maybe," he says, looking ahead. "If it still has the last card you put in it."

"You think they might still be around? Or will they have gone now?"

He shakes his head but doesn't answer and starts the ATV again. They drive toward the stream, neither trying to speak over the engine.

Anna can't hear the water when they get close, but she recognizes the area and clutches at the game warden's arm. They get out of the ATV, and she leads him to the tree with the trail camera in it. She gestures toward where it is mounted and waits while he reaches for it.

He squints against the bright sky, feels all around the shaded trunk, then shakes his head. It's gone. The entire camera this time. "There's nothing here," he tells her, frowning. "Are you sure this is the right tree?"

"Positive. Here's the log I stood on to change the card."

He looks appraisingly around at the other trees nearby while Anna waits.

"Well, then," he says. "It seems like it's been stolen."

"No," Anna says. "That camera was a gift. I can't believe it."

"Show me this baiting station," he says.

Anna expects the barrel to be gone, too, but it is still there, though less bait remains. "I don't think it's been refilled," Anna says. They look down at it, blue and rusted, sides drilled full of holes close to the bottom so that rain doesn't stand in it. Bees and bottle flies buzz around the hard pastries, lifting and resettling as Anna and the game warden move near them.

"Should we go ahead and put it in the trailer?" Anna asks. She begins to rock the barrel to loosen it from the dirt.

"Wait," the game warden says. He is looking from trunk to trunk at the nearby trees. "Stay right there." He walks in a semicircle, gazing up, reaching and running his hands over the bark in places. He comes back to her holding something tightly against his chest. He shows it to her.

"Another camera," Anna says. "Not mine. Mine was more of a green color. My friend Ben looked for another one when we were here, but he didn't find it. What does it mean?"

"It means a few things. It was pretty well hidden—it would have been easy to miss. This is how the poachers determine the habits of the bear they're baiting," he explains. "Since this stuff is still here, they might think another bear might be in the area. Or maybe there isn't another bear and they just haven't had the chance to remove their trap yet." He pauses. "We can also assume that they've seen you, though they must not have thought they had anything to fear from you. For some reason, it didn't occur to them that you'd call me."

"Well, they were wrong," Anna says. "What are you going to do with the camera?"

"I'm taking it with me. For one thing, unless they have been careful to stay out of its range, it probably has a photograph of whoever set it up. And it's evidence. Along with the barrel and the bait. Maybe there are fingerprints."

"Should we leave the baiting station?" Anna asks. "You know, like a sting operation?"

"We don't have enough manpower for something that drastic," he says. "And I would rather take the stuff with me while I can. If I don't, it will disappear. And we might risk losing another bear, too."

He offers to take Anna back to her house, but in reply, she digs a black plastic bag out of a box in the ATV and starts picking up the stale doughnuts and cinnamon rolls.

It doesn't take long, between the two of them, to clear the baiting station. The barrel bounces and clatters in the little ATV trailer all the way back, and Anna imagines the wildlife for yards around scattering as a result, birds lifting into the sky, fisher-cats diving into burrows, deer slipping into thickets, rabbits pressing their fast hearts against the ground.

The game warden leaves her on her porch with a warning. "We might have just made some ruthless people very angry. Leave all of your exterior lights on tonight," he says. "And have a shotgun on hand, if you own one. I would really rather you stayed in town or had someone come out here with you."

"I'll be fine," Anna tells him. "My husband will be home any time, and I'm tougher than I look."

"I'm sure that's probably true," he says, with the bare hint of a smile. "But if you do have any trouble, don't call me first. I won't get here in time. Call emergency services. Hide somewhere and stay quiet until the sheriff gets here."

"I will."

"I should give them a head's up, actually. One of my good friends is a deputy. I'll see if he'll patrol out here tonight. Maybe for the next several nights."

"That's really not necessary," Anna says, "though I appreciate it."

"I'll keep you posted," he says. "Be careful and keep alert."

Anna enters her house cautiously, listening for the wolf, which has been locked up for hours. The cat, which doesn't come out in the open much now that the pup has started to take an interest in it, stretches and yawns from the center of the kitchen table. Anna shoos it onto the tile and goes to the cellar door. Opening it a crack, cringing when the old hinges creak, she peers down the stairs into the darkness. She can hear scrambling, digging, and panting—primal, animal sounds—and goose bumps prickle her arms. She opens the door wider and whistles.

There is the sound of claws clicking on stone, and then the wolf pup appears out of the darkness to stand in the slant of light on the stairs just in front of Anna. It seems happy to be released, loping past her as she makes her way to the den to rest.

After dinner, while Anna watches television, the pup frustrates her by worrying something hard, chewing loudly as it lies on the rug beside the chair. It must have carried something from the cellar up in its mouth. Anna doesn't have the energy to try to take whatever the object is away; she waits until the pup rises and trots to its bowls in the kitchen, where she can hear it lapping water.

She bends to see what it has left behind. Something small, jointed, off-white. She picks it up, puzzled, then throws it away from her in surprise—it slides under the TV cabinet.

The pup had been chewing on a bone, but she hadn't given it one.

29

A t twilight, Anna carries a blanket, an electric lantern, and the rifle to the barn. She had retrieved the gun from the sugarhouse without pausing to enjoy, as she usually would, the warmth and welcome of the familiar, well-used tools, the air earthy with the fragrance of leather and wool. She had locked the sugarhouse again quickly once she had the rifle, abandoning it to shadow.

The wolf pup trots at her heels, snapping at the edge of the blanket that has escaped her hold and drags in the long grass behind her. Despite the growing darkness, she can see the house clearly when she stands in the walk-through barn door and looks back. The blinds and curtains are closed, but yellow shines around the perimeters of the windows in bright bars; she had turned on the lights in every room and left them blazing, like a lighthouse casting its hope into the forest instead of the sea.

Anna does not expect the poachers, if they come, to attack her but to attack her horse and mule. That is where they could hurt her most, and she works on the assumption that they will know it, too—it seems so obvious. She has slept in the barn before, when she and John had a mare that expected a foal, or a horse had colicked. Spending the night bundled against the evening cool while the horse and mule drowse and chew their hay isn't a prospect that seems either especially difficult or undesirable. It might even be cozy.

She causes a small commotion coming into the barn with the wolf pup; Keeper doesn't mind the young predator, but Charlie snorts and stays wide-eyed and stiff, watching its every move and keeping his long ears pointed at it as long as he can see it. He huffs and paws when they walk past him. His reaction puts Anna on edge, but there is no help for it. If he paws too much or charges the stall door, she will have to hold him. She hopes he'll grow used to the wolf quickly and calm down.

Exhausted by the long day, Anna spreads some fresh straw in the corner of an empty stall and nestles into its prickly sweetness with her back against the rough wood panel. With the half door closed, no one will be able to tell she is there except by the glow of the lantern at her feet, which shouldn't carry up high enough to be obvious. While Anna settles in, the pup stalks the stall's perimeter, burying its nose in the straw and sneezing. Once it has satisfied itself that nothing interesting has been hidden there, it lies against Anna's outstretched leg and goes to sleep.

Holding the rifle across her knee, Anna waits. The horse and mule rustle in their stalls and rattle their buckets and sigh, then stand still. There is no wind or rain outside. But for the snoring pup and chirping frogs and crickets, there would be silence. Anna tries to stay watchful, but she is warm under the blanket and the lantern emits a soft circular glow, as soothing as a nightlight in a child's bedroom. Anna's head lowers several times and she jerks back to alertness, only to nod off again.

She is awakened around eleven by the yip of a coyote outside the barn. The thickness of the night around her makes her shiver; the air smells of dew. She sits still and can hear the coyotes brushing against the outside wall with swishes and thuds as they trot past. They snap at each other and growl just beyond where she leans. The wolf pup groans and turns over onto its side, eyes open. The coyotes must have just gotten into the trees when they begin to sing. First a howl, lonely and sharp, that thrills along Anna's neck and raises goose bumps on her skin. The howl lingers, caught by the canopy, then falls. It hits the damp earth and disintegrates into a cacophony of whines and barks that bound along the ground in all directions, then die out, leaving the darkness empty. The wolf pup whines and sits up. Anna pulls it nearer her and strokes behind its ears.

In her exhaustion, Anna soon falls asleep again, and wakes some time later with a cramp in her neck. *Some guardian I am.* She doesn't know what has awakened her; she holds her breath and listens. There is the grind of tires turning on gravel, and light spills through the loft window, increasingly bright, only to ebb and just as quickly almost vanish. A car has pulled into her driveway. She waits. Whoever drives it doesn't get out, but stays inside with the engine running.

Anna has left the barn door cracked so that she has a way to see the yard. She pushes the pup off her lap; it rolls in the straw and looks at her appraisingly. Quietly as she can, she opens the stall door to let herself out into the aisle. She holds the gun along the length of her leg, pointing down. Keeper snorts at her in surprise when she goes by, but Charlie only stands watching her with eyes that glitter with reflected points of light. Near the door, she crouches and tries to steady herself.

If the poachers have come, she might only have one chance. Taking a deep breath, she looks toward the house.

She can tell the car is white. Because the headlights are on, she has trouble making out anything other than that and its shape—a coupe or sedan, not a truck, as she had expected. She waits, and the driver waits.

Anna's palms grow sweaty where she grips the gun. She begins to count under her breath to pass the time. She sits so long that her legs go numb. It occurs to her that she has become a person John wouldn't recognize.

Another vehicle finally drives down the road. It slows going by Anna's house but doesn't stop; its headlights swing through the yard, illuminating the side of the car, and Anna relaxes. The car in her driveway is that of a sheriff's deputy. This is the game warden's doing. She had forgotten. She wonders what he told the deputy about her, what he had said to get the deputy to agree to stay so long.

Relieved, she sinks back into the cool dust, dropping the rifle beside her. Once the sting of returning circulation in her legs passes, she makes her way back to the stall where the wolf pup lies snug in the bedding, twitching with dreams. After settling in beside it, she closes her eyes.

But she doesn't sleep again—not yet. The car stays outside with its headlights burning ahead, unwavering. She can picture the man who sits there, faceless, listening to the radio, perhaps. She can picture the animals, all in their places—her horse and mule, helpless (she has trapped them in their stalls, but they are unaware they are trapped)—the heavy bear sinking into the grass hollows; the deer listening from the thickets, knee-deep in fog. The Kingdom gets to be too restless around her. It clamors.

Anna feels in her pocket for the bone that she had retrieved from the wolf pup and kept because she didn't know where to put it. *Funny how things follow you.* She turns it in her fingers. She has been tempted to throw it back into the basement, listen to it rattle off the stairs she can't see, but something has stopped her. Now that she knows of this bone, she doesn't want to throw it away. She wants to know exactly where it is. She does not want to be surprised by it again. The dirt floor of the stall has been packed hard by years of horses, and is too hard for her to dig. But there is a space behind the wooden post she leans against, hidden by slats. No one will ever see behind it, not unless the barn is torn down someday, taken back to the ground, long after she is gone. She drops the bone behind the post and hears it hit the soft dust at the base. Then she sleeps.

The sun comes through the barn in stripes. Charlie nickers when he sees Anna stand and stretch; he wants breakfast. Keeper paws impatiently at his wooden partition, then raises his head when Anna tells him no.

Anna brushes the hay off her jeans and unlatches the door of the stall where she slept. The wolf jogs past her, showing the oiled, easy motion of the carnivore even at its young age, on its too-big paws. It tracks Anna as she feeds the horse and mule, pausing only to sniff around the edges of the aisle. Charlie has grown used to the wolf smell overnight and is no longer very worried by its antics. Anna wonders briefly if she might have reason to regret desensitizing the mule to the odor of an animal that will grow to be so dangerous, but it doesn't matter, it has been done.

She has just dumped the feed into the bins when voices catch her attention. The noise of feeding—knocking against buckets, the water sound of pouring grain and beet pulp—and the concentration required for measuring out the oats and supplements had distracted her. She pushes the pup back into the stall with her foot, leans the rifle against the barn door, and looks out.

Though she expects to see the deputy again, or maybe the game warden, it is the sheriff himself on Anna's porch. He is talking into his radio. She comes up behind him as he is knocking. Though she isn't quiet, he doesn't turn, so she takes a moment to smooth her rumpled clothing and untidy hair. With his back to her, he doesn't notice her until she speaks. She clears her throat.

"Good morning," she says. "Is there something I can do for you?"

The sheriff, a man she hadn't voted for, turns and touches the edge of his hat. "Yes, ma'am, I believe you can. Is this your property?"

"Yes," she says, and gives him her name. "My husband John and I own the Northeast Kingdom Saddle Company, operated out of our old sugarhouse over there. Are you here about the bear poacher?"

"Bears? No, ma'am," the sheriff says.

"Oh," Anna says, confused. "I thought the game warden must have sent you."

"We do work with him quite a bit, but I'm actually here about another matter." He clears his throat. "We received a tip about some suspicious activity."

Anna looks at him, her mind blank, unsure how to respond. He meets her look steadily. "What does that mean?" she asks. "Could you be more specific?"

"Yes, ma'am. It seems there might have been some kind of accident that didn't get reported," he says. "Were you aware of a repossessed vehicle hidden on your property?"

Oh, my god. Anna had somehow allowed herself to forget the black truck. The deer poachers who had never left the clearing. The mule's shoulder, which had bled real blood. "No," she says evenly. "My car and truck were both paid off a long time ago. What kind of vehicle? Where was it?"

"On your eastern boundary, not far inside the fence line. The fence isn't down, so the driver either came in another way, or someone repaired the fence."

"I had no idea," Anna says.

"No? Well, apparently, the payment for the truck was on some kind of automatic draft. When it started bouncing, the truck was repossessed, and the car lot tracked it with the GPS it had hidden under the dash."

"I'm surprised they could even do that," Anna says. "Do all cars have it? Seems an invasion of privacy."

"A lot of them do."

"And the car lot people can just come and take it back? It's not trespassing?"

"Unless it's in a closed garage, if the paperwork's in order, they can take the car back, yes."

"That's incredible," Anna says. "I can't believe it. But what does any of this have to do with me? I don't mind if they take it, of course, as long as they don't bother anything else. Do they need help getting it out?" She swallows. "You mentioned an accident."

"Yes, ma'am," the sheriff says. "The repo guys thought something seemed weird about the truck's having been left in the middle of the woods, apparently for months. The payments on it had stopped only three months back, but it's been there for a long time. It's covered in a lot of dirt and debris and a window is broken out. They found a couple of coolers inside filled with unopened beer and empty beer cans, some old food. The bed of the truck had organic matter in it."

The buck. Bones. Leaves. And once some maggots, probably. Decayed meat. She hadn't opened the coolers. "Go on."

"It turned out to only be the remains of a deer, as we had suspected from some other evidence," the sheriff says (*Probably the antlers*, thinks Anna), "but the repo guys thought something seemed wrong, and it bothered them enough to give me a call. As it would happen, the man who owns that truck has been missing out of New York State since at least last November or December. His employer assumed he didn't want his job anymore. He was reported missing only after not showing up for his final paycheck. He and a friend apparently told people they were going on a hunting trip, and they never came back."

"That's awful," Anna says softly.

"Yes, ma'am."

"So you think something happened to them? On my land? If they were here, they would have been poaching."

"We don't have much information yet," the sheriff says guardedly. "But I need to ask you a few things."

While Anna stands uncomfortably rubbing her shoulders against the early chill, wishing she could sit down, he poses questions.

Did you notice anything unusual in late November to early December? *No, everything was normal. The birds singing. The bills coming due.*

Do you remember hearing any gunfire around that time? *Yes, during hunting season, I often hear it.*

How often do you check that part of your property? *Not very. Once or twice a year, lately.* When was the last time you did? *Last fall, I believe. To the best of my recollection.*

Have you ever had trouble with poachers before? *Yes. Always. Poachers, neighbors, and dogs.*

Is your husband available? *He isn't here right now, but I'll tell him you need to see him.*

Anna is instructed to stay close in case the sheriff's office needs to reach her; they intend to return with cadaver dogs, which will arrive soon with their handlers from Burlington and Montpelier. She assures the sheriff that she will help in any way she can.

After he has gone, she goes into the house that still has the lights on in every room and sits at the kitchen table, forgetting about the wolf pup she has left in the barn, the horse and mule waiting to be let out of their stalls, and the rifle loaded and ready, propped against the rough-hewn wall. She hadn't been able to ask the sheriff what she really wanted to know: *If your mule kills a man, and you don't throw yourself in front of the mule to stop it, have you broken the Good Samaritan law?* And, *What sort of math is used to determine that kind of responsibility?* And, *Does a person have to report the dead?* Families can bury their loved ones on their own land, though she doesn't know what is involved in doing so. What about burying strangers?

How long do I have left?

30

The road opens before Anna with depth of field, trees flying past the window in a blur of blue and brown and green, but those still before her stand sharp against the sky, inviting her progress. This is an effect of tunnel vision. Edison had been surprised to get her call, but pleased that the saddle was finished. He hadn't understood her urgency with regard to its delivery, but he'd agreed with some surprise in his voice to accommodate her at Moose Hollow despite the short notice. As Anna drives, the twists and turns in the road behind her grow darker and more confusing, like a storm building at her back, pressing her ahead. She tries not to look in the rearview mirror. Her forest lingers there in an impenetrable mist where strangers threaten to uncover what the land intends to hide. She hasn't been able to think, so close to it all. She has to get away from the shabby house, the overgrown green yard.

She approaches the convenience store, her hands still shaking and sweating on the steering wheel. She stops as before for coffee there, and to stretch her legs, comforted to a small degree by having created her own routine so far from home. She allows herself to be glad that she will soon see Edison and Julie and the little golden mare that will wear her saddle, the one she has made herself.

In less than an hour, she will know for sure if her project has been successful. She has grown too close to judge, can even see the saddle's stitching and tooling in red outlines when she closes her eyes, as though they have been burned into her vision. She loves the saddle but in some ways has no confidence in it. The craft evident in Anna's work might be almost as good as that of the work John had done. It should be; it has taken her several times over the amount of time it would have taken him to complete the same task. But surely such skill as John's would be impossible, coming from her limited experience. It is possible that she is fooling herself regarding its quality, and will look like a fool to Edison.

Still, she has ridden in a saddle she made with her own hands, and there is no taking that from her.

Anna had run a dust cloth over the saddle one last time before loading it in the trunk of the car on a clean sheet to protect it from bits of dust and hay, lingering as she polished again the tooling on the supple leather. She had decided several times over in the days after she had completed the saddle to cancel the order and keep it for herself, especially after she had ridden in it, but in the soft white morning light, the idea that she'd even considered going back on her contract with Julie had shamed her.

The fields and arenas at Moose Hollow brim with activity. Anna slows the car to study the powerful, balanced movements of well-trained, expensive horses while they school. All of the dressage horses are immaculately collected under saddle by lithe riders; necks arched, weight set back on muscular haunches, the horses lift at invisible signals, and the jumping horses are rangy and farsighted until they are asked to work, when they flow into the canter and spring into the sky as if unbound from a counterweight. It is beautiful, all of it.

After she has parked, Anna stands outside for a while and watches a class of beginning jumpers in the oval ring, children riding a colorful mixture of short sturdy paints and chocolate Shetlands and dappled Welsh ponies that pop over crossrails at the kicks of small legs and then pin their ears and try to graze once they have landed. Is it possible? Surely she has never been as new as that. She can't picture it anymore.

Anna carries the saddle into the barn. She sees the Haflinger in the crossties, silhouetted by the light that comes through the open overhead door behind it; Julie grooms it with quick sure flicks of the brush, and dust lifts from its coat in a pale mist to hang just over the mare and the woman and catch the sun. Julie greets her, but doesn't stop her work.

"You've brought it, then?" Julie asks. "The enchanted saddle that's to solve all of my riding problems?"

"Yes," Anna tells her, "made special just for you and Honey."

"Well," Julie says, "I've got to tell you, I have pretty high hopes after all this time."

Edison comes out of his office smiling. "Anna!" He claps her on the shoulder so hard that she flinches. "Good to see you again. Is that it?"

She nods and holds the saddle toward him. He looks it over while she holds it, rubs the leather tooling and runs his hands along the cantle, then takes the saddle from her and cradles the channel along his arm, peering down the middle, judging its balance. Anna, not wanting to miss anything he says or does, holds her breath. "Nice, soft, good leather," he says. "Exactly the quality I'd expect. How much does it weigh? About twenty pounds?"

"Eighteen. It's not going to break anyone's back to carry it around."

Edison turns it again, starts to say something, but changes his mind.

"It really is lovely." Julie has finished grooming the mare and comes around to join them. "Shall we see if it works?"

"Yes, let's," Anna says. "This is the most rewarding part." *I hope.*

Julie lifts the saddle onto the Haflinger's back without a pad and slides it into its sweet spot, where it rests naturally in the dip behind her withers but in front of her loin. "It fits her just right, doesn't it?" she says to Edison, and he steps beside her and checks, feeling underneath the tree.

"No bridging," he agrees, "and it's short enough, and off her shoulder and her spine. The girth hangs straight down in her groove. Looks good so far."

"I think I'm going to go ahead and tack her up and then lunge her to get her used to it. Do you mind waiting?"

"That's what I do with new tack, too," Anna assures Julie. "Better to have any wrecks happen before you get up there."

Anna and Edison lean on the rail while Julie lunges the mare in a circle around her. The mare snorts as she warms up. She's fun to watch, the way she lifts her short thick legs in a trot far too fancy for a draft horse masquerading as a pony. Her hooves are twice the size of those of any other horse her height.

"Hard to picture her pulling a plow for the Amish, isn't it?" Edison says. "That's what she probably did before she wound up on her way to slaughter."

Anna nods and smiles. In a way, yes, it is hard now to imagine the energetic, intelligent little horse thin and tired and broken-spirited, as she must have been as she waited in the kill lot, though when the mare had stood still and lowered her head in the crossties while being groomed, Anna could see the old white marks left by a harness collar that didn't fit, and could glimpse then how such an animal could have turned the earth to earn a living.

After several minutes of warm-up, Julie stops and leads Honey toward them. "It must feel okay to her," she says. "She didn't act like she wanted to buck, and the saddle hasn't slid forward at all. I'm ready."

Julie bridles the mare, tightens the girth, then takes her to the mounting block. "Here goes nothing!" she calls. They watch her buckle her helmet before swinging onto Honey's broad back. The mare stands still, waiting for Julie to pick up her other stirrup and get settled. Julie finds her seat and nudges the mare's sides with her heels. Honey steps off into a swinging walk.

Anna tries to gauge what Julie might be thinking, but her expression as she goes around the arena is blank. At least the mare is moving well. "Does she like it or not?" Anna asks Edison.

He shrugs. "Julie can actually be a little abrupt," he tells her, "which can hurt people's feelings. But she'll definitely let you know how she feels once she's made up her mind. I'm just impressed that her leg is in the right place in this saddle. We've had a hell of a time the last few months trying to get it underneath her and keep it still. And the mare is moving out well."

Julie cues Honey into a trot, and the mare transitions into the quicker gait with a little hop; perhaps, as a former workhorse, she throws her weight forward to move some kind of burden that no longer exists. They go clockwise, then counterclockwise around the arena, then in serpentines. Julie passes them again, grinning broadly, and then she starts laughing, and Anna laughs too.

"This is wonderful!" Julie calls. "I love it. I don't even know how to thank you. I have no pain, and I'm so secure in the seat. I could ride all day." She rides to the rail and halts, still smiling. She pats Honey's neck; the horse has worked up a light sweat and huffs softly. "Do you want to try?" she asks Anna.

Before Anna really understands what has happened, she too is on the little Haflinger, trotting in the perfectly leveled and layered sand while the long flaxen mane bounces in front of her, and Julie and Edison blur by at the fence. The mare goes faster and faster; it doesn't frighten Anna, but makes her feel like a little girl, like she has gotten away from the adults and can ride her pretty horse however she likes without anyone watching or caring. She doesn't worry about anything but herself and the horse. But she too quickly grows tired from posting the bouncy trot. It's with real reluctance that she rides back to the rail.

"Honey is pretty green still, isn't she?" Anna asks breathlessly. "What a fun mare, though."

"She won't stay green for long now that I can ride her for more than fifteen minutes at a time," Julie says. "What do you think, Edison?"

"I think you'll be able to do anything you like with her by fall," he says.

Anna dismounts and hands the reins to Julie. "I'm guessing you'll want to ride some more?"

"Gladly. First, I have this for you." She digs in her pocket and pulls out a folded check. It is made out to the Northeast Kingdom Saddle Company; the memo line says "Miracle Saddle." Anna thanks her.

"Maybe this isn't something you'd know," Julie says, "but how in the world did your husband manage to create a narrow twist on such a wide tree without making me feel like I'm perched over my horse?"

Anna beams. "He's an expert." *It has to do with how I arranged and shaped the padding. It wasn't easy.* She bites her tongue to keep from saying so. The triumph is hard to hold in.

Edison says, "He's more like an artist. Please tell John this might be his best work yet. They've always been good, but this one has such attention to detail. You don't think he'll do any more custom orders?"

"I'm afraid this was the last," Anna says. *And I still can't believe it worked. There must surely be some mistake.* "Unless, of course, he can spare time to build me one. I probably told you this, but that's exactly the saddle I would have wanted."

"I'm sure he'll do it, if you ask nicely," Edison says. "You are, after all, the love of his life, aren't you?"

"I suppose that's true," she says.

Anna leaves them in the arena, Julie riding her mare and Edison calling out instructions: soften your hands and push her into the bridle, lengthen that stride. As she walks, she can feel the thin rectangle of the folded check through her pocket. Even allowing for the materials she'd had to buy to complete the saddle, it's the most money she has ever made herself. But more than that, she has made one good thing in this world.

31

Though the morning has sapped her energy, Anna is tired only in body, not in mind, and she doesn't want to return to the bewildering and uncertain life in the little house just yet. Her home ought to be safe enough in daylight. It won't hurt anything if she enjoys her success just a little bit longer. Maybe the saddle is the last triumph she'll ever have, the only meaningful thing she'll ever do. She pulls into the bank parking lot in Belbridge and studies the check that Julie has given her, relishing every curled letter of the amount written on the second line.

She lets the teller know she'd like to cash it, not deposit it. The teller raises an eyebrow but turns to her screen. "Do you know your account number?"

"No, I'm afraid not," Anna says. She digs her driver's license out of a wallet filled with receipts and expired credit cards. "Can you look it up with this?"

"Yes, just a second while I find your account." The teller's manicured fingernails are so long, Anna wonders how she manages to type, but after a few quick taps, she looks up.

"You're wanting to cash it through the Northeast Kingdom account, correct?"

"I suppose so," Anna says. "Can you tell me the balance?"

"It looks like it's just under fifteen thousand dollars right now," the teller says pleasantly.

Anna freezes. She asks carefully, "What did you say?"

"Just under fifteen thousand?"

"I don't understand. How is that possible?" Anna asks.

The teller looks at her with a quizzical expression. "Well, it looks like it hasn't had much activity in quite some time. Only a few small automatic withdrawals. Is something wrong?"

"No, it's just . . . I thought I only had a few hundred dollars at most," Anna says.

Tap tap tap. The teller studies the monitor. "Yes, in your personal accounts. This is notated as a business account."

Anna can feel her hands start to shake, so she puts them under the counter where the teller can't see. "This might sound like a stupid question, but how many accounts do I have, exactly? My husband usually does the banking."

"Just three. Checking, savings, and business. Checking and savings are tied together, business is separate."

"Can I access the business account online, too?"

"Sure, but you need a separate access code. Would you like for me to set it up for you?"

"Yes, please," Anna says, dazed. She usually just has clients make checks out to her. The first time she'd gone to the bank, the teller must have deposited the Northeast Kingdom check into the wrong account—personal instead of business. So that's the account Anna had kept using. All these months. She has really been far better off than she imagined. She could have done more, taken care of more, eaten better food, lived better. She hadn't known in time.

The teller hands her a card with an account number and a PIN. "Do you still want to cash this?" she asks, holding up the check.

"Yes. Actually . . ." Anna wavers. "Can I withdraw more from that same account?"

"Sure," she says. "But you should know that any cash transaction ten thousand dollars or over involves a lot of paperwork. It's supposed to fight terrorism."

Anna laughs. "I'm not a terrorist," she says. "Just an old woman who likes to buy horses." That is true, or had been at some point.

Anna leaves with $9,500 in a zippered bag with the bank's logo centered on the front. She isn't sure what impulse has driven her to withdraw such a ludicrous amount of money; when she had decided to cash the check, she had had a vague notion that it would be nice to have cash on hand, easily accessible in an emergency. And besides that, it might be fun to spend a little while she still can. Who knows what will happen next? She has a vague idea of going to lunch in town, somewhere nice. Having a glass of wine with lunch, even. But she changes her mind. She doesn't want to take the money into the restaurant with her or leave it in the car.

It should be secure enough at home. There are a thousand places there that she can hide it. But she regrets having it as soon as she walks out of the glass doors of the bank with inches and feet in numbers beside the frames, there to mark the height of someone fleeing after a robbery. Walking to her car, she tucks the bag under her arm to hide it, and is sure she will be mugged, though such a thing probably hasn't ever happened in Belbridge.

The arthritis in her knees flares up again when she slides into the seat, and her head pounds. Anna isn't sure of herself or what else she should do. She is tired. She has left the wolf pup in the basement again in case the sheriff shows up early with his cadaver dogs. She worries about the wolf. But there is no reason for anyone to enter her house just yet, to look anywhere but in the woods near where the truck had been found.

There's still a pay phone in front of the grocery store—one of the few left anywhere in the country, perhaps. She parks close to it. It has a laminated yellow phone book in its small, clear plastic cubicle, the way they had all had in the old days, attached there with a blue cable through one corner. Anna pushes the bag of money under the passenger seat and digs in the dash of the car for change. How much does it cost to make a call these days? She finds two dollars in grimy quarters at the bottom of the glove box—probably stashed there by John for the air machine in case the tires get low—and puts them into her pocket.

The town is big enough to accommodate its own funeral home, but only one. Someone picks up the phone on the second ring. A cheerful voice says, "Belbridge Funeral Home. Kelly speaking. How can I help you?"

"Hello," Anna says. "I have a question about home burials. How do they work? Can you set up something like that?"

"We can certainly help facilitate the process. Have you recently lost a relative?"

"I have an aunt in hospice," Anna lies, "and we want to bury her on the family land when she passes."

"I'm sorry to hear about your aunt, though I'm glad you thought of us to assist you. We would be happy to help. When the time comes, there's some paperwork you'll have to fill out with the Vital Records Office and the town clerk."

Anna half-listens to several minutes of instruction that don't really have much to do with her situation anymore. Once the voice finishes, she asks, "And what happens if we forget to file the paperwork? With all the other arrangements we'll be having to make?"

"This isn't something you should try to do alone. We are here to keep you from being overwhelmed," the voice says firmly. "But no matter what you decide to do, make sure you file the paperwork and get permission first. If you don't, and you bury your aunt anyway, you could face up to five years in prison, a fine of one thousand dollars, or both."

"That sounds pretty serious," Anna says into her shirt collar.

"I'm sorry?"

"Thank you for your help."

"Of course," the voice says. "I would be happy to meet with you to discuss this in detail. Call us—"

Anna puts the phone back on its receiver. How long will it take them to bring the dogs, how long will it take them to realize that she has something to do with the bodies in the woods? They will find the two men quickly. She hadn't buried them deep; she had grown tired after only a foot or so, hacking at the muck with a snow shovel and a pickaxe that had been in the black truck, the only tools she had been able to find at short notice since John kept many of the regular maintenance tools in the basement, where she never went. She had dragged the bodies into the hole using the horse, which had been skittish at first—covered them with what dirt she could, and leaves and rocks, and piled the jump standards over them. She had done the right thing. They would probably have wanted to be buried. But it could cost her ten years and two thousand dollars. And whatever consequences she might face because she hadn't been a Good Samaritan, tried to save them in the first place. The fine won't be any problem now, but the rest will be.

And what about John? She hasn't buried John. Hasn't even told anyone about him. He lies where he fell because she can't bear to move him, to cover him over. His body will have been opened, by now, cleaned by animals and weather. He had always been most at home in the woods.

Before pulling into her driveway, Anna stops in the road and studies her house. It would look neglected to anyone else and sometimes looks that way to her. It is true that it sometimes confines her. The overgrown yard, the paint chipping off the siding, the outdated fixtures, the shaggy butterfly bush hanging over the porch, the bare wooden barn that leans a little to the left—they belong to her irrevocably, are a part of her whether she likes it or not. But except for her parents' house when she was very small, when the central heat would come on and she would pad on the soft carpet to the kitchen where her mother would be up, stirring hot chocolate in her nightgown, it has been the place she has known best, felt safest, most herself.

Being sick used to be simple, not like now when she has to

arrange her entire life around it; it used to mean lying on the couch in a sleeping bag watching television while the smell of chicken noodle soup drifted from the stove. Now, being ill is complicated, difficult, lonely. But in the close walls of the house in front of her, she has often recovered nonetheless. Has often even been comfortable, content.

Anna longs suddenly, painfully, for someone to care for her.

She parks the dusty car and steps into the mudroom, which she hasn't cleaned; last autumn's soil still sits in the shapes of soles along the wall. The wolf pup hears her unlock the door and yelps to be let out. Anna releases it from the cellar. It gambols in circles around her on its lanky legs, tripping sometimes on its own paws. It is growing quickly; it becomes more wolfish every day. You can almost watch it happening. It pounces on the light that comes through the window and snaps at it as if at flies. It looks through her when she bends to rub behind its ears.

Anna puts the zippered pouch of money into a drawer and covers it with old appliance manuals, then makes tea. It's early afternoon. She sits with a novel at the kitchen table trying to read, but she doesn't have enough concentration for it; the words mean nothing, and she keeps looking over the edges of the pages at the drawer with the money.

It helps to have it close by, now that she can see no clear way forward, and she doesn't know what will happen when the cadaver dogs arrive. They will find those men and the sheriff will know someone buried them. It won't take them long to figure out that it was her. Who else could it have been? She had to do right by human remains, didn't she? It is her land.

And there's more. Won't the sheriff want to search her house after finding the secrets she has kept in the woods? They will arrest her. And the horse and mule—have they served her and John so faithfully all these years, only to be run through an auction by a disinterested sheriff's office and sold to slaughter? Anna can't stand the thought of such betrayal.

Then, what about the wolf? No matter what else happens, they will take the wolf from her, she's certain.

Anna is stuck. Everything that lives in her world requires her to provide some kind of protection. The proximity of the money now, instead of comforting her, spoils her focus, makes her anxious. In her situation, what good might it really do? She would give all of it to change what had happened.

"Anna!"

Anna drops the teacup with a clatter and feels her skin prickle; someone outside is calling her. She sits tense, listening, her pulse a panicked flicker. The sheriff already? Or could it be Ben?

The man knocks again.

"Open the door. I know you're there. I saw you go in."

They know. Will they break down the door? She wills herself to stand. The man peers through the panes; with his hand shading his eyes, his face is in shadow. He lowers his hand to knock again. Anna is washed with relief, and then irritation. It's only her neighbor, Hank.

She interrupts his knocking by opening the door. Anna starts to ask what he wants, but loses the words when faced with what leans against his leg, its smoothworn stock resting in his palm. She hasn't seen it in so long, but it is so familiar, the scratches through the black paint on the barrel, the initials carved crookedly into the wood. John's rifle.

32

Hank sees her looking at the gun and nods. Anna stares at him, trying to make sense of it. Overcome by some emotion she can't name, she covers her mouth. She is outside her body, can feel her lips open as she tries to speak. She is trying to understand, keeps trying to say something, but can't. Then she meets his eyes and knows everything.

Soundlessly she retreats back into the house, nearly tripping over the wolf in her haste; she reaches for the edge of the door and slams it with all her strength. But he has stuck his foot into the open space, and it only bounces off his thick hiking boot. He throws the door back so hard that the knob sticks in the sheet-rock and stays.

Anna backs down the length of the mudroom, the pup whining and cringing just behind her, worried at her behavior. Hank matches her stride for stride.

They watch each other for several minutes with the kitchen table in between them.

"It was you," Anna says finally, hating the trembling in her voice. She puts her hands on the table and leans against it to steady herself. "You killed John."

"Now, hold on. We're about to have a little talk about that," Hank says. He sets the rifle on the table and turns it so that the barrel points just off to the side of where she stands. Anna feels a cold rock settle in her stomach. "First, why don't you go ahead and tell me why the game warden's been messing around out here. His truck's in your driveway every other week. I'm thinking you must be great friends by now. What exactly does he know?"

The game warden? "I don't know," Anna says. "Just that there was a baiting station on my property, and he knows someone killed the bear that attacked my dog. Why do you care?"

"I care because someone took my trail camera."

"*Your* trail camera?" Anna asks. Her body hums. *Think.* "Oh. Of course. You're the poacher."

"I don't like that word," Hank says. "It makes it seem like I don't have certain rights." He gazes out the window, but keeps his hand on John's rifle. "I've lived here for a long time. Long before you ever did. I made a living off of the land around here, hunting and fishing. All I needed. No one bothered me. Then people like you came with your fences and city laws." He spits onto the kitchen tile.

"Are you going to kill me?" Anna asks. "Why are you telling me this?"

Hank laughs. "The way I see it, we're in a unique position. Neither of us can turn the other in. So you know that I killed some bears and deer, so what?"

"And my husband."

"Now, that was self-defense."

"You were trespassing. Exactly the way you are now." Her voice gets louder; she is close to losing control of it. "He was defending our home. Trying to stop an animal from suffering. Protecting us from people like you."

"That sounds awfully high and mighty, coming from someone like yourself," Hank scoffs. "What about your husband's many misdeeds? You think no one saw? Where do you get off judging an animal's life is worth more than a man's?"

"What are you talking about?"

"I saw him. I have trail cameras all over these woods." The wolf pup, still cowed, has slunk up to him to investigate and smells his boots; he kicks it and it yelps. It backs warily into the corner.

"Stop it."

"That's not a husky," he tells her.

"What are you trying to say?" Anna asks again; she tries to swallow, but the lump in her throat remains. "What do you mean about my husband?"

"Aren't you keeping up the good work yourself?" he asks. "Those two hunters with their black truck didn't exactly make it out alive, did they?"

"That wasn't all my fault," she says. "If you really were watching, you know it wasn't."

"You didn't do anything about it, though, did you?"

"There was nothing I could do."

"There might have been. But that's neither here nor there. A lot of people have died out here, haven't they? A mysterious amount, the sheriff might think."

"Just say what you mean," Anna says, exasperated.

"You can't turn me in because I know what John did. And I think you know what he did, too. But I'm going to say it, just for your benefit. Every time he took that rifle out to clean up some mess a poacher had made, what he really went after was the poacher."

"What?" Anna is shaking. "That's not true."

"How many did he kill over the years? Five? Six? He was pretty smart, really. They're hunting illegally, so no one knows exactly where they are. Hard to trace them when they disappear."

"You're crazy," Anna says. "John never—"

"Bullshit." Hank slams his hand on the table with a crack that makes Anna jump. His wedding ring leaves a chip in the wood. "You forget, I've watched you both for years. You knew enough to stay well inside the house when your husband came back from those little outings with a dead man slung over the back of his mule, didn't you? The only thing I don't know is where he put them." He gestures behind him. "He carried them right in that door I just came through, over his shoulder like a sack of feed. Where are they, Anna? The cellar? The crawl space? Hidden in a wall somewhere?"

"Oh, my god." Anna, on the verge of collapsing, just manages to pull out a chair and sink into it. Her thoughts are like water going over boulders, with no anchor, nothing to attach them. They blur into shapes. *When is John coming in?* A young horse running in a green pasture, a neighbor's dog barking just past the mailbox, her clothing stained red and brown and pushed to the bottom of the laundry bin, her gentle husband sitting at the end of the bed slouched under the weight of what they are helpless to change, telling her they should move. Deer bleeding into snow in bright drops of red, the sewing machine under its dark cover, the scratches in the stock of the rifle, the hard hate-filled eyes of the mule. John's soft manner and strong hands, the crow's feet at the corners of his eyes, the way he looked down and shuffled to his shop to spend hours creating something good and beautiful with his own hands to replace all the bad. Had she seen it? She is good at lying, and she can't trust herself.

Yes, maybe it is true, and maybe she had known, once. And maybe it just didn't fit her idea of what their lives should have to be. What she and John should have to be. Are people responsible for the actions others drive them to? She can make herself forget like that, she can live around things. She had known enough not to try to figure it out, at least, not to ask any questions. She had known enough to realize she didn't want to know more. The wolf had found a bone she didn't return.

She is in the tower of a castle that is falling, stone by stone. She fights to hold it together, but there is too much of it.

"So you see," Hank says, "you can't turn me in because I know about all the bodies you've collected. I can't turn you in because you know about mine." *He doesn't know about the sheriff and the cadaver dogs. That I'm already lost.*

Anna puts her elbows on the table and buries her head in her hands. She doesn't care that John's old gun is aimed toward her. "What do you want?" she asks. She hears—and Hank does, too—that it is a concession.

"What do I want? I thought you knew," he says. "I want to live my life." Then he yells, pounding on the table until she thinks it will break, "I want my fucking trail camera back!" Before Anna can react, he is beside her and squeezing her neck between his bicep and forearm, holding her head back so far that she wheezes and almost chokes. "You're going to fix this," he says while she struggles against him. "You got the game warden involved. It didn't have to be this way."

If he finds out I don't have it, that he's practically already been caught, it's all over. It's over for both of them; it's too late to change anything. This is what their lives have come down to.

"It's . . ." she says, but can't get enough air to speak. He loosens his hold. She rubs her neck and gasps for breath.

"Tell me."

"It's on a shelf in the cellar," she says. "Against the wall."

He picks up John's rifle and points it at her. "Take me to it," he says.

Holding her hands against her hot throat to soothe it, still coughing, Anna walks toward the cellar door with the cold tip of the gun in her back. Her own rifle now lies uselessly on the floorboard of the backseat of the car, covered with a blanket. She has never even fired it.

The cellar door creaks as Anna pulls it open to reveal the darkness that falls away down the stairs. Hank looks over her shoulder. Anna trembles.

"Well?" Hank says, nudging her with the gun.

Anna swallows. "I have to turn on the light up here," she explains, "and then turn on the next light at the bottom. Otherwise it's too dark to see." She reaches up and pulls the chain that turns on the bulb at the head of the stairs. The chain snaps back against the bulb with a loud clink. The dim yellow light flickers, then shines down the first half of the stairs. Hank steps forward, knocking her with his shoulder, and peers into the shadows.

"What in the hell?" Hank says in a constricted voice beside her. Anna has been watching his face, but at his tone, turns to look down. She stifles a scream and staggers back. There are bones strung along the stairs. A barely joined radius and ulna, scored by sharp young teeth, leans between the third and fourth. Smaller ones that might have belonged to fingers scatter down until the shadows hide them.

"The wolf," Anna says. All the time it had been locked in the darkness, it had been busy digging, drawing out what had been hidden. Excavating. "It's true."

Hank turns to her, face grown pale, and opens his mouth to say something, but before he makes a sound, Anna drives her shoulder and elbow as hard as she can into his gut. He groans and stumbles backwards, looking at her with wide eyes, like the eyes of the man who had fallen under the mule, and then he trips. He slides on his back down several stairs, grunting, gun clattering beside him. He stops sliding and lies still.

Anna stands frozen at the top. "Hank?" she calls. "Hank?"

He is dead. No, his leg twitches, and the black rubber tread of his hiking boot thrashes in the air. He makes a strange, strangled sound and sits up, panting. He lurches to his feet, then forward onto the loose bones.

They slip out from under him, and he falls again, onto his ribs this time. He slides until he disappears down the lower stairs, his face swallowed by the darkness. After the noise of the fall ceases, the small bones that scatter like pebbles being dropped, all is silent in the damp cool air except for the dripping that has always been there.

Anna pulls the chain to turn off the light and closes the door and locks it, struggling to snap off the key in the heavy old knob. She lodges one of the wooden kitchen chairs underneath. Maybe the door opens the wrong way for it to help; she doesn't know. It doesn't have to hold forever, just long enough.

Anna calls the wolf pup to her, and it comes with its tail tucked between its legs, but that will soon change. It is growing fast and will grow strong, too.

33

Sheriff Smith has no reason to be concerned yet about the saddlemaker's absence. No one is sure exactly when he and his wife left, but it can't have been long before; the house doesn't have an abandoned look, though it could undeniably use some upkeep. The porch light is off. He can't tell if lights inside are on. There is no buildup of mail or newspapers. But it does seem unusual the woman, at least, isn't there when they arrive. She should have been expecting them; she had been asked to make herself available if they had questions or needed direction. She had seemed like she welcomed their help. They still haven't spoken to the husband.

They don't have a warrant to search the home or any reason to ask for one yet. There has been some danger to the homeowners, the sheriff understands, from poachers, but there isn't any sign of foul play anywhere around the house. The only thing that moves is a cat that meows at him through the window. It stands on the sunny kitchen counter next to large bowls full of cat chow and water. The sheriff studies the room behind it. A folded paper with the name *Ben* written in bold letters is stuck to the fridge with a magnet, along with assorted business cards and Post-its with writing too small for him to read. Signs, he thinks, of normal, busy lives

The barn and garage sit quietly, the chicken coop door is flung open as though it hasn't been used for some time, though the sheriff somehow formed the impression that it had been full of hens before. Then again, he hadn't really looked closely at it.

Sheriff Smith searches around the house and yard just long enough to convince himself that the woman and her husband really aren't there before starting the planned work in the woods with the cadaver dogs. They have been granted use of the dogs for a limited time; there is a possible missing persons case in Burlington that also demands them. He will return to the house with a warrant later if he needs to.

The sheriff has no real reason to worry yet, but he does. He can't shake the feeling that something doesn't add up, that he is missing something important. Long years of experience have taught him to give credence to his instincts. He doesn't know exactly where the feeling comes from, so he keeps two dogs in the clearing and sends one of the dogs to comb along the trails just in case it hits on something randomly. He has long believed luck is what happens when you put yourself in the right place at the right time. His few deputies have learned to trust him.

He believes he is good at his job, but he hates assignments like this one. These are the sort of woods you could get lost in, the sort that hold secrets in the hollows like a mist that never gets warm enough to rise. Unfamiliar stretches of forest disorient him, give him the creeps. He is prone to attacks of claustrophobia, though he hides it well. He slaps the mosquitoes off his arms with no regard to how hard he hits.

At a tip from one of his deputies, he has spoken to the game warden about the homeowners' situation with the bear poachers, thinking it might be related to the disappearance of the two men in the black truck. The game warden explained with eagerness that he had retrieved a trail camera from the area not long ago. Game wardens can make cases stick so seldom that he seemed almost happy it has become serious enough for the sheriff's office to get involved. Maybe poaching can't get a conviction, but murder . . . ? They plan to meet at the office later to look at the grainy photographs and see if the man in them can be identified.

Belbridge is, after all, a small town. It's true that it has pockets of deep isolation that can make the sheriff's job more difficult. Still, if the man in the photographs is a local, someone will know him. Unfortunately, the only fingerprints on the camera reportedly belong to the game warden himself.

Small towns. Months of nothing, when you get so sick of writing speeding tickets you think of robbing a bank yourself just for a change, then poaching and, possibly, murder, all at once. A man and his wife, possibly missing. And just that morning, another married man had been called in missing, too—a neighbor of the saddlemaker's. None of it can be coincidence, can it? The sheriff frowns. The neighbor hasn't been gone long enough for anyone to worry except his wife, not even long enough to file a report; they'd had to tell the wife to call back in several hours. She hadn't been pleased.

It's a lot for his small office to handle.

One thing at a time. The sheriff walks heavily around the clearing near where the truck had been found, scuffing his feet, waiting for something to happen; he is ready to wait all day. It could be worse, considering. It is clear and warm, nice enough out if you can ignore the bugs.

His radio crackles. "Go ahead," he says.

It's the deputy he had sent off with the extra dog. "We've found some remains, sheriff," he says. "They appear to be human."

"What condition? Recent?" the sheriff asks, thinking of both the missing couple and the missing neighbor.

"No, I would say months old. They're just bones. Picked clean and spread around."

One of the two missing New Yorkers, then? Sheriff Smith sighs. "Where are you?"

"In a clearing maybe a quarter-mile southwest of you."

"I'm on my way," the sheriff says. He takes his time getting his bearings and is about to head into the forest in that direction when he is interrupted.

"Sheriff!" One of the handlers waves; his German shepherd strains at its leash and whines, pawing next to a stack of white-washed landscape timbers. "We've got something here."

He hands the deputies their shovels, and they pull away the lumber and start to dig.

They don't have to dig far.

34

One day the illness will kill her. The doctors had told Anna long ago how her organs had been weakened by it, corkscrew-shaped bacteria spiraling through the soft tissue into the heart, the brain. Something will set off a chain reaction and weaken her. Fatigue, exposure. A sore throat that has its root in spring allergies, a common fever could become a real danger for someone like her.

One day the arthritis will make getting around too difficult, and she'll be helpless. One day, the disorientation will lead her far away and lose her there. She has long known, to some extent, how she will die. She lives with that knowledge in the back of everything she does.

But today, she is still herself, and she has a good horse, a good mule, two weeks' worth of supplies (maybe more), a map, a compass, some matches, a rope, and a bag full of cash. She feels like an outlaw. She pats Keeper's neck and recites the old Frost poem to calm her nerves, what she can remember: *It seems to me / I can't express my feelings any more / Than I can raise my voice or want to lift / My hand (oh, I can lift it when I have to).*

What she would have given for an adventure like this when she was young. She wouldn't have been afraid at all then, of not having anywhere specific to go. That would have been the best part.

And you like it here? / I can see how you might. But I don't know! / It would be different if more people came, / For then there would be business.

The horse and mule pick their way over trails she has never gone down before. It is what horses are meant to do. She gives Keeper his head as they come to a rock fall. The wolf pup trots up ahead of them and waits at the top, scenting the breeze. It limps a little; its pads haven't hardened yet. The horse noses the boulders, gauging them, then scrambles over. Charlie, loaded with gear, follows sedately behind. They are all free; the Kingdom is theirs.

We didn't change without some sacrifice . . .

Overhead, a hawk cries *scree*. It is good and right; it is what wilderness sounds like. Soon, the trees will begin to turn gold and red. After that, the hard winter. It's the winter Anna fears most of all, the cold and the days that are short and difficult, when the shadows of the trees will stretch like bars and bleed together until they become a long, empty night. There will be nothing to do but listen to her teeth chatter and wait for the sun to rise. She will have to melt snow as drinking water. If she makes it through the winter, she can make it.

Somehow the change wore out like a prescription.

There is no one left to ask anything of her. *If this is what it comes to*, she thinks, but doesn't finish it; there isn't a reason to finish it. She can't live in one place and protect what is her own, but she might if she lives in many places. She reaches behind her leg to feel the rifle in its scabbard. The safety is off; she has made certain of it.

I've lain awake thinking of you, I'll warrant, / More than you have yourself, some of these nights.

And at the end, whenever it may be, if her bones rest where no one ever goes, it really doesn't matter. Let the sky inhabit her ribs; she can hold it as well as John had. Let her body feed the growing wolf's, if it must. Let the horse and the mule live the rest of their days in the green mountains, following the deer after she has gone. It is the way of things.

Still, her heart had almost filled to breaking when she had looked back at her little house with its yellow windows shining, the door that held in the last mysteries of the lives of two imperfect people, who had nonetheless known as much happiness as anyone could be allowed.

ABOUT THE AUTHOR

Chera Hammons holds an MFA from Goddard College in Plainfield, Vermont, and serves as writer-in-residence at West Texas A&M University. The author of four books of poetry, including *Maps of Injury* and the 2017 Southwest Book Award winner *The Traveler's Guide to Bomb City*, she lives near Amarillo, Texas, with her husband, three cats, a dog, a rabbit, a donkey, and five horses.

TORREY HOUSE PRESS

Voices for the Land

The economy is a wholly owned subsidiary of the environment, not the other way around.
— Senator Gaylord Nelson, founder of Earth Day

Torrey House Press is an independent nonprofit publisher promoting environmental conservation through literature. We believe that culture is changed through conversation and that lively, contemporary literature is the cutting edge of social change. We strive to identify exceptional writers, nurture their work, and engage the widest possible audience; to publish diverse voices with transformative stories that illuminate important facets of our ever-changing planet; to develop literary resources for the conservation movement, educating and entertaining readers, inspiring action.

Visit www.torreyhouse.org for reading group discussion guides, author interviews, and more.

As a 501(c)(3) nonprofit publisher, our work is made possible by the generous donations of readers like you.

Torrey House Press is supported by the National Endowment for the Arts, Back of Beyond Books, The King's English Bookshop, Wasatch Global, Jeff and Heather Adams, Suzanne Bounous, Diana Allison, Kirtly Parker Jones, Kitty Swenson, Jerome Cooney and Laura Storjohann, Heidi Dexter and David Gens, Robert Aagard and Camille Bailey Aagard, Kathleen and Peter Metcalf, Rose Chilcoat and Mark Franklin, Stirling Adams and Kif Augustine, Charlie Quimby and Susan Cushman, Doug and Donaree Neville, the Barker Foundation, the Sam and Diane Stewart Family Foundation, the Jeffrey S. and Helen H. Cardon Foundation, Utah Division of Arts & Museums, and Salt Lake County Zoo, Arts & Parks. Our thanks to individual donors, subscribers, and the Torrey House Press board of directors for their valued support.

Join the Torrey House Press family and give today at
www.torreyhouse.org/give.